CO[illegible]AL

CONSCRIPT: BOOK 4

Scott Bartlett

Mirth Publishing

High River

Cover art by Tom Edwards (tomedwardsdesign.com)

Library and Archives Canada Cataloguing in Publication

Bartlett, Scott

Corporal (Paperback Edition) ; Scott Bartlett; illustrations by Tom Edwards

ISBN 978-1-988380-88-9

Contents

Chapter 1

Everyone on Nibiru was a veteran, now.

Po could see that on the faces of his fellow Marines as he patrolled Gomorate with his fireteam, whenever their visors were up or de-polarized.

Their eyes weren't just bloodshot from exhaustion, with dark bags of skin bunched beneath them. They were hollow. He noticed a lot of men shuffling, too—and when he caught himself doing it, he vowed never to let himself walk that way again, or his team.

"Look alive, Hill," he said to the Marine who'd made a return to Fireteam Echo, this time to replace Gomez while he was recovering from the brain injury he'd suffered in Karakata. "Walk like a Marine."

"Yes, Corporal."

It still felt weird, being called corporal. His promotion to lance corporal had come down not long after 131st Platoon had returned from killing To'sheth Rin. It had taken less than a week, and Po had gotten the sense that the short delay came down to officers on the ground feeling out GEA's reaction to what Po and his fellow Marines had done before they rewarded him for it. Gunny Emery had been vocal in his support for Po, and even Colonel Coleman had seemed favorably disposed toward him. But none of that would have mattered much if the Global Equity Accord had decided for some reason that he'd acted outside orders and counter to their grand strategy.

But while there was increasing talk of splintering factions within humanity's highest governing body, this time things had shaken out in Po's favor, and he felt grateful for that. He knew he'd been luckier as a Marine than he had any right to be, pretty much since bootcamp.

Although, I wouldn't count getting conscripted as lucky. He'd seen too much, done too much, to make a case for that anymore. But he'd gotten promoted faster than he'd ever expected to, and he'd earned the respect of men *he* respected, like Gunny Emery.

And Sergeant Young. A lump rose in his throat as memories of his old squad leader resurfaced, and he forced them back down into his subconscious. *Snotting up on patrol is the last thing I need.*

Losing men like Young was part of what ripped a front-line Marine's heart out, and gave him that hollow-eyed look, which gradually calcified into a hardened stare. It was what had given pretty much all of boot battalion that look—although, no one called them that. Not anymore. The moniker "boot battalion" had stuck longer than it probably should have, but by now, no Marine would ever accuse the men of Po's battalion of being boot.

Either way, these days he thought more about his company than his battalion. 131st and 129th held the men he'd suffered and bled alongside, and while he didn't know the men from 130th as well, he suspected that would change soon enough. They'd filed the paperwork to have their company named "Raptor," and to Po, Raptor Company felt most like home now.

"Krik, what did that sign we just passed say?" he asked without warning.

"Fresh Adelqo meat," the other Marine answered right away, as he no doubt knew Po would want him to.

"Very good." Po faced front again, rifle at the ready while he made sure to keep his own head on a swivel.

Lately, he tried to keep his Marines on their toes with questions like this, and he always wanted an immediate response. The point was to see how alert they were keeping, and how observant. If they had a few seconds to respond, then they could just replay their Circuits' footage, and find out the answer from that.

He wasn't surprised Krik had aced his question. He'd grown close with the Marine lately, who'd been with him when he shot To'sheth Rin. They'd stared death in the face together and lived to tell about it—the two who'd delved deepest into the Janus base, and who'd walked away with the kill of a lifetime. Krik was a professional, and while Po would trust almost all of his brothers with his life, with Krik, it was at another level.

Unfortunately, Krik's vigilance wasn't matched by a lot of the Marines in Gomorate. Plenty of men were getting complacent, these days. With Rin dead, the general expectation was that the war was all but over, and the Corps had little left to do but punch in, punch out, and collect paychecks. That had led to some embarrassment for one patrol, which had failed to notice a Nibiran who managed to sneak in and steal from a Marine supply cache, right in front of their noses. According to rumor, their Circuits had incriminated them pretty badly—apparently, two of them had been looking right at the thief.

Po didn't want that for Fireteam Echo. So he saw to it personally that they stayed frosty.

It felt good to be back to leading only a fireteam, after commanding all of 131st Platoon during the raid on Rin's underwater compound. Jumping over being put in charge of a squad and straight to a platoon had been weird. Maybe he'd find himself permanently in that position someday, but for now, he was glad to be back with his Echo boys.

He was also grateful to be only one short of a full fireteam to command. Plenty of units in Gomorate had multiple holes waiting to be filled, after all the deadly battles they'd been through. Po knew GEA had been pressuring the Corps to accelerate recruitment and training since before he'd been a trainee, and under normal circumstances they'd be flooding across the system to replace the dead on Nibiru. But Janus' swift destruction of every satellite in orbit had put paid to that. The resulting orbital debris prevented any shuttles from landing on or leaving the planet, and it had made communication with the rest of the system a lot harder.

I wonder if Nicky wrote me again.

He couldn't decide whether he wanted that or not. If she had, it would be in violation of him telling her not to, which he'd done after the revelation that she'd decided to have contact with their father again. But after months on this oven-like planet, with insurgents hiding under every rock eager to kill him, he missed her desperately. Marco, too—and sometimes, he even found himself wondering what Lorenzo was doing.

I hope Nicky knows about what's happening here on Nibiru. She must. It would be big news back in Psyche Colony. *There's no way GEA could cover up an entire interplanetary war. Is there?*

Of course, there *was* the fact that GEA had always preached friendship and accommodation of the Nibirans, prior to their attack on Cycler 3. The war had to be embarrassing for them, on some level. But surely they wouldn't cover it up. They *couldn't.*

At least, Po hoped they couldn't. Without the satellites, he wasn't able to access his crypto account to manage his funds, and he'd been stupid enough not to set up automatic transfers to Rosa, his mother, to pay for Nicky's meds. If they didn't know about the situation on Nibiru, then they wouldn't know Po was stuck here and unable to access his account, which meant they probably thought he'd intentionally cut off payments along with his letters.

The thought that Nicky might not be able to afford the treatment she needed was most excruciating of all. But he couldn't control that, so he tried his best not to think about it. The most he could do was be the best lance corporal, the best team leader, he could be. To contribute as well as he could to restoring full functionality to the Marine units trapped on this awful planet.

A message pinged his implant, louder than a regular one, and his vision flashed red. That meant it was from an officer, since only they had the privilege to send enlisted Marines priority alerts. If he hadn't been on duty, it simply would have opened automatically, and wouldn't close until he'd read it. But the implant was smart enough not to impede his vision under circumstances where a fight could technically break out at any moment.

He took a quick look around to confirm there were no threats in the area, then he opened the message, dialing back its opacity even more than it already was. As always, the priority alert was bordered in red.

"LANCE CORPORAL PO ABBATO, CHANGE INTO A CLEAN SERVICE UNIFORM AND REPORT TO BATTALION HQ AT 0400."

Po blinked at the message, surprised it hadn't ordered him to at least wait until their patrol was over. He didn't have even a half hour until 0400—there'd be just enough time to sprint back to the apartment building Raptor Company was using for a barracks, get changed, and then move just as fast to HQ.

Are the officers getting complacent, too? Taking away my team's leader during a patrol? Or am I actually just paranoid?

Maybe there really was nothing to worry about anymore on Nibiru. Maybe Po really had ended the war with the rounds he'd put into To'sheth Rin. But somehow, he couldn't quite bring himself to believe that.

"Krik, you're in charge. I just got called to HQ."

The other Marine glanced at him, eyebrows raised behind his transparent visor. "Now?"

Po nodded. "Right now. Hopefully the higher-ups haven't changed their minds about the Rin kill."

"No." Krikorian shook his head. "They love you now, Abbato. I'm sure they will give you a medal or something. A backrub, at the very least."

Po shrugged his shoulders. "You know, I *am* kind of stiff." He grinned at Krik, nodded at the others, then turned and jogged back to the barracks. He stowed his suit with the help of the supply officer overseeing the pop-up armory in the basement, and then he ran to the apartment where Fireteam Echo slept, there to wash up and get into a clean uniform in record time.

Feeling fresh, and hopefully looking it, he made for the temporary battalion headquarters that Colonel Tuffin had ordered set up where an indoor Nibiran market once had been.

***

Po arrived at the temporary HQ with minutes to spare, and he was immediately directed to a makeshift office that had once been some Nibiran vendor's market stall. Curtains had been hung along the sides to give the illusion of privacy—no one could see you in there, but anyone nearby would hear you sure enough.

Isn't that just like the Marines. Rough and ready solutions for a multitude of problems.

It made sense: no one knew how long they'd be in Gomorate, or when the next attack might come, or how long the war would go on. If the Nibiran capital became a longer-term home to the Marines, they'd set up something more permanent. For now, everyone was still making do.

Inside the stall-turned-curtained-office, a first lieutenant was sitting at a squat metal desk that looked like it belonged in an old-timey schoolroom. Po saluted him.

"At ease, Corporal."

The lieutenant got to his feet and stuck out a hand, which surprised Po. But he recovered quickly, and managed to execute a firm handshake.

"Take a seat," the officer said. "I'm First Lieutenant Melvin."

Po did, and thanked him, already feeling slightly relieved at the warm welcome. It seemed he probably wasn't about to get chewed out for some of his more...*creative* choices in the op to get Rin.

What was more, the lieutenant didn't have that cocky air a lot of officers did who'd never seen combat. Instead, he had a quiet confidence about him. Lieutenant Melvin had shot at an enemy on more than one occasion, and had been shot at in kind. Po was sure of it.

"Why'd you choose Rifleman as your MOS, Abbato?"

Po furrowed his brow, momentarily knocked off-guard by the question. He shrugged. "That's the job I recognized most, from the books I'd read about the Marines."

"But your GASVAT scores *did* qualify you for a more advanced MOS. A lot of them, actually."

Po just shrugged again.

"Were you always a big reader?"

"I enjoyed reading as a kid. These days...well, sometimes. Mostly I'm on duty or sleeping. This war has been a little..."

"I get it," Melvin said. "I understand you also dropped out of high school. When you were in level one."

"Yes, sir. I decided I was better off working, instead of finishing my last three years of school. My family debt was pretty monstrous. Still is."

"When you were in school...would you have considered yourself a leader, there? Among your fellow students?"

Po laughed. "Definitely not."

"How about as a worker in the Psyche Docking Cylinder, where I understand you operated a mech—a W-200 Powered Loader."

"I wouldn't say so, sir."

"You have three siblings. Do you think it'd be fair to say you were a leader to them?"

Po paused. "To two of them, maybe."

"And how are you liking the Marine Corps, so far?"

"Honestly, sir...it's a lot better than I expected."

"And your unit?"

"I love those men. They're brothers to me, now. They're some of the best people I've ever met, which is crazy, because I knew a lot of them back in Psyche, and I never would have said that about them then. I guess they just kind of grew into it."

Lieutenant Melvin was nodding slowly. "Abbato, I'll tell you why I'm here talking to you today. Obviously, losing all our satellites made communicating with high command trickier, but we do have a few large ground antennas whose sites we've managed to secure. What we've been getting from them is that the Corps is in short supply of officers, especially good ones. We're pumping new recruits through bootcamp in record numbers, and we need Marines to command those boots—preferably, officers with combat experience."

Melvin folded his hands atop the bent metal desk. "We sent the higher-ups the footage from your Circuit, and from every Marine who went with you to infiltrate To'sheth Rin's compound. It's all been carefully analyzed. Based on that analysis, I'm here to offer you the chance to go to Earth and start a college degree so that you can qualify to become an officer. The degree would be fully paid by the Corps. You'd also be paid a living allowance. The only requirement would be that you'd need to agree to become a Marine Corps officer afterward, for two terms of service. And yes, I'm aware you've been sentenced to serve three terms—your education would count as your completion of the first one."

"I...wow." Po stared at the office's bulkhead—he was conditioned to think of even a curtain as a bulkhead, apparently—as he contemplated Melvin's offer.

It was a chance to enjoy some peace for a while. Maybe forever. He didn't know how much this living allowance would be, but if he cut back on expenses as much as he could, he might even still be able to carve some out to send back to Psyche for Nicky. And when he finally finished school, and whatever training came after, then he'd be an *officer,* and much higher paid than he was now.

It would work out even better for her, in the long run. And for me, too.

But something was missing from this conversation, he realized. Zanth.

During an encounter like this, with an officer who was offering him the world as a direct consequence of the Emplor's assistance, the alien would normally be standing in the corner behind Po's superior, preening and gloating.

Why he wasn't here, and why he hadn't appeared since the day 131st Platoon had inadvertently slaughtered a Gomorati Army unit, Po didn't know. But what he *did* know was that the alien's help had brought him here. If it wasn't for the Emplor, he wouldn't have come this far. Not nearly.

Then he thought about Sergeant Young, who'd died as he fought alongside them, right on the front lines. He thought about Zapletal, taken out by a Janus RPG. He thought about Corbin, and Suzuki, and about all the Marines they'd lost since coming to this forsaken planet. He thought about Gunny Emery, and Navarro, and Gomez—all still recovering from the wounds they'd taken.

And he thought about his fireteam, who he'd be leaving behind. Who, maybe, he'd never see again in his life.

He shook his head. "No, sir. I'm sorry. But I can't become an officer."

With that, he stood up, saluted the surprised-looking Melvin, and walked out of the makeshift office.

Chapter 2

"So you really are a nutcase," Taylor said through a mouthful of chewy Adelqo meat. The lack of shuttles making planetfall had finally forced the Marines to switch to local fare for chow—an unpopular but necessary measure. "After everything we've been through here on Nibiru, you decided what you'd really like is a second helping."

Po shrugged. "Things seem pretty quiet right now." Not that he believed for a second they'd stay that way.

"Abbato," Zhang said, on the verge of chomping down on his own Adelqo-meat sandwich. "You could have been an *officer*. That was a really big opportunity." The Chinese was looking at him with wide eyes.

"And have to deal with a bunch of Earthers, for years? No thanks. Who actually wants to be an officer, anyway? Way too much responsibility. Always checking maps and herding cats. That's not for me. I'd rather just engage the enemy. Keep it simple."

"You have to do a certain amount of map checking anyway," Krikorian put in. "And you'll only have to do more, going forward. They *are* going to put you in permanent charge of a squad at some point. You know that, right?"

"Cross that bridge when I come to it," Po muttered. He gestured with his sandwich, and tried to change the topic. "I wish this could be that same meat we found in Eremus, spilling out of that cart." He still didn't know what it had been—he just knew it was delicious.

His attempted topic change quickly took root. "Those sausages were the best thing I ever ate," Taylor said sincerely.

"You guys found a *sausage* cart?" Zhang said in disbelief. "And you didn't share with the rest of us?"

Po and Taylor exchanged looks, then cracked up.

"Nah," Taylor said.

Gomez and Paisley were with us that day, too. He missed Gomez. *I'll have to visit him again when I get a chance.* The Marine was on the road to recovery, but he still had memory lapses, sometimes asking the same question two or three times in the space of five minutes.

As for Paisley...Po couldn't muster up any positive feelings toward the guy. Their relationship had always been rocky, but there had been a time, after Po had saved his life in the fight for Eremus, when things had been looking up between them.

But he could never bring himself to like someone who deserted the Corps. Who deserted his brothers. Disagreeing with a superior was one thing...but being insubordinate and then leaving his unit to go who knew where, and do who knew what...that was a completely different thing.

Po hated him for it, and he definitely wasn't alone.

"Hey," Taylor said. "You guys hear about those signals out of Sovran?"

"Sovran?" Po repeated. "What's that?"

"Sovran Station. It's that cycler that went dark a few decades back—they completely cut off contact with the outside world. You seriously haven't heard of it?"

"That *is* ringing a bell, actually."

"Well, this is just RUMINT, and I have no idea how it started circulating among us Marines here on this backwater blister of a planet. But apparently, people have started picking up signals coming out of there. All encrypted, so no one knows what they say. Still, though...kinda spooky, right? Broadcasting, after all this time? I wonder what they say."

"What happened on Sovran?" Hill asked.

Taylor shook his head. "No idea. Something crazy, I would think. Whatever it was, GEA managed to cover it up completely. There's plenty of theories floating around the nets, but I don't think anyone really knows."

There was a commotion at the door to the mess hall, which used to be a food court shared by the apartment building's residents. Po turned around to see Ara Darshim arguing vehemently with the Marine posted there. He had an arm across the entrance, barring her from entering.

Po stood wordlessly and walked over. "Stand down, Private," he told the sentry. The Marine didn't look happy about it, but he complied, retreating to his post against the bulkhead just outside the door.

"Ara. Where's Calik?" Calik was what Darshim had named her son after he'd hatched from the translucent egg Paisley had nearly hurled over a cliff.

"I left him with a friend. Po...I have to tell you something."

"What?"

She glanced at the sentry, then continued in a hushed but urgent voice. "There's going to be an attack. On your garrison in Valta."

He shook his head slowly. "Janus has been totally quiet since we took out Rin."

"Well, that's about to change. They know your ships will be here soon, to clear out the debris in orbit. Which means this is their last chance to inflict real damage on you—striking when you least expect it, because you think that killing their leader was like chopping off Janus' head. But it wasn't like that. Janus is a many-headed hydra."

Po raised his eyebrows. Darshim had talked like this several times during the journey back to Gomorate, where she'd decided to settle down with her son after the op in Morati Firth. And *he'd* believed her. Unfortunately, not many others had.

No one wants to even think about more fighting. We all need a break from it, badly. And Janus will know that, too.

"I thought you were out of the espionage game," Po said. "Too many people know you now, you said."

"I still have contacts, Po. And they still tell me things."

"Why are you coming to me with this?"

"Because you're the only one who knows me well enough to listen. Look, we Nibirans need you Marines now. We become more dependent on you each day. If Janus gets the upper hand against you, where would that leave us? With them in power, probably. We don't want that, and I know humans don't want it either."

We can't afford *that,* Po reflected. He nodded. "All right. Come with me to the field hospital where Gunny Emery's recuperating. We'll take this to him, and if he takes it seriously, he'll pass it up the chain."

"We don't have time for all that, Po. They're attacking tomorrow!"

"Tell that to the Marine Corps chain of command. Let's go."

He led Darshim down the hall, abandoning his Adelqo sandwich half-eaten on his tray. *No big loss there,* he decided.

***

"Still happy with your decision not to leave and become an officer?" Taylor asked him as they loaded their gear into the back of an AC-900 gunship—a task made much easier by the strength enhancement afforded by the SERAPH suits they were all wearing.

Po shook his head. "I wouldn't have left yet even if I'd said yes. The orbital debris from all those blown-up satellites stops even officer candidates from leaving."

"Yeah, but they probably would have kept you back at base and fed you caviar," Taylor said. "To get you used to the officer life."

Po snorted, but didn't bother answering. Taylor knew just as well as any of them that their officers were eating the same Nibiran slop they all were. But the Marine seemed to be afraid he'd seize up if he didn't have a quip of some kind to deploy at all times, and it was usually simpler just to let him run his mouth.

They finished loading their gear and lifted the loading ramp to form a seal with the rest of the ship. With that done, they strapped in for the two-hour flight to Valta. All of Raptor Company was in here—129th, 130th, and Gunny Emery's 131st Platoon—with another sergeant rotated in, Rowe, to temporarily take Emery's place while the gunny healed up. As for Po's squad, Second Squad, Corporal Flores was in charge for the time being. If the company hadn't lost so many Marines across multiple battles, it would be a pretty cramped shuttle ride. Even as things stood, there was little room to spare.

Two companies were being sent to back up the Marines garrisoned in Valta: Raptor and Mike. Mike Company was in another gunship. They hadn't come up with their own name yet, which was why they still had the standard designation taken from the phonetic alphabet. Some companies never came up with one, which Po chalked up to lacking the sort of esprit de corps that Raptor Marines had.

Neither company was officially garrisoned in Gomorate, which made them easy choices to send as backup for the forces in Valta. Emery had warned Po that Raptor probably would be sent, since the company contained 129th and 131st Platoons, which were becoming popular options for sending into the least pleasant situations on Nibiru.

"That's called being a victim of your own success," Emery had said, grinning at Po and Darshim from a sitting position, with his mattress raised to prop him up. With that, he'd grabbed Po's bicep. "Hey. Are you good for this?"

"Yeah. I'm good."

"Are you good?" the gunnery sergeant asked again.

"I'm good, Gunny."

Emery nodded. "Okay. Keep a clear head, and watch out for your boys."

"I will."

Po used his implant to hook into one of the AC-900's exterior sensors, opening a floating window in front of him so he could watch the jungle canopy whip by below them. That was something the gunship pilots usually let the enlisted men do, although there were a few ornery ones who didn't allow it.

Flying over the jungle outside Gomorate reminded him of returning from their failed DA to capture or neutralize Shiv Horan, only to find FOB Longhorn overrun by Janus, and their fellow Marines hiding out in the hardened bunkers scattered throughout the base. The insurgents were doing everything they could to get at the sheltering Marines.

We got you in the end, didn't we Shiv? Po had been the one to shoot him, which felt almost as surreal as being the one to get To'sheth Rin. Back in the days before the battle for Gomorate, Shiv Horan had seemed like a big, important target. But on the day 131st Platoon came for Rin, he was little more than a barrier between Po and getting his Nibiran. A barrier that had been dispatched with relative ease.

He'd gained a certain amount of notoriety for those back-to-back kills, especially outside of Raptor Company. The Marines in his company knew him too well to treat him with much reverence—or with any, really—but he often got nothing but respect from men he ran into from other units, now. For some reason, they brought up the way he'd dispatched Horan even more than his taking out Rin.

I owe Navarro one for that. He still hadn't thanked the other Marine for sending him those Nibiran phrases to memorize. He'd visited him in the field hospital twice since getting back to Gomorate, but their relationship was still basically on the rocks. They had a lot of air they'd yet to clear lying between them. *Hopefully we get the chance.*

The jungle gave way to the blue waste of the Sodalite desert, before turning into mostly barren plains—certainly nothing like the lush ones 131st Platoon had trekked across in the continent's southeast, on their way to smack Rin in Morati.

The news came when they were a half hour out from Valta. The pilot received the alert, then forwarded it to their platoon leaders, who distributed it to their subordinates. Po had been studying a map of Valta, while trying not to think about Krik's comment about doing just that, when the alert superimposed itself over his vision:

"ATTENTION ALL LOCAL UNITS, THE GEA MARINE GARRISON AT VALTA FELL UNDER HEAVY ATTACK BY JANUS INSURGENTS AT 0213. REQUEST IMMEDIATE BACKUP."

"*What?*" Taylor said over Second Squad's internal channel, his eyes on Po. "I thought Darshim said the attack wouldn't happen till tomorrow!"

"Insurgents must have caught wind that we're on to them," Corporal Flores said. "That, or they got paranoid. But it doesn't matter. Either way, we're going to be in the thick of it the moment we touch down."

Chapter 3

"Go, go, go!" Sergeant Rowe ordered the Marines of 131st Platoon, even as the dust was still settling from the AC-900's landing.

Fireteam Echo was closer to a side hatch than the rear ramp, so they poured out of that, weapons raised and thermal on to spot any hostiles through the kicked-up dust cloud.

"You have our objective, 131st Platoon," Rowe said. "We head west, curving through the neighborhoods there to come at our target from the north. Spread out—each fireteam will find its own path. Don't lose track of where you are in relation to the objective."

Po led his team, still diminished to four, to a nearby shed where no other Marines were. A low brick wall ran parallel to it, to the east. It seemed like a good spot to get their bearings, with a little cover and concealment if they needed it.

Valta was divided into four quadrants, and its flatness reminded Po of Eremus. The dust was just brown here instead of blue. The structures looked similar, too—though there seemed to be more of the cracked-egg variety he'd seen in villages scattered throughout the Sodalite Desert, and fewer of the long, angled buildings that looked like towers that had fallen over onto their sides.

According to intel that had continued to pour in as the two gunships approached the city, insurgents had come from everywhere, popping out of the ground like they had in FOB Longhorn and also pouring out of buildings where civilians had been thought to live.

Whether that meant they'd dug tunnels into those structures' basements, or there were simply more insurgents hiding amidst the Valta populace than they'd thought, it didn't really matter. Not at this moment, anyway. The upshot was that Janus' numbers were shocking and overwhelming, and most Marines in the city were in pinned-down positions, trading shots with insurgents as their numbers slowly dwindled.

Po's team would now make their way toward the largest of those positions: a bazaar with four entryways to defend.

No one was firing on the Raptor Company Marines as they spread out from the shuttle. That didn't come as a surprise, since the pilots had purposefully touched down in spots they knew from intel held few or no insurgents. But it *was* kind of nice when something went according to plan.

"Let's go," Po said over his team channel, and they continued to push through the tiny yards surrounding the egg-like dwellings, weapons raised and eyes sweeping their surroundings constantly.

Mike Company had been ordered deeper into the city, where their gunship would deposit them at a position southeast of the same target. In Po's opinion, Raptor should have been sent there, given things were more likely to have changed deeper into the city since the intel they'd received had been collected.

Ours are the more experienced Marines. We *should have been sent deeper in.* But that hadn't been his call to make.

He had a map of their immediate surroundings open in a transparent overlay, and he kept having to up the opacity to check where they were in relation to other teams. He was doing his best to keep properly spaced out from the Marines to their west and east, but it was proving a challenge. The platoon was still too bunched-up.

Thankfully, Sergeant Rowe spotted it too. "Spread out more, Marines," he ordered over the platoon-wide.

As they moved from house to house, hopping walls and fences low and tall, Po noticed eyes peering at them through a crack in one of the white-dome houses' exteriors. He tensed, nudging his rifle's muzzle in that direction in case he needed to return fire, but the eyes' owner seemed to mean them no harm. At the next egg-shaped house, he spotted two more pairs of eyes tracking their movements.

"Anyone else seeing these Nibirans watching us from inside the eggs?" Taylor asked from his position at the last house, as he and Krikorian covered Po and Hill while they advanced to the next.

"Pretty sure they're civilians," Po said.

"What makes you say that?"

"Because I've been seeing them almost since we left the gunship, and none of them have shot at us." He frowned, though no one could see it through his polarized faceplate. "That said...stay frosty."

Any one of these 'civilians' could turn out to be an insurgent in hiding. After all, it seemed pretty likely that many of those fighting Marines in the streets had been pretending to be Valta residents before the battle.

Probably they've all been activated now. I doubt any of them are still hiding like that.

Even so...he put nothing past Janus, who was known to keep multiple cards up their sleeves, for playing at the worst possible times for the Marines. According to intel, that kind of sly trickery had mostly been To'sheth Rin's work. But no one truly knew how the Janus would show up on the battlefield, now that Rin was dead.

Either way, it was quickly becoming clear that Valta wasn't like Eremus. The residents there had known a battle was coming, and those with the wisdom to flee in advance had been able to do so. This time, Janus had struck without warning.

This must be terrifying for the Nibirans who live here. It also made things extremely dicey for the Marines. This planet was turned against them enough as it was. Catching civilians in the crossfire definitely would not improve the situation.

As they neared the covered market where the platoon they'd been sent to rescue was pinned down, Po's implant was able to populate his map with known enemy positions, at greater and greater levels of accuracy. If the satellites had still been up, he could have known those positions back in Gomorate. But as things stood, he had to rely on the SERAPH suits' short-range capabilities as they sent the latest intel along a daisy chain formed by each suit's transmitter and receiver.

"Check out the house I'm highlighting," Po said to his team, using his Circuit to place an indicator on their shared map as he spoke.

"Looks fancy," Taylor said. "Compared to living in an egg, at least."

"Even better," Po said. "It should offer us a good position against the insurgents giving our boys in that bazaar so much trouble."

"You think we should take it for our own?" Krikorian said.

Po chuckled. "Well, I'm not looking to invest in the Valta real estate market. But I do think we should borrow it, temporarily. Looks like there's a back entrance we can come in through here." He made a smaller mark at a higher resolution. "I'll take Hill in and give you the go-ahead if it's looking viable. We'll clear it in two pairs."

"Sounds fun," Taylor said.

They reached the house in a couple minutes, and from an alley mouth, Taylor and Krik put their crosshairs on the upper-level windows to cover Po and Hill as they entered the backyard. They each leapt the brick wall one-handed, rifles in their other hands. As one, they reached the back door. Po didn't slow—he used his momentum to kick it in with the suit's heavy boot.

The door was high-quality, as he figured it would be. Still, it was not built to withstand the suit's raw might. It burst open, slamming against an interior wall with a cracking sound, sending plaster dust puffing out from behind it.

He moved inside with rifle raised—only to find a frightened-looking Nibiran family sitting on cushions arranged in a circle near the corner opposite from him. They wore expensive-looking robes, except for two of them, who wore aprons and stood against the wall with folded hands. Po took those two for servants.

All seven of the Nibirans huddled together as he aimed his rifle at the floor just shy of them, a few of them pushing themselves back against the wall as if trying to melt through it. The aliens bayed and croaked in terror.

"It's okay," Po said in his best Nibiran, which wasn't very good. At any rate, it didn't seem to do much to calm their nerves. He lowered his rifle more, so that it pointed at the floor near his feet, and held up a placating hand. That didn't seem to do much, either.

Hill was already checking rooms leading off of this one. Po got back on the team channel. "Krik, Taylor, get in here. There's a family. Taylor, I want you to stay in this room to watch them."

Taylor cursed. "Honestly, Abbato? At this point, you're just trolling me. You take *every* opportunity to keep me out of the action. Every last one."

"Trolling is my prerogative as team leader. Shut up and watch them."

Po and Hill were already pushing through more rooms by the time Taylor came in to begin his babysitting. Krik joined them in clearing the rest of the house. In less than two minutes, it was theirs.

The house, which by Nibiran standards might as well have been a mansion, followed an L-shape, with the small arm projecting toward the insurgents who Po and his teammates wanted to shoot. But before they could get set up, he had to see to it that no unwanted guests could sneak in and ruin their day.

Taylor would be able to watch the back entrance as he guarded the Nibirans, but that still left the front. Po opened that door, and found it opened inward.

That's a plus. He cast a contemplative eye over the rest of the front room, which he would have called a living room, though he had no idea what the aliens called it. He dragged over a tightly upholstered armchair while he ordered Krik to bring some plates from the kitchen. Hill was already upstairs on overwatch.

"These our new home security system?" Krik asked as he came in carrying a nice, big stack of tottering plates. The suit's strength allowed him to carry them with one hand on bottom and one hand on top, despite how many there were.

"You better believe it."

Krik already had the idea, so Po let him balance the plates between the armchair's back and the front door without further direction. If someone tried to come in, the plates would fall to the floor and smash, which their suits' enhanced hearing would definitely pick up, even from upstairs.

"What about the windows?" the Armenian asked once he'd rigged up their new home alarm.

"They'll try the door first," Po said. They didn't have time to booby trap the entire house. As always, "rough and ready" was their watchword.

They joined Hill upstairs, where the Marine had taken up position at the end of the short arm of the L.

"Get going," Po said, jerking a thumb down the hall. "Set up down there somewhere."

"What? Why?"

"Because that's the best spot, and I want it."

"Lame." Even so, Hill got up and headed to another position.

Po chuckled. "You're a Canadian. Don't talk to me about being lame."

He knelt at the window where Hill had been, which he found to be a fantastic position indeed. From where he crouched, he could already put crosshairs on two separate insurgent positions—a group of them firing on one of the bazaar entrances from behind a fence, and another from a house whose front was perpendicular to both the market and the house Po and his team had taken.

The insurgents were careful not to stay visible for long...but they were still plenty visible, and so far they were apparently unaware of Fireteam Echo's presence.

He settled in and waited for the order to commence firing to come from Captain Haldane, who was commanding Raptor and Mike companies during this op. The plan was for both companies to start firing at the same time, which should result in the greatest number of dead insurgents.

In theory.

The plan made sense to Po...but then again, since becoming a Marine, he'd already watched plenty of sensible plans fall apart the moment battle was joined.

Without warning, a pair of boots swung into the room from above the window, knocking Po back and sending his rifle clattering across the floor.

He staggered backward, managing to catch himself against the wall and keep his footing. A figure in SERAPH armor was standing silhouetted against Gnara's dim light. Po had IFF tags switched on by default, but his implant couldn't bring up anything for the Marine who'd attacked him.

His assailant surged forward again, and Po sidestepped, intent on tossing the Marine against the wall—and probably through it. But his opponent ducked, redirected his momentum, and sent a fist into Po's side, hard. He stumbled again, but recovered quickly.

"What's going on up there?" Taylor asked. "Sounds like someone let in a herd of Adelqo."

But Po had neither the time nor the mental bandwidth to respond. The other Marine was pressing the attack, raining blows onto his head and torso. Po blocked as many as he could, but his opponent was quick, and seemed to know exactly where and how to strike. Many of the blows got through.

His armor had already suffered multiple dents, but even the strength boost afforded the Marine by his own armor could do little to truly hurt Po inside the SERAPH suit. Still, it was force against force, and he was feeling plenty rattled. Then, without warning, his attacker swept his feet out from under him with his leg, and in less than a second, he was on top of Po, straddling him with Po's own rifle pointing down at him.

The assailant's visor lowered to reveal Paisley's grinning face. "I could kill you," the former Marine said. "You need to remember that. If I chose to, I could kill you."

"Then why don't you," Po grunted.

"Because they still think you have potential. For some reason. I'm only here to give you a message."

"What?" Footsteps were approaching rapidly down the hall—no doubt Krikorian or Hill come to check on him.

"I've already delivered it. Remember, Po." Paisley tapped the rifle muzzle against Po's closed visor. With that, he dropped the weapon and stood to sprint toward the window, diving through it.

Chapter 4

Krikorian appeared in the hall almost simultaneous to Paisley's vanishing out the window.

"What happened to you?" he asked.

Po was in the middle of pushing himself to a sitting position. He shook his head as he grabbed his rifle and gave it a quick check over. "Forget it. Get back to your position. The sergeant's going to give the order to start firing any second."

With a curt nod, Krik complied, and Po returned to his window. Adrenaline coursed through him, making him feel alert in the way only almost dying could. To his shame, his body trembled, and he forced himself to take several deep breaths so he could draw a steady bead on the insurgent positions he'd already identified.

He fought just like I fought Freddie, behind that supply shed on Cycler 3. Ghostly red prompts had appeared in his vision during that fight, helping him to land his blows in a way that perfectly neutralized everything his opponent did. The same thing had happened in Shackleton, in his fight against the Janus sympathizers.

Paisley knew just what to do to disarm me and get me on the floor. Po had already begun to suspect back in Gomorate that an Emplor was helping the other Marine, just as Zanth had helped him. He'd even confronted him about it, but Paisley had pretended not to know what he was talking about.

Well, this confirmed it. The Emplor *were* helping Paisley...and now he'd gone rogue.

Was that the path Zanth had planned for Po, too? He resisted the urge to shake his head again. He couldn't begin to think how the Emplor might be planning to use Paisley, now that he'd deserted the Corps here on this far-flung alien planet.

But the scariest question was what he'd do if Paisley came back. He'd tried to put in extra training ever since infantry school, to win some independence back from the

Emplor, who'd helped him advance so much. But now he knew what that training was worth. If he was up against an opponent who had alien help, he stood no chance.

He said they still think I have potential. But what would happen if Zanth decided Po was a lost cause? That he wasn't going to be useful in advancing whatever agenda the alien had after all?

They'll dispose of you, a voice told him from the back of his mind, which sounded like his brother Lorenzo. *Just like you'd get rid of any liability.*

"All Raptor and Mike Marines prepare to commence firing," Captain Haldane said over the shared channel.

Po settled his scope over a Nibiran currently framed by a window as it fired on the pinned-down Marines in the bazaar.

Then, a few seconds later: "Fire!"

He did. The rifle jolted in his hands, and his target went down.

All around him, M37 rounds snapped and popped, and surrounding the bazaar insurgents fell where they stood, by the dozens. Po's Circuit let him see the moment of their probable deaths: their red indicators turned to black as the implants' AIs determined that they had died, based on observed impact and also on where each shot had been placed. Most of the Nibirans had multiple Marines firing on them simultaneously.

With most of the Nibiran insurgents laid out, either dead or dying, Raptor and Mike closed like a fist and initiated cleanup.

***

Po and his team were among the first to reach the bazaar, and so they got to see firsthand the fresh gratitude on the faces of the Marines they'd saved, who had their visors up to greet them.

"Look at that," a fellow corporal said, grinning toothily as Fireteam Echo filed in, with Delta not far behind. "A crowd of angels come to save us. I'd kiss you, if you weren't a bunch of big smelly Marines."

"Won't be necessary," Po said. "Did you lose anyone?"

The corporal's face fell. "Three dead, five wounded. We've had bad luck. One of the Marines they killed was a corspman, and another corspman's wounded. It's just Gupta left, and he's got his hands full."

"Our corpsman's right behind us." Po switched to Second Squad's channel, not wanting to waste time to set up a two-way. "Drobnic, get up here! We need you."

"On my way," the Slovenian said.

"Two of the wounded are up that way," the corporal said, waving toward the north. "We were spread pretty thin, trying to keep them from getting in here with us."

Po nodded. Soon, Second Squad's corspman was inside the covered marketplace, helping see to the injured Marines. As he worked, Po's eyes wandered down the broad tunnel that stretched northward.

Both walls were covered with goods—everything from fabrics, to knitted garments and dolls, Adelqo jerky, and wooden toys—right up to where the wall began to curve to form the arch of the ceiling. Up there, arched, open-air windows perforated the tunnel every couple meters or so. In between, patterned fabric runners spanned the ceiling from wall to wall—mostly royal blue, but segmented by white and red chevrons at regular intervals.

Seems like a tactical nightmare. Those windows looked ripe for tossing a grenade inside—or launching one. Indeed, not far down the hall, a fabric vendor's wares were on fire, with many of them already burnt to a crisp. So far, the neighboring stalls hadn't caught fire, but that could change.

"Sergeant, suggest we move out of here as soon as we can," Po said over the platoon-wide. "I'm thinking the insurgents would love nothing more than for us to bunch up together in here." He fed what he was seeing through to Rowe, so he could see for himself from his rearward position.

"Yes," Rowe said in his clipped, perfunctory manner. "Agreed. Let's make that happen."

Before long, Drobnic and the other corspman, Gupta, had the injured Marines stitched up enough to get medevaced out by one of the gunships. 131st's First Squad stayed behind to secure the LZ and make sure the injured and dead were safely collected, but the rest of Raptor pushed north through the tunnel, along with the platoon they'd rescued.

They met up with Mike Company where they were guarding the northern two entrances along with the remainder of the platoon whose bacon they'd pulled out of the fire. Now that the platoon was freed up, they joined both companies in pushing north, to the next major position where Marines were pinned down.

***

The fighting for Valta's streets was fierce, and the enemy clearly knew the terrain better than the Marines did.

They took casualties, but by rescuing the pinned-down groups of their brothers, they swelled their ranks, slowly becoming a small army. Insurgents still took pot shots at them from concealed locations, but after losing their third RPG operator to a rifleman before he could get off a single round, they seemed to grow more cautious.

After liberating their third group of Marines, the joint force was becoming far too large and unwieldy, especially since the streets were narrowing as they gradually pushed northwest. Captain Haldane gave the order to split up, with Mike veering off north and Raptor continuing as they were, and the remainder pushing due west.

It was a good order, and a necessary one. Po didn't blame Haldane for not foreseeing what came immediately after.

Insurgents began pouring out of houses, in numbers unmatched by anything they'd yet fielded in Valta. The first surge they encountered, Po and his squad were driven into a warehouse across the way, thankfully finding access to the rooftop quickly and holding back the mounting alien tide from below and above.

Just like that, *they* were the ones pinned down and waiting for rescue. Po took up a position on the corner of the warehouse roof and began suppressing two different enemy positions at once. It wouldn't have been possible without the help of his Circuit warning him whenever a Nibiran at the position he wasn't covering popped up to take a shot. When they did, he quickly shifted his muzzle that way and drove them back down with a burst of rounds. Thankfully, neither position seemed to realize he was dealing with both of them at once, as they didn't seem to make any effort to coordinate with each other.

The gunships in the area—five in total—were ordered to start patrolling the city's outskirts, firing warning shots from above at any Nibirans attempting to enter from the surrounding roads. But the insurgents were still coming from somewhere.

There must be tunnels. Valta wasn't like Gomorate, which was built on rock, and where Janus operatives had *still* managed to appear where they shouldn't have been.

This city was far more vulnerable to that type of infiltration. Since Raptor and Mike had arrived, Po doubted the enemy would have had time to dig tunnels from far enough away to escape the Marines' notice. But there could easily be existing tunnels, which had never come to the Marines' attention. In his experience, the locals weren't exactly forthcoming with humans, and for the most part they also seemed to live in abject fear of Janus.

The sense Po got from the planet's natives was that they knew the Marines would be gone one day, and Janus would still be here. Helping the Marines was viewed as opposing the insurgency, which would almost certainly mean death—if not now, then later, when the Marines finally left Nibiru.

"We like the stability you bring," a Nibiran had told him back in Gomorate, who he'd chatted with using his implant's translator. "It's nice. But you don't belong here. One day you will leave. As for Janus...Janus is rising."

That wasn't supposed to be true any longer, with the death of To'sheth Rin. Killing the insurgent leader was supposed to be like cutting off a chicken's head. Sure, it might run around for a while after, but in the long-term, without it the creature couldn't operate.

Are we looking at a headless chicken here? Or something else?

This didn't *seem* like the flailing of a doomed animal. It seemed much more like a cobra that had been waiting for its prey to drop its guard before going for the kill.

But if Janus wasn't in its death throes, then what had been the point of coming to Nibiru at all? What had they actually accomplished?

Captain Haldane's voice spoke into his mind via the implant. "Marines, I have some news. The first ship assigned to clean orbital debris and exfiltrate Marines has just arrived. It's currently positioning itself in geosynchronous orbit over Valta to lend us a hand. It can't help fight, since firing from orbit would likely take us out too. But it'll give us eyes in the sky. The ship is one affectionately known by some of you as the S.S. *Gear Issue.*"

Whooping came over the squad channel at that. Po exchanged glances with Taylor, who was positioned a little farther down the rooftop, to his left.

The other Marine risked taking his eye off his scope long enough to look at Po and grin through his de-polarized visor.

"Hear that, Abbato? The good ol' *Gear Issue*'s back!"

Chapter 5

The *Gear Issue*'s arrival was a game changer. The word was quickly disseminated that, in addition to a major laser upgrade for the purpose of clearing the millions of pieces of debris created by the satellites' destruction, the building-turned-ship had also been outfitted with a state-of-the-art orbital recon sensor suite.

Back in Psyche, it had never occurred to Po to wonder just how granular modern image systems got, or whether a satellite could monitor someone from orbit, since on the station where he'd grown up nothing had ever been far away enough to affect its visibility. He vaguely remembered a bootcamp class on the topic, but he'd apparently somehow managed to zone out for it, despite Sergeant Doyle's extensive efforts to hold his and his fellow recruits' attention.

As it turned out, sensors had advanced enough to enable high-resolution video of practically anything that happened on a planet's surface, even from high orbit. After the battle, Po became interested in how that was possible, and found that his implant held all the information he should have been paying attention to during Doyle's class.

According to it, the *Gear Issue*'s new system approached the theoretical limits of what an optical system could achieve, which involved a 100-meter-diameter dish antenna with uniformity of shape down to the nanometer, affixed to an ultra-sturdy frame equipped with actuators to adjust the dish's curvature.

But on the ground in Valta, with insurgents firing on him from multiple positions, there was no time to dive down the rabbit hole of orbital surveillance systems. The basic upshot was enough: the *Gear Issue* could now tell them exactly which structures the Janus operatives were pouring out of.

Captain Haldane worked with the other commanders on the ground to quickly divvy up targets between infantry units and the five AC-900s, and they got to work. The *Gear Issue*'s arrival also afforded them a more complete picture of where Marines were deployed, filling in the gaps that had been unavoidable when they had only daisy-chained Circuits to rely on.

The trusty ship's crew wasn't being stingy with their intel, either. They granted access to every fireteam leader, and Po quickly picked out a roaming platoon six kilometers north-north-east of the warehouse where they were pinned down—currently unengaged and with a clear path to Second Squad's position.

"Sergeant Rowe," he spoke over a two-way channel. "Looks like 9th Platoon could do good work by coming south and helping us flank the Janus that have us pinned here."

"Acknowledged. I'll contact their commander."

Within minutes, 9th Platoon was on its way.

Now we just need to hold out.

But Delta and Foxtrot were doing good work on the ground floor securing the warehouses' ingresses, while Echo pulled out all the stops from the rooftop to keep surrounding enemy positions suppressed. Krikorian was using his M126 sniper rifle to make any insurgent who lingered in the open regret it, and Po had brought his grenade launcher to bear, using his Circuit's telemetry to arc rounds into windows and behind walls. Taylor and Hill were patrolling the rear of the warehouse with their M37s, their eyes on the alley that ran behind it, where no hostiles had yet dared to show themselves.

Then 9th Platoon arrived, and promptly engaged the largest insurgent position from behind. That made all the Janus in the area scatter, freeing 131st's Second Squad to start hunting again.

How quickly the battle for the city turned from there was a testament to just what a devastating blow Janus had struck in destroying their satellites during the battle for Eremus.

Once we get a few more ships in orbit, we'll own this planet again.

But what the actual result of that would be, Po was a lot less sure than he'd been even just a few weeks ago. What purpose would it serve to own a Nibiru-sized hornet's nest, whose occupants were getting angrier and more murderous with each passing day?

Humanity couldn't let Janus take power on Nibiru—the threat to the system at large would be too great, especially with their apparent ties to the Emplor. But how long a war would they have to fight to stop that from happening? In the end, each Marine victory only seemed to anger and radicalize the planet's civilians, driving the insurgency's recruitment. It felt like every Janus they killed was replaced by ten more.

Could a war like that ever end?

***

They began withdrawing from Valta almost immediately upon retaking it from the insurgents.

The decision had a lot of Raptor Company men asking what the point of the op had been. The point was obvious, of course: to save the garrison that would have been overrun without their help.

Even so, leaving the city felt like its own defeat, and it was prompting broader questions about the war on Nibiru as a whole.

"What's it all for?"

Po heard more than one of his platoonmates say something along those lines.

"What's the point?"

Plenty of Valta's residents seemed happy enough to see them go as they turned out to watch the Marines line up and file aboard their gunships for exfil. That was to be expected—but the ones who made leaving hardest were those who looked at them with fearful and even tear-filled eyes, who held their children close as Po and his brothers left, and who didn't leave the LZ even as the gunship took off and flew out of sight. He knew, because he watched them through the AC-900's exterior sensors until the plaza fell out of view.

They know what comes next. The Marines had left a vacuum in Valta, and power abhorred a vacuum. Janus would be only too happy to step in and fill it.

It quickly became clear that both Raptor and Mike companies were slated to head into orbit, which seemed to mean Po would once again find himself aboard the S.S. *Gear Issue*. The revelation led to more questions, at least it did for him:

Why couldn't they have left for orbit straight from Valta? Wouldn't that have conserved more fuel?

But he knew as well as anyone how pointless it was to question Corps logistics.

No one had yet revealed where they were actually going, but Po found he already had enough to think about while he waited to find out. He'd been on Nibiru for long enough that it had become his reality, and as the gunship took them back to Gomorate, he thought back over everything he'd experienced here.

Ranging out from FOB Longhorn on patrol, then returning to base to eat like kings and feel invincible.

Corporal Richards' and PFC Gregory's capture, and their broadcast execution.

The assault on Eremus that had provoked.

The destruction of the Marines' satellites...and the unending sense of danger and uncertainty that had followed, like the mother of all rug pulls.

FOB Longhorn's fall...and their salvation at the hands of a company of Gomorati Army soldiers.

The battle for Gomorate.

And the long hunt for To'sheth Rin. The hunt that had taken Corporal Young and Zapletal from them.

And Paisley, for that matter.

Rooting insurgents out of their cave base to liberate Ara Darshim. Infiltrating Karakata, and the disaster that had followed. Finally, tracking Rin down in his underwater lair in Morati Firth.

Returning to Gomorate.

And now, this.

Looking back at it now, with the knowledge that he'd soon be leaving it all behind—knowing, or at least hoping fervently, that he'd never look at anything by Gnara' ghoulish light again—the memories all blurred together to form a single, months-long nightmare. A relentless exercise in killing, and almost getting killed.

Humans weren't meant to be subjected to the horrors of war for this long, he knew. In the normal course of things, Marines were usually rotated out before this level of combat fatigue could set in.

But Nibiru hadn't *been* the normal course of things. They'd been fighting for their lives here, from the moment the satellites had gone down.

Without warning, he began to tremble, like he had after the fight with Paisley, except worse. He did his best to stop himself, and his cheeks burned as he wondered if the others could see. He decided the SERAPH suit was probably masking it. Which was good, because he couldn't stop. It was as if his body was processing all at once the trauma he'd undergone these past months.

***

More details came out shortly after their return to Gomorate—about their departure, and about where they'd be headed next.

Apparently, the capital city would become the main staging area for the Marines who'd remain on the planet. Structures were already being rebuilt with the help of Nibiran builders, to serve as more permanent facilities for housing and feeding Marines and for storing and maintaining hardware like Torres tanks, APCs, and AC-900s.

The population of Gomorate was staying surprisingly stable. Plenty of civilians had fled the city before and after both battles for it, and more were leaving with the revelation that the Corps had chosen Gomorate as its main base of operations. But that also seemed to be attracting a raft of new residents, who were finding accommodations throughout the city at prices that ranged from cheap to free. These Nibirans seemed to be fleeing Janus, and were probably hoping for the Marines to stay a good, long time.

More of them would come, Po knew. But he did wonder how well they would be served by their decision, in the long term.

During the days leading up to their departure from Nibiru, Fireteam Echo was intercepted by Ara Darshim while patrolling the lower streets. With some hesitation, Po called a halt. Technically, he was supposed to make himself available to Gomorati residents who needed his help. He just wasn't sure his superiors would think chatting with Darshim counted.

"Ara," he said, his head still on a swivel, and his rifle held at the ready. "How have you been?"

"How have *you* been, Po? What happened in Valta?" She wore a hooded red cloak, with her face cast partially in shadow.

He grimaced, which the Nibiran couldn't see, since his visor was polarized. Come to think of it, he had no idea how Darshim had identified him. *Maybe she's learned to recognize my walk. Or the particular way my suit has been banged up.*

He was hesitant to reveal intel to a Nibiran, even Darshim, who'd led him to To'sheth Rin. But he supposed the events in Valta were no secret.

"We nearly got steamrolled," he said. "But we pulled it off in the end."

"Most of your brothers were saved?"

He nodded. "Yeah. Most."

"I am glad for it." Darshim's eyes fell to the ground, and she remained silent for several long moments. Po checked the time on his implant, trying to gauge when it would start sending him prompts that his team should be farther along their patrol route.

"We've become too reliant on you," she said at last, meeting his eyes once more.

"Oh? Well, I guess you're happy to see us pulling out of this planet, then."

"No, actually. Without you Marines here, the government will crumble. The Gomorati Army will fail. And Janus will take possession of this planet—their designs fulfilled, at long last."

"Not if people like you stick together, Ara. Not if you work toward a better future."

"Please do not offer me empty words. You humans have created a monster, here. You've given Janus the pretext to fill its ranks like they've always dreamed of. You've driven thousands of Nibirans into their arms. The Army cannot deal with what has arisen. And as I said, the government has already become too dependent on you. When you depart, the cracked and hollow shell you leave behind will collapse on itself."

Wow. Would it kill her to show some positivity? "We're leaving men behind to *train* your soldiers, Ara. We'll teach them to fend for themselves."

"You will have your work cut out for you. The Army is still riddled with traitors, and many of the rest are lazy ones who believe in nothing. If they're not lazy, they're incompetent."

Po tilted his head to one side. Based on what he'd witnessed of the Gomorati soldiers, he found it difficult to disagree with her.

"Where will you go?" she asked him.

"That's need-to-know, Ara," he said softly. "Do *you* need to know?"

"Hm," she said, and then threw herself against him without warning, extending her furred arms around him as far as they would go.

Awkwardly, he hugged her, patting her back while being careful not to do it too hard. Interacting physically with unarmored beings was always a little risky, while in the SERAPH armor.

"I will never forget you, Po Abbato. I will always remember you as the human who saved my son. Calik will know all about you, once he reaches the age of understanding."

Sometimes, I'm still not sure I've reached that age myself. "I'll remember you too, Ara. I hope Calik does better than I did, without a father in his life. But considering how mine is, he might be better off without one."

"How can you say such a thing?"

"Uh—sorry." His cheeks flushed. "Just—just don't lose hope, okay? There's always hope."

She pulled back, peering at his darkened visor from beneath her cloak's hood. "How do you know that?"

"I don't, actually. But a friend of mine does. His name is Navarro. Maybe...maybe you should talk to him, before we go. He's resting up in the field hospital."

"Maybe I will. Po...can I see your face? One last time? Perhaps I will have it carved, someday."

He stiffened. "You can see it," he said slowly. "As long as you promise *not* to have it carved in anything."

Her eyes widened. "You are an odd individual, Po Abbato! Very well. I do promise."

He lowered his visor, and she stared at him solemnly, for longer than felt comfortable.

Finally, she nodded. "Yes. Your face is etched in my memory, now, and your name will ever ring in my ears."

His teammates had begun to snicker over the team channel. He ignored them.

"I'll...uh, I'll miss you too, Ara."

She held up a hand. "Farewell, Po Abbato."

He held up a gloved hand back. "See ya, Ara."

Chapter 6

"Zhang, so help me, if you don't get out of my way I'll clock you one in the jaw."

The Chinese Marine turned to blink down at Taylor, whose hands were balled into fists as he waited for enough people to leave the head for him to finally reach one of the sinks to wash his hands.

Po was fighting down the urge to laugh as he tried to decide if Taylor was tall enough to effectively punch Zhang in the jaw. "Calm, Taylor. You've got nowhere urgent to be."

Taylor's head snapped toward him, his lips a tight line, but he said nothing.

"Zhang, can you shift over a bit for him?" Po asked.

"Sure thing." The hulking Marine turned sideways in line for one of the urinals, and Taylor managed to squeeze past him.

"See?" Po told him. "Problem solved."

No one seemed happy to be back aboard the S.S. *Gear Issue*—not even Taylor, who had always loved her dearly. Everyone was on edge as they left Nibiran orbit.

Memories were fresh of the day Janus had destroyed three warships in orbit over the planet, along with every single satellite. That had been accomplished with missiles launched from concealed facilities on Maw, and while the higher-ups assured them the moon had been thoroughly searched before they sent Marines back into orbit, no one truly believed it.

At least we have plenty to distract us.

Three warships was a lot for the System Fleet to lose, and on top of that, RUMINT said GEA was getting increasingly nervous—what with the recent nuclear threat from the moon, Janus on the rise on Nibiru, the Emplor gradually revealing themselves as an adversary, and even the Allies of the Kuiper Belt making some noise, apparently. And so, the Council of Hegemons had pulled most of their warships back to Earth, to watch over humanity's homeworld from orbit.

That meant there weren't nearly enough ships to allocate to getting Marines off of Nibiru. Which in turn meant only a lucky few got actual berthing compartments, while everyone else had to make their racks in cargo bays, escape pods, between rows of seats in the auditoriums, and even next to live munitions.

Raptor Company found itself bedding down at the end of a dead-end corridor, pretty close to a well-trafficked one. And "bedding" was a strong word—especially considering that, for the most part, they didn't have any. Marines were rolling up utility trousers and shirts to use as pillows, and that was about it. What was more, a couple officers had their offices nearby, and their comings and goings might as well have been a herd of stampeding Adelqo to a bunch of hair-trigger Marines fresh from months in a combat zone.

To round out the morass that morale had plummeted headlong into, every enlisted man was operating under the assumption that they were headed straight for Emplora, whose orbital space the hyper-advanced alien species that lived there had warned humanity never to violate. As far as anyone knew, they would be among the very first to be tossed into what seemed certain to prove a meat grinder, and no one was particularly happy about that either.

"Does this chow seem strangely good to you?" Krikorian asked in the mess later that day, around a mouthful of butterscotch pudding he'd just squeezed past his lips from a tube.

Po narrowed his eyes as he squeezed his own pudding down his gullet. The tubular desert was the sort of thing you'd expect to get in microgravity, even though they were still accelerating. But the steak and eggs he'd just polished off definitely *hadn't* been your typical shipboard fare.

Generally, good chow was a cause for happy Marines, but it wasn't hard to tell Krik wasn't happy.

"Yeah, it is pretty good," Po said slowly. "Why?"

"Hasn't anyone told you that the better they feed you, the worse a death trap they're about to throw you into? Think how good the chow was back on the moon, before they packed us into *Gear Issue* to send us to Nibiru."

Po thoughtfully depressed the last of his pudding onto his tongue and swallowed.

"Huh," he said. The theory did seem sound.

Across from him, Gomez was staring warily down at his own tube of butterscotch, as though it had become a snake and he was trying to decide whether it was poisonous or not. The Marine was still suffering some aftereffects from his brain injury, but apparently the docs had promised he'd be fully recovered by the end of the voyage.

Ever since the trip from Cycler 3 to the moon, the *Gear Issue* had had a proper crew of spacers, unlike the ill-suited jarheads she'd suffered to operate her during her maiden voyage. During the journey to Nibiru, the Marines and Fleet personnel had seemed to basically understand each other, but since picking up the Marines at Nibiru, the spacers seemed to treat them with a mixture of bewilderment and fear.

Po thought he might know why. Fighting Janus by the angry red light of Gnara for as long as they had, most Marines had acquired a certain wild quality. Many of them spent too long making eye contact, or staring at the bulkhead, or into space. Others had a glint in their eye that said they didn't care whether they saw the end of the day or not.

A change had come over them, and there was nowhere it was more obvious than in the gym, where the Marines' brutal approach to sparring gradually drove the Fleet personnel out of all shipboard martial arts competition. Po didn't hear any of the Marines comment on their exodus—none of them seemed to care. They just carried on with their overly exuberant matches, physically working out neuroses they'd picked up on an alien planet, while the spacers relegated themselves to the sections with free weights and strength machines.

Po regularly caught Fleet personnel staring at him like he was a caged Emplor, or one of the Scourge, or something. They quickly averted their gaze when Po returned it. One morning, he asked a petty officer what he was looking at.

He hadn't meant it to be as threatening as it sounded. But the spacer quickly answered, in a strangely squeaky voice: "Nothing! Sorry." With that, he turned to perform a rapid exit down a side corridor.

In a past life, Po might have felt bad for scaring the poor guy. But at this point, his emotional barometer was pretty much busted—at least, when it came to normal human interactions. The graph of his feelings had all but flat-lined. Outside of a combat zone, it seemed he just took everything in stride, with the same flat affect and lack of reaction. He wasn't sure whether his detached state of mind would wear off or not as his memories of Nibiru receded.

Probably it won't, if they're throwing us at Emplora. Probably I'll be numb like this for a good long time.

That, or I'll be dead.

As it turned out, the Corps *wasn't* throwing them at Emplora. Or rather: GEA wasn't.

But that still didn't adequately describe the situation. The full picture was that *part* of GEA was throwing *part* of the Corps at Emplora...but as it turned out, the jarheads aboard the S.S. *Gear Issue* had lucked out. They wouldn't be among those sent to violate the Emplor's orbital space.

Not yet, anyway.

"The truth is, GEA is fracturing," Colonel Tuffin said as he paced back and forth along the edge of a tarmac platform, beyond which a sea of fluffy, golden-brown clouds stretched to the horizon. There, a thin haze gave way to the star-strewn vault of space, with the sun outshining all other lights. "The Global Equity Accord has always been composed of disparate factions united only by their lust for power. But like the elites of any society throughout history, they mostly distrust each other, and each one stands ready to drive a blade into his fellow's back the moment he judges the risk low enough and the payoff high.

"Why am I saying this to you? Well, who are you going to tell? Your Circuit severely limits your access to the system nets, and even if you wanted to relay your CO's frank assessment of GEA to the public, it would detect the topic and prevent you from posting it in real time. Sure, you could blab about it when you finally get out, and you probably will, to whoever will listen. Problem is, beyond your fat, middle-aged loser who spends his days skittering across the nets' bloated underbelly, posting and consuming conspiracy content, no one *will* listen. No Earther, anyway. An Outer might, but they don't need much convincing about GEA anyway, so it'll be status quo all the way down."

Prior to this briefing, Colonel Tuffin had ordered every enlisted Marine aboard the *Gear Issue* to sit or lie somewhere secure, where they weren't likely to have to move out of some spacer's way. Ten minutes later, he took over their Circuits and brought them to this simulation, which looked suspiciously like a set of bleachers set up near the side of one of Venus' cloud cities.

Although, if it was a real cloud city, then in real life they wouldn't all be able to sit out here without some sort of suit on, not to mention a breather, since Venus' atmosphere was mostly CO2. But of course, in a sim anything was possible.

Tuffin had also removed their ability to talk using com channels, so that they'd only be able to ask questions by raising their hands, or chat with their actual neighbors inside the sim. And Po couldn't help noticing that neither the Marine on his left nor his right belonged to his company. That was probably by design, to cut down on the chance of men chattering while Tuffin was talking. Not that anyone was likely to do that anyway. Every

Marine Po had ever discussed Tuffin with had seemed to have the utmost respect for the colonel. And right now, he figured everyone here was particularly interested in what he had to say.

"But I digress," Tuffin said. "I didn't call you here to talk politics, or to stare at pretty clouds. Suffice it to say that there's been some infighting within GEA concerning how to react to the revelations that have been stacking up, about how us and the Emplor maybe aren't the besties we thought we were. While the Emancipation Doctrines are still going strong, even as the aliens' betrayal leaks out to the public as though through a sieve, some on the Council of Hegemons seem to think we should throw the entire Corps at Emplora, while others consider that a bit reckless.

"Would we win if every Marine hit the Emplor at once? I honestly have no idea. But that's not what has some people in GEA worried. What's more concerning is the unrest that's been cropping up on Venus, which is not exactly known for instability. There was that one time the AKB took over one of the cloud cities, but that was an isolated incident. As a rule, the rich folk living on Venus are fat and happy, and even the grease monkeys who keep everything running are well-paid. Every job that might have been low-paying enough to make someone irritated was long ago given to a bot.

"And yet, there's been trouble. First, it was malfunctions in life support, which might have been explained away by bad luck, incompetence, or neglect. But the more they cropped up, across multiple colonies, the more suspicious they became. And by the time the 'spontaneous' fires started, followed by the outright explosions, everyone began to feel pretty sure someone was up to something."

That brought a few snickers from the Marines, but for the most part everyone was still too engrossed in what Tuffin was saying for humor.

"And if there *are* bad actors on Venus—sophisticated actors, with access to sensitive areas, not to mention resources, and spread across multiple floating colonies—well, it's not a stretch to imagine such an enemy might be able to set up a launch facility on one of them, for sending missiles into orbit. From there, they could easily strike targets *near* Venus. Such as, for example, a System Fleet ship full of Marines headed toward Emplora. When the Emplor's rogue planet conveniently barreled into our system to get caught on our sun's gravitational pull, it settled into an orbit nestled just underneath Venus'. And as it happens, the two bodies are drawing nearer each other. Starting in five months' time, there'll be a period of about four months where terrorists launching from a Venus cloud city would have a pretty easy time reaching out and touching Emplora's orbit, even with a relatively primitive missile system.

"*Why* would such a group help out the Emplor like that? Who knows. But the aliens have already proven to possess allies in unlikely places, so it seems...*prudent* to resolve the situation on Venus first." Tuffin gave them a tight smile. "Like I said, there are geniuses in GEA who'd like to send every available Marine at the Emplor right now, even in spite of what's been going on in Venus. Thankfully, more level heads have prevailed, and you people drew the right lots. At least for the time being, you'll be heading to sought-after Venus instead, there to play hide-and-seek with some terrorists and be generally hated by the locals, who consider jarheads hanging around the neighborhood harmful to their property values. And hey, who knows, maybe you'll even get some leave. Any questions?"

Chapter 7

It was still hard to accept he was finally off Nibiru.

After the constant stresses of combat, reality had assumed the quality of a dream. Plenty of his fellow Marines complained about the cramped conditions aboard *Gear Issue*, but Po didn't really care. After everything he'd endured on the alien planet, being stuffed on a spaceship hundreds of billions of miles away from everything felt like the lap of luxury.

But it *was* his reality, and there was one implication of that reality he found increasingly difficult to escape:

He could write Nicky, now.

She'd written him. Multiple times. Not long after boarding the ship, his Circuit flooded with her letters—short but fervent pleas for him to write as soon as he was able. To let her know he was safe. In them, she said she knew about the war on Nibiru, and about the destruction of the satellites in orbit there. But she didn't seem to know that their destruction would have prevented him from sending the payments he'd been sending back to Psyche prior to Nibiru. Instead, the conclusion she'd drawn was that he was injured or dead.

He started writing a reply, multiple times, over the months-long trip from Nibiru to the cloud cities of Venus. But he could never bring himself to write more than a sentence or two before deleting what he'd written.

Every time he tried, images of his father poured out of his subconscious: first, of him sitting beside Nicky's bed, just as Po had once done—accepted back into the Abbato family like nothing had ever happened.

Then came the memories. Of Luca sending Po's mother against the wall. Of him shaking Po until his teeth rattled when he said something about it. Of Marco crying.

Stuff like that.

And when those memories came, he just couldn't fathom how Nicky could accept Luca back into her life. How any of them could.

I wonder if he's started hitting them yet. I wonder if he's reigning over them like the tyrant he is, all while the admins turn a blind eye. We were lucky to get him put away the first time. There might not be another chance.

So he didn't send Nicky anything back. The memories made him too enraged to put anything together. What he did do was resume the crypto payments to Rosa's account, starting with a big lump sum to make up for all the payments he'd missed on Nibiru.

The idea that Luca might get a hold of that money, or Lorenzo, kept him up at night. But he couldn't not send it. Not when his sister's sickly face surfaced in his mind's eye, momentarily blocking out all those memories of grief and rage.

It was enough to let them know he was still alive. And it was the most he could bring himself to do.

***

"Zhang?"

The big Marine started beside him, then looked at him. "Yeah, Po?"

"Were you asleep?"

Zhang grinned. "Yeah. I think I was."

Po stared at him for several seconds. "Bro...we're heading into Venus' atmo."

"Oh. Cool." He closed his eyes and rested his head back against the seat.

"Zhang!"

The Chinese jolted again. "Yeah, what?"

"Open up a window in your implant and check this out. This might be the only time you ever to get see this!"

"Ah. Right. Okay." Zhang's eyes fixed on a point in the air in front of his face.

Po furrowed his brow as he studied the other Marine for several seconds more, which he didn't seem to notice.

He has to be the only one on the shuttle who wasn't watching this.

Shaking his head, he returned to watching the golden-brown orb as it slowly grew larger, and more and more detail became visible. The planet looked like it was shot through the middle with lightning, except the 'bolt's' angles were softer than that, and less angular. Smaller instances of the swirling 'lightning' were visible all around the main one.

The patterns were created by varying densities in the clouds that covered the entire world. Some spots were a dark brown, while others, like the lightning patterns, approached white. At the very top of the planet, the clouds formed what looked like a sickly smiley face.

He felt almost hypnotized by the planet as it blossomed before him, becoming more intricate the closer they drew. Soon, it filled the entire sensor's view which he'd patched into. And not longer after that, the shuttle began to tremor with greater and greater violence as it plummeted deeper into the atmosphere.

Po had done some reading about Venus on *Gear Issue* during the dull moments between drills, briefings, and working out. As far as extraplanetary bodies went, Venus was apparently the easiest on fuel when it came to reentry, thanks to how its thick atmosphere facilitated aerobraking. That, combined with its proximity to the sun, made importing goods cheap. Unfortunately for Venus' economy, the reverse wasn't true. The climb out of the system's gravity well was more expensive. On the other hand, the atmosphere was mostly carbon dioxide, which could be captured and converted into propellant. So he guessed it evened out.

The shuttle dove into the clouds, which enveloped it completely, so that the orange miasma was all that could be seen from any of the shuttle's exterior sensors.

"Pretty cool," Zhang said. His eyes unfocused, indicating he'd closed the window.

"Zhang, people pay millions to live here."

"Hm."

***

Thanks to the clouds, there was no view to be had of Aeolia on approach, though Po saw plenty of 3D representations after, on deck-to-overhead murals scattered throughout the colony.

As it turned out, the sim Colonel Tuffin had brought them into on the way here was a lie, in more ways than one. There was no colony in existence that you could stand on the edge of and stare up into space from. Each floating balloon colony on Venus was completely enveloped in billowing, orange-brown cotton candy.

Every day was overcast...but that didn't mean the colony wasn't stunning. The Teflon-coated, liquid silicone rubber dome rose to over four hundred meters at its apogee, and the sky was a roiling shroud lit by countless lights suspended from the colony's metal superstructure, which were programmed to follow a day-night cycle.

The colony, which some people (especially its inhabitants) called the unofficial capital of Venus, was a proper city. It was shaped like a perfect circle, with a downtown core complete with skyscrapers, which gave way to suburbs, commercial districts, and industrial districts, with greenspaces running all along the twelve-and-a-half kilometer circumference.

Gravity was a comfortable ninety percent of Earth's, but anyone not up for walking could use their implant to rent one of the scooters or motorcycles docked in neat rows at evenly spaced charging stations. The vehicles swept through the streets silently, like ghosts, but Po had the opportunity to learn that they *did* emit a shrill beep when about to hit someone—the pedestrian didn't actually get hit, since the onboard AI brought the thing to a pretty quick halt.

There were also a number of satellite colonies, which rode Venus' high winds in formation with Aeolia, in case residents felt like taking a day-trip to enjoy their various offerings and getaways. Airships ran on a schedule to ferry people back and forth between them, with one-person and two-person craft also available for rent.

Everything looked like it had been built last week—every surface polished to a gloss and clean enough to eat off of. Though, for a Marine to say that wasn't saying much.

All the same, even the lowest-income residences looked immaculate. In size and aesthetics, they screamed unbelievable luxury, especially compared to anything anyone lived inside of back in Psyche. Each neighborhood here was perfectly cultivated with evenly spaced trees, and an occasional breeze even ruffled their leaves. Po had no idea how they accomplished that.

Unfortunately, none of the luxury seemed to extend to the Marines. Every jarhead who stepped off the shuttle was immediately granted leave, since arrangements for their lodgings had apparently fallen through approximately two minutes after the shuttle touched down in one of the landing bays, which extended off the city proper.

Colonel Tuffin was now apparently "working out new accommodations" with Aeolia's admins, but as far as anyone could tell, these admins belonged to one of the GEA factions that believed every last Marine should have been sent straight to Emplor.

Po and his brothers were ordered to leave their weapons aboard the shuttle, and then, in not so many words, to go find something to occupy themselves in the city. Preferably nothing that would disturb the locals.

As it happened, the mere sight of uniformed Marines walking around their streets seemed to disturb the locals deeply. The Marines would have been wearing plainclothes, except none of them had expected to be granted leave the second they stepped off the shuttle. Aeolia's residents openly gawked and glared at Po, Taylor, Krik, and Zhang as they strolled around the shining boulevards.

For their part, Po and his brothers gawked right back.

Because of Aeolia's size, all of Raptor Company had been stationed here, but Po knew smaller units had been sent to dozens of other floating colonies. He wondered if they were running into the same treatment they were.

"Too bad we didn't bring civvies," Zhang said.

Taylor snorted. "Why?"

"The people here don't seem to like our cammies."

"Who cares? They can learn to like 'em. We're gonna be around for a while."

"I wonder how long our 'leave' will last," Krikorian said. "Seems like it could be days."

"Ever think you might get sick of leave?" Taylor said.

The Armenian shrugged. "Without a rack to lie down in, shouldn't take long."

"I'm sick of it already," Po said, returning the glare of a well-dressed elderly woman who'd had too much cosmetic surgery, at least in his opinion. It gave her an unnatural look, he thought, unsuited to her age.

The only ones to greet them warmly were the bots that could be found on practically every street—and Po liked that even less. They reminded him of the touchy-grabby cop-bots back in the asteroid colony he'd grown up in, bringing back memories of them chasing down petty thieves and tackling them brutally to the ground.

"Good evening, sirs," one said, who was holding an actual broom while sweeping a plastic bag into a dustpan attached to a hinge at the end of a stick.

"Shut up," Po said.

"Absolutely," the bot answered. "I'll keep quiet until your next instruction. In the meantime, if you need anything, just ask."

They continued toward downtown, wandering aimlessly, and looking for an excuse to spend some credits. It had been so long since any of them had had the chance to actually buy anything—other than back at FOB Longhorn's MCX, not to mention aliens selling weird Nibiran stuff from their stalls—that Po figured they were a pretty easy mark for anyone interested in making some money.

But instead, they found something to hold their interest that was completely free. It was a public park nestled in a deep bowl, the bottom of which was transparent, so that the swirling clouds were visible below. It felt like they were walking on vapor, and it was enough to hold their attention for the better part of an hour as they walked the park's paths, which wound around cultivated gardens with oak and cherry trees that reared from their midst, casting dappled shadows on the thick orange-brown mist below. They could also see dark cylinders that extended below the colony's floor, which Po concluded each housed a tree's roots.

He found himself staring into the endless swirling beneath his feet, wondering how long it would engulf him if he were to break through the floor and fall through it.

Taylor challenged Krik to a race around the park, and Po and Zhang watched them, Po with amusement, Zhang with a strange look of wistfulness.

"Hey, Po," he said. "Thank you for including me today."

"Including you?"

"Yes. For bringing me along."

Po shot him a look. "We're just killing time, Zhang. They don't have anywhere for us to stay."

"Yes, but back in Shackleton, you and the others went out without me. I think because I was too boot. After I got kept behind in bootcamp."

Po felt his cheeks reddening. *Kept behind after getting injured saving me.* "None of us are boot now, Zhang. Not after everything we've been through. We're brothers now, thicker than blood. Nothing can change that. So of course you're with us today. You're family."

The size of the grin that sprouted on Zhang's face after Po said that only made him feel more awful about ditching him when their battalion was stationed on the moon.

"I didn't *do* anything!" a man yelled from somewhere to their left, abruptly slicing the park's ethereal peace to ribbons.

"Stop resisting," a bot said in its bland voice, like a carved-wood table with all its interesting features sanded off. "You are charged with attempting to incite violence. Stop resisting."

"I'm just going to visit my mother. You don't have any proof against me!"

By now, Zhang and Po were jogging toward the altercation. By the time they reached the scene, the bot was pumping tens of thousands of volts into the man it had accused, using its built-in TASER. An agonized cry tore from the man's throat as he sunk to his knees, and then fell forward onto his face. A few other pedestrians, two men and a woman, had been passing on the street when the confrontation began. Now, they were backing up against storefronts across from the park, the color draining from their faces.

"Hey," Po yelled at the bot sternly. "You didn't give him a chance to explain himself."

What he and Zhang could do against a cop-bot without any weapons, Po didn't know. But all the old anger was resurfacing, from how brutally the bots had policed him and the other residents of Psyche when he'd lived there. It surprised him, how hot that anger still burned, on seeing it happen again before his eyes.

The bot ignored him, since it was busy jerking the man's hands behind his back and slapping a pair of restraints onto his wrists, which snapped shut automatically.

"Stop resisting," the bot said, even as the man was still spasming from the electrocution. It grabbed his neck from behind and slammed his face into the asphalt.

"*Hey!*" Po yelled, stepping forward with his fists clenched.

"He is a disturber of the peace," the bot said, rising to its feet, facing Po. "He is inciting violence."

Without warning, the bot turned to face the civilians cowering against the storefront, then began to stride toward one of the men. "You are attempting to incite violence," it said in its not-quite-human voice, a quality Po had heard was by design, to instill uncertainty in anyone who interacted with the cop-bots.

The man held up his hands. "No I'm not—what are you talking about?"

Like lightning, the bot's hand darted toward the man's neck, and with that he was sinking to the ground too as current caused his body to shudder and jerk.

Krik and Taylor ran up, Krik holding a pickax in one hand and a shovel in the other, while Taylor held a rake and a spade.

"Some gardener left his tools in the park," the Armenian said, tossing Po the shovel while Taylor handed Zhang the rake.

Taylor gestured toward the bot with the spade he now held in both hands, even as the cop-bot was advancing menacingly on the woman as she backed away from it, hands held in front of her.

"Shall we engage in a little reprogramming?" the Marine asked.

"Sounds good to me," Po growled, raising the shovel and stepping swiftly toward the bot.

Chapter 8

Po swung the shovel with all his might, putting his weight into it and anticipating where the bot's dome would be by the time he followed through with the shovel's head. The tool hit the bot's cylinder with a satisfying *clank*, sending it staggering sideways a moment before it would have reached the woman.

It caught itself against the front of the store, deftly whirling around to face Po before using the glass to propel itself at him. Po shoved the shovel's haft sideways at the bot to fend it off, but the thing grabbed it in both silicon grippers.

His strength was no match for the bot's, and his arms yielded steadily as it drove the shovel handle toward his face.

That was when Krik's pickax swung overhead to puncture the thing's shoulder plating, immediately causing the wiring and circuitry underneath to spark.

Krik wrenched the pick toward himself, yanking the bot with it and causing it to lose its grasp on Po's shovel. He immediately readjusted his grip and started jabbing his adversary in the face with the tip, but he couldn't get a good angle to do much damage.

The bot twisted sideways, yanking the pickax from the Armenian's grasp and causing it to become dislodged from its shoulder, to fly into the storefront window, which cracked.

Not bulletproof, then. It was a strange detail to note in the middle of a fight, but he'd found that the more time he spent in combat, the more his detached mind was able to absorb.

Taylor advanced on the bot, jabbing at it with his spade in an apparent effort to drive it back. It wasn't deterred by the attack in the slightest, not even flinching away as Taylor's strikes rained down on its face. Instead, it stepped inside of the Marine's reach, grabbed him by the front of his pants and the neck, and flung him clear across the street and into the park, where he landed in a heap.

Roaring, Zhang rushed at it with his rake, driving the butt toward it. But in a blur of motion, the bot sidestepped, grabbing the handle and pulling, which caused Zhang to stumble forward. As soon as the big Marine came into range, the bot swung an arm, batting the Chinese away and sending him reeling back across the lane, to land on his hands and feet.

Krik was coming up behind it with his recovered pickax, and he swung it even as the bot started turning to confront him. Too late—the pick found the place where the bot's back met its neck, biting deep into its torso. It twisted, but Krik still held on, even though his feet skittered across the pavement with the effort as he was shifted back and forth by the bot's thrashing.

"Now, Abbato!" Krik yelled.

Po didn't need a second invitation. He brought his shovel down on the thing's face as hard as he could. A high-pitched whine emanated from it, and he repeated the act. The bot seemed to be having trouble raising its arms to block—maybe Krik's second attack with the pickax had damaged its actuators, or something. Either way, its movements grew more and more sluggish as Po continued to dent its face and head, creating rents that emitted sparks and fluid. At last, it was moving only feebly, and Krik tore his pickax free, causing the bot to fall over onto its back. With that, the Armenian proceeded to savage the thing with the ax end of the tool, all up and down its torso.

"Okay, Krik," Po said after a couple minutes. "I think it's, uh...dead, or whatever."

"I want to make sure." The Armenian drove the ax into the bot's torso once again.

"You've made sure. Now knock it off."

Krik extracted his pickax from the thing, still holding it at the ready and eyeing the felled machine warily. By now, Zhang was standing nearby, and Taylor too, though he was cradling one arm in the other.

"Now what?" Zhang said.

Po pressed his lips together. "Now, we get to see how the admins feel about us after we did that." He gestured toward the bot with a knife hand, a tic he'd picked up from Sergeant Mitchell back in bootcamp. Something caught his eye, and he redirected the gesture. "Look."

The others turned, and Krik's and Zhang's fingers tightened on their makeshift weapons. Three other bots were approaching from down the street, but nothing about their demeanor suggested they were acting erratically, like the other one had.

Yet.

As for the people the rogue bot had terrorized, they'd already picked themselves up and cleared off.

***

After hearing Po's account of the cop-bot's erratic behavior, the newly arrived bots' AIs were apparently smart enough to know not to arrest the Marines on the spot, since something unusual had clearly gone down.

They *did* insist on the four Marines accompanying them to the central security station. "If you do not comply, you will be arrested," the bot standing closest to Po said.

It took a few hours of sitting around while bots stood by to make sure they didn't go anywhere, followed by questioning by some admin's aide who was at least an actual human being. More waiting followed that, before the conclusion was finally arrived at that something unusual had indeed happened—and that Po and his teammates had been justified in intervening as they had.

With that, they were released.

"That was the finest example of bureaucratic redundancy I've ever seen," Taylor said as they left the station to walk down a street at random. "And I used to *work* for an admin."

"Seriously?" Krik asked. "You worked for an admin?"

Taylor nodded. "Back on Psyche. Until I was caught deleting surveillance files on residents they deemed dissident. *Then* they decided I'd make a much better Marine. Well...after a couple months of simjail, they decided."

As they walked away from the station, their implants were automatically released from the locks the bots had put on them, which had prevented any signals from being received or sent. With that, a message popped up in Po's vision, from Gunny Emery to all of 131st Platoon.

Apparently, during their hours at the station, accommodations had finally been found for the Marines at some warehouse in the southeast. A blue line appeared in his vision, showing him the most efficient route to Emery's location, accompanied by an order to head there at once.

When they arrived, they found their lot hadn't improved much from the sleeping arrangements on the *Gear Issue*. Saggy-looking cots were arrayed around the perimeter of a dusty storage room. Emery stood near the end of the room. Marines of 131st Platoon were arrayed around him, some leaning against bulkheads, others sitting on cots or on the deck.

"Ah, you're here," the gunny said when he spotted Po, Taylor, Zhang, and Krik filing in through the entrance.

The rest of the platoon turned and broke into applause, led by Emery.

"You're clapping...because we beat a bot with gardening tools, Gunny?" Po asked when the applause started to die down.

"We're clapping because *you're* why we have somewhere to sleep," Drobnic said, grinning.

"Huh?" Zhang said. "How?"

"It was only after you took out the rogue bot that we managed to convince this geothermal company that maybe having Marines around isn't such a bad thing after all," Emery explained. "They're feeling the unrest as much as anyone. And they know it's bad for business. If people end up leaving the cloud colonies—and the exodus *has* already begun—then their customer base shrinks. So they lent us the use of this warehouse where they keep replacement parts."

Po shrugged. "Makes sense, I guess."

"The Corps already has a presence here on Venus," Emery continued. "We have our own floating bases here, with locations not publicly known. But we don't typically show up in the civilian colonies. That's what's rubbing these rich people the wrong way. Thing is, that's *their* problem, not ours." He pointed toward Po. "What Fireteam Echo did is exactly what I want the rest of you doing. Patrol Aeolia's streets. Look into anything that seems strange. Ask questions. Do what needs to be done. We have a battalion of Marines headed for Eremus as we speak, which means we don't have time to mess around. If there's a threat here to our brothers—if there's a chance someone might launch missiles at that ship full of Marines—then we need to get to the bottom of that, fast, and put a stop to it before it begins. In the meantime, we'll be training in crowd control, because our intel says to expect riots any day. There's already another city on the other side of the planet that's in chaos as we speak.

"Unfortunately, chaos isn't limited to Venus. We got word while we were on approach to this city that back on Nibiru, Janus is more active than ever—littering the roads with IEDs, attacking our supply lines, and using guerilla tactics to hit our outposts and keep everyone on minimal sleep. They've taken out plenty of Gomorati Army assets, too. We all know what it means for Janus to take Nibiru...a lot more risk for the rest of the system.

Meantime, on Earth, Lebanon's managed to install another rogue government, and at the same time, Venezuela's managed to get it together enough to start causing GEA trouble. It's possible the EPA can handle it, but it also wouldn't surprise me if Army calls uncle and admits to their bosses they need the Marines to come in and clean up the mess. The Corps could get called to deal with any of these crises, at any point. So don't get too cozy. Consider this your vacation—and enjoy it as much as you can."

Taylor raised his hand.

"Go ahead," Emery told him.

"Our platoon's full of holes. All of Raptor Company is. Are we gonna start collapsing units, or are we getting some replacements?"

Emery smiled. "Funny you should ask that. We can expect to get our first infusion of boots, fresh out of bootcamp, by the end of the week. I'm sure you'll all help them feel right at home."

***

It felt good to be inside his SERAPH suit again, especially after the fight with the bot. Other than a handful of exercises he'd taken part in at the squad, platoon, and company levels while aboard the S.S. *Gear Issue*, he hadn't worn it since they'd left Nibiru. But with how cramped the ship had been, the drills they could reasonably schedule had been limited. Either way, he always felt more confident inside the suit. There was more he could get done, wearing it. And it commanded a lot more respect, even from Aeolia's hostile residents.

Regs said they couldn't wear the suits off-duty, and for the most part, he wouldn't want to...except that no one trusted this place. As a result, most Marines just hung around their so-called barracks during their time off, playing cards, pranking each other, or messing around on their implants.

Based on what Po experienced on patrol over the next few days, stopping the rogue bot hadn't endeared them to the local populace as much as they might have hoped. Glares still followed the Marines wherever they went, and most residents refused even to speak to them. But at least no one yelled at them. Certainly not while they were wearing their suits.

Of course, it was also possible most people in Aeolia hadn't heard about the incident with Fireteam Echo and the berserker bot. The admins in charge all seemed against the Corps, and it would have been fairly straightforward for them to suppress the incident.

Po had heard the admins were being pretty tight-lipped about where that particular bot had been manufactured, and they also wouldn't let anyone from the Corps look at its code, with the justification that its protocols were proprietary to GEA. Never mind that the Marines *worked* for GEA.

The admins of Aeolia obviously wished the Marines would go somewhere else. They'd also clearly been ordered to tolerate their presence by a higher-up in GEA—one who wanted them here. But the admins didn't do much more than tolerate them. And that, barely.

Maybe the admins' stonewalling them about the bot meant nothing. Maybe its going haywire had been a random, isolated incident, unconnected to anything. But Po tended to doubt it, and he wasn't alone. Either way, it was the only lead they had so far, and no one knew how much time those Marines headed toward Emplora actually had.

And so, with Zanth nowhere to be found, Po turned to the man who'd helped him the last time they'd dug up intel about the Corps' enemies, back in Shackleton Colony.

As much as he hated to, he turned to Navarro.

There was no privacy to be had in the supply-room-turned-barracks—at least one off-duty fireteam or two was always hanging around. So Po contacted Navarro using his Circuit's private messaging function.

"*Hey. Navarro.*" His eyes were on the other Marine's face.

Navarro's eyebrows shot up. "*Po. It's been a while.*" The flat reconstruction of his voice wasn't quite in line with his facial expression, though it was *kind* of close. "*You finally ready to believe me that you were imagining those things back on Nibiru?*"

"*I didn't imagine a thing. I have footage of you harassing that FOBBIT. And calling me scum.*"

Navarro paused. "*Wait, seriously? Then someone overwrote your Circuit. Because I'm telling you, that never happened.*" He shook his head slowly. "*Po, if you think you have footage of that happening, then we have bigger problems. We need to figure out—*"

The message continued, but Po wasn't listening. His attention was on the door, which had just opened. Gunny Emery was stepping through.

"The day has arrived, Marines," Emery said. "Raptor Company's new members are here. Abbato, I believe you're already acquainted with one of them."

Another Marine stepped past the gunny, his eyes locked on Po.

Po stiffened, then automatically rose to his feet, staring back at the new arrival.

Standing beside Gunny Emery was Lorenzo Abbato.

Po's brother.

Chapter 9

"You're off duty, so why don't you show him around a bit?" Emery said, a little less enthusiastically than he'd spoken before.

He saw how I reacted to it being Lorenzo. Po swallowed, then forced himself to walk over to his brother and extend his hand. "Welcome aboard," he choked out. "Brother."

Lorenzo grinned, his eyes glinting the way they had a million times, growing up together. "Glad to be here." He spread a hand toward the corridor behind him. "Won't you lead the way?"

"Gunny," Po said with a nod toward Emery, before leaving their berth, such as it was. Lorenzo followed close behind.

They walked in silence through the warehouse proper, which was bisected with great, rearing shelves stuffed mostly with spare parts for geothermal power plants.

Take away the gravity, and this could be the Equipoise warehouse where the cop-bots got me.

He normally avoided thinking of Psyche whenever possible. Except, it was difficult not to, with his brother behind him, stepping so close to him that he walked on the back of Po's boot a couple times.

There was a decent chance that was intentional, but Po ignored it. He'd learned to ignore plenty of things, during his time in the Corps.

How well did you *learn in bootcamp, Lorenzo?*

"They assigned you to 131st Platoon?" Po asked the moment they exited the warehouse into Aeolia's outskirts, without looking at his brother.

Lorenzo quickened his pace, until he was walking level with Po. "Nah. 129th."

A quiet sigh of relief escaped Po's lips. "Then why did Gunny bring you to our berth?"

"I dunno," Lorenzo said, grinning toothily. "Because we're brothers?"

Po didn't answer, and they walked in silence for several blocks through the industrial park, as it gradually gave way to more aesthetic neighborhoods.

Aesthetic or no, there are bots in every part of this city. The bots made him more wary than they ever had, even the ones not assigned to security. Seeing more of the system—and experiencing some things no one should have to—had given him some perspective on certain things, even though he'd never been looking for it. It had also made him more attuned to potential threats.

"Did you hear about the bot going rogue?" Po asked, his voice coming out tighter than he'd meant it to. His instinct definitely wasn't to be *nice* to Lorenzo, or to *help* him. It was to stand ready for attack. That was what he'd learned to do, during the years and years they'd spent together.

"A little," Lorenzo said. "That was you, huh? That took it out?"

Po nodded. "Me and my fireteam. Most of the guys don't leave the barracks now, during leave. No one wants to be caught out without their suit on, when the next bot goes nuts."

"And yet, here we are."

Po spun toward him, unable to contain himself any longer. "Weren't you a member of the Obsidian Angels?"

His brother paused for several long moments before answering. "I was *accused* of being one. But how did you know that?" he asked in a tone that was almost a growl.

"You were *convicted* of being one. Otherwise, you wouldn't be here. And there are a lot of things I know about. Like the letter you sent my instructors while I was in training, trying to get me smoked."

Lorenzo stopped in his tracks, in front of a highly cultivated soccer field. "Nicky told you. Didn't she? So she's been sending my dirty laundry out across the solar system."

"How is she?" It was the wrong question, and he should have known not to ask it. But hearing her name, spoken by none other than his own brother, sent a pang of worry and longing for his ailing sister. "How is she adjusting, to...to..."

"To dad getting released?" Lorenzo's grin returned, wider than before, though no more maniacal than the way he'd smiled during their shared childhood. "Oh, she's adjusting just fine, Po, don't you worry about that. I mean, the bruises *do* eventually fade, and once you've been smacked across the face enough times with the back of a hand, you *kind* of start getting used to it. Do you know what I mean?"

Po's entire body tensed, like a coiled spring. Lorenzo was trying to bait him, he knew. He was still trying to get him smoked—probably even discharged. And if he attacked his brother first, then Lorenzo would actually have decent grounds for getting that done.

But even knowing that, it took every ounce of Po's willpower not to lash out at him. Visions of pounding his face into the sidewalk danced through his head, and his eyes blurred and pulsed with his rage-quickened heartbeat.

As it turned out, Lorenzo was experiencing about as much hatred of Po as Po was of him, and he did him the favor of attacking first.

Without warning, his brother turned and rushed him, just as he had so many times when they were kids.

But Po wasn't a kid anymore. He deftly sidestepped, then executed a push kick as Lorenzo stumbled past, a move he'd perfected during Muay Thai matches with the other Marines aboard the *Gear Issue*.

Lorenzo recovered quickly, coming at him again. This time, Po sidestepped the other way, to deliver a low kick to his brother's shin. Envisioning his leg as an ax, he followed through, eliciting a cry of pain from his opponent.

Lorenzo crumpled, and Po soccer kicked him in the side, flipping him over. With that, he straddled him, and backhanded him across the face. Blood and spittle flew.

"Think you could get used to that?" Po snarled down at him. He raised a hand to pop his brother square in the face, and Lorenzo flinched.

But he didn't follow through. Instead, he stood and stared down at his brother, who stayed on the ground.

"Don't *ever* try that with me again," he said. With that, he walked back toward the barracks.

***

Gunnery Sergeant Emery sat on the opposite side of a wood-paneled desk normally used by some middle manager, Po imagined. The gunny was frowning across the desktop at him.

"I guess I shouldn't have brought your brother to you," he said. "I thought...I don't know." Emery shook his head. "Brothers are normally happy to see each other."

"Have you spent much time on Psyche, Gunny?"

Emery stared back at him blankly. Then, he shook his head. "Point taken, I guess." He sighed, loud and long. "Did you know I've been agitating to get you a Fleet Cross?"

Po blinked. "Huh? Me? Why?"

"Because you deserve it, after what you pulled off with To'sheth Rin. You did me proud, Abbato. You did us all proud. But this stunt with your brother...that's going to complicate my efforts."

"Gunny, are they going to discharge me? He attacked me."

"Well, you didn't seem all that reluctant to attack him back. Did you?"

"No, Gunny."

Emery pressed his lips together. "Realistically, neither of you are going to get discharged. The Corps is desperate for Marines, so the bar for getting fired is higher than it's even been. But you didn't hear that from me. In fact, you didn't hear it at all."

"Yes, Gunny."

"This will be characterized on both your records as just a squabble between brothers. Brothers *do* squabble, and you...definitely squabbled. Pretty enthusiastically."

Po nodded slowly.

"But you're in two different platoons, and if needed, your brother will be relocated altogether. But I'm confident that won't be needed. And I'm justified in that confidence. Aren't I, Abbato?"

Po paused for a few seconds. Then: "Yes, Gunny."

"Good. In the meantime, it seems we may have a lead on someone who can tell us where that bot came from that attacked you and your teammates. Guess who's being tapped to chase down that lead?"

"131st Platoon?"

"Good guess. But it's just Second Squad. We're not expecting a fight, and a full squad is probably already overkill. Better safe than sorry, I guess. I'll be commanding the mission."

"Sounds good."

"It's outside Aeolia, in what you could call a house boat. Floating alone out there on the sea of clouds. As you might guess, it's not exactly cheap to live in your own little cloud colony, and this is someone who's high up the corporate ladder of a local bot manufacturer. Apparently, he's concerned enough about what happened that he's willing to talk to the likes of us, against the wishes of the executives and admins who control the company he works for."

Po raised his eyebrows as he tried to remember the last time he'd heard of someone being that selfless. "Wow. Couldn't he get fired?"

"Easily. But sometimes, people really do make that kind of sacrifice for the good of others. That shouldn't come as much of a surprise to you, Marine."

Po thought about the quote Navarro shared with him, back in FOB Longhorn. About a true soldier fighting because he loves what's behind him, not because he hates what's in front of him.

Then, he thought about how he hadn't written Nicky.

What am I fighting for? he asked himself.

***

Gunny Emery wasn't expecting an engagement at the exec's house boat, but even so, Second Squad was sitting inside the shuttle in full SERAPH armor, all toting M37Cs and a few other toys besides. Po tried to imagine the look on their new contact's face when he opened the door to find fifteen hulking Marines, all armed to the gills.

But he supposed there would be no "answering the door"—a place like that had to have an airlock of some kind. Which realization helped him to realize just how much the gunny had meant it when he'd said this place wasn't exactly a poorhouse.

"Hey, Abbato," Gomez said over the Fireteam Echo channel. "You okay?"

"Yeah," Po said. "Why?"

"I heard your brother's one of the Marines filling in the gaps in Raptor Company. And he attacked you."

Po snorted. "Did *you* attack me, Gomez?"

"Huh?" Gomez furrowed his brow at him through his faceplate, looking genuinely confused. According to the doctors, he'd completely recovered from his brain injury. But it had still left him with some gaps in his self-confidence. "No. Of course I didn't."

"How about you, Krik? You attack me?"

The Armenian just grinned back at him. "Nope."

"Taylor?"

"Not this week."

Po didn't bother turning to the new Marine assigned to fill the gap in their team, Private Vacca, since this wasn't meant for him. Not yet.

"Did anyone in Second Squad attack me?" He looked at Gomez again.

"No," the other Marine said slowly. "I don't think so, at least."

"How about anyone in 131st Platoon?"

"They didn't. Did they?"

"No, they didn't. And that means that no brother attacked me."

"I'm still not getting it," Gomez said. "*Your* brother—"

"I have no brother that I trust more than the men on this team. This squad. This platoon. I would trust every single one of you to die for me, just like I'd die for you if it came down to it. That's a bond no blood can touch, Gomez. So, no. A brother didn't attack me. Just some idiot I know from Psyche."

Gomez was nodding, now. "Got it, Abbato. Glad you're okay."

Po grinned, and bonked the other Marine on the helmet with his glove.

The channel fell silent, and Po opened up a window to an exterior sensor, just to stare into Venus' perpetual orange fog. The shuttle pilot was guiding them to the exec's private residence using "dead reckoning," which was one of the things Emery had briefed them on before leaving Aeolia. It was a navigational method that used gyroscopes, magnetometers, and accelerometers, along with known data about their destination's last observed location, plus its speed and the distance it should have covered.

As it turned out, dead reckoning was the only way to find anything that floated inside the planet's thick clouds, since satellite signals couldn't get through them to make GPS function, and radar was useless too.

After learning that, Po understood the exec's willingness to help them a little more. If things went south for him, he could always just abandon the established course his personal floating island followed. Every floating structure on Venus, with the exception of Marine bases, was *supposed* to follow a course that was kept on the public record. But if one of them chose not to, who could stop them? Provided this exec had the supplies, and a good-enough water filtration system, he could stay off the grid indefinitely and probably never be found.

The trip only lasted about a half hour—for now, at least, the exec apparently kept his itinerant home pretty close to Aeolia. The shuttle first smacked against bumpers installed around the floating house's perimeter, then followed its edge until it found the airlock it was supposed to dock with.

The Marines exited into an atrium filled with leafy, tropical-looking plants and windows that began at the deck and curved over them to form the overhead. Through the fronds and leaves, the ever-present golden-brown miasma could be seen.

Second Squad was on high alert. There'd been no response from the occupant as the shuttle approached, despite their pilot radioing him repeatedly. And it was strange that he wasn't waiting to greet them at the airlock.

The floating home was spacious and luxurious, but it didn't begin to approach Aeolia's size. It took Second Squad less than five minutes to clear the entire structure.

It was even before that that they found the exec's body, dangling from a length of rope attached to the central shaft of a ceiling fan in the master bedroom, his face a swollen, blackened mask. It was protocol while clearing a structure to breathe only the oxygen they'd brought with them, and so they hadn't smelled the body's stench, which otherwise surely would have hit them like a collapsing wall the moment they stepped out of the airlock.

Chapter 10

Po was sitting at a bar next to Krikorian, in a place called Infusion. For Po, it was the first time he'd ventured into Aeolia's city center while off-duty, since the bot's attack. He was pretty sure it was Krik's first time since then, too.

They each had their hands curled around a pint of lager, which they were both nursing. They hadn't come here to get drunk, and anyway, their implants would tattle on them if they tried.

The cloud city had proven a dangerous place for Marines on the very first day they'd gotten here, with its abundance of bots that could apparently go haywire at any time. And with the 'suicide' of the exec who'd been about to spill the provenance of the rogue bot, Venus had only shown itself all the more dangerous.

The suicide had borne multiple signs of not actually being a suicide, such as the ceiling fan only being high enough to achieve a slow and torturous strangulation, and the lack of a kicked-over chair or any other object he might have stood on to do the deed.

It was a sloppy job, but pretty much everyone on Second Squad was in agreement, including Gunny Emery: the exec had been *suicided.* Someone had obviously identified him as a liability, intercepted his communications, and gotten to him before Second Squad could. And whoever had done it hadn't seemed all that bothered about concealing the foul play.

Po wasn't sure how far the news had spread through Raptor Company. But he knew several men in 131st Platoon were feeling desperate. No one knew how much time they might have to detect and thwart a missile attack on the *Magnolia*, the ship currently carrying a battalion of Marines ever-closer to Emplora. And no one wanted their brothers' deaths on their conscience, especially when they had a chance now to prevent them.

And so, he and Krik had asked around, till they'd managed to extract from a reluctant civilian that Infusion was one of their best bets for running into the seedier element on

Aeolia. Descending into the bar from the street, Po had quickly come to believe it. The place was low-ceilinged and dim, and at the bottom of the stairs the floor was sticky with a spilled beverage no one had bothered to mop up. Who knew what else the poor lighting concealed?

He leaned slightly toward his teammate. "Krik."

"Yeah?"

"That group in the corner. They don't look like meshminders to me."

Krikorian nodded slowly. "Agree. Too much personality."

The five men sitting around the corner table were as raucous as Infusion's clientele seemed to get—slapping each other on the back, elbowing each other, exchanging wry grins, and chuckling frequently, albeit fairly quietly.

"Think they could be AKB?"

"Why don't you go ask them?" Krikorian sprouted a wry grin of his own, to indicate he was joking.

"Honestly, I might just do that."

"Seriously?"

Po shrugged. "I'm not good at this sneaky, subtle stuff. And I'm sure they know what we are, anyway. Maybe the direct approach *is* the best approach."

"If you say so. Want me to come over with you?"

"Nah, I don't think. I want to look as non-threatening as possible. Just keep an eye out."

"I got your back."

With that, Po slipped from his seat, taking his pint glass with him, which was still about half-full.

The group's eyes were on him almost from the moment he left his bar seat. Their gazes didn't leave him as he crossed the room, and by the time he'd reached them, they'd all fallen completely silent.

"Is there room for me?" he asked, nodding at the bench seating that ran along the wall.

"What do you want, Marine?" asked the man sitting farthest from him, who wore earrings and a goatee that tapered to a point, which looked sharp enough to be dangerous.

"I want to know if any of you would like to enlighten me as to who's behind all the unrest on Venus. There was a riot a couple weeks ago in Laputa, on the other side of the planet. Word is it nearly brought the city down. Do you want that to happen here? Or would you like to help me prevent it?"

"How do you figure it's your business?" a woman asked, whose hair was styled in tendrils that seemed to defy gravity as they emanated out from her head.

Po glanced over his shoulder at Krik, who nodded. He stepped closer to the man on the end of the bench seating. "Move in, would you?"

With obvious reluctance, the man shifted down, and Po took a seat at the table. He leaned over it, his hands folded.

"We have a ship full of Marines who are going to be within missile range of Venus' cloud cities pretty soon. We're afraid that if a bad actor creates enough chaos, they'll be able to launch missiles from a platform somewhere in the clouds."

"We aren't the ones causing the riots, Marine," the first man said. "If you're smart enough to know who *we* are."

"I think I have an idea," Po said. *AKB. Allies of the Kuiper Belt.*

"Hopefully you do. Because I'm not going to say it out loud. But you just tell your other superiors that we aren't to blame, for any of this. Tell them to leave us to our business, and we'll leave you to yours."

"Then who is responsible?"

"GEA."

Po screwed up his face. "Huh? GEA is inciting violence against GEA?"

"Elements within GEA. To cover something up."

"What?"

"Don't know for sure. But you ask me, it's something to do with the bots. Something strange is going on there."

You're telling me. "Anyone you can introduce me to, to help me get to the bottom of it? So you and your friends can enjoy...peace, here in Aeolia?"

"I'm not introducing you to anyone, Marine. Get going. Just tell your officers to leave us be."

He beheld only stony faces, now, and he could tell the conversation was over.

"All right, then. Thanks for the information."

None of them answered. Po returned to the bar, where Krikorian looked at him expectantly. "Well?"

Po shook his head. "We've gleaned everything we're going to, here. Better move on."

"Got it."

Krik stood, and they headed for the exit together.

***

They headed further into the center of the city then, delving deeper into Aeolia's downtown in search of another establishment they'd managed to learn about, called Gala Gala. It seemed like an odd name for a bar where the city's underbelly went to drink, since as far as Po knew, a gala was a big fancy party for people like politicians and corporate executives.

Maybe the name is a joke.

"You sure we shouldn't just head back to barracks?" Krik asked as they drew nearer the block where Gala Gala could apparently be found. "I could see word spreading pretty easily that there are two Marines in plainclothes walking around asking questions. Could attract the wrong kind of attention."

"I'm sure we *should* head back," Po said. "And I'd go to my rack right now if it weren't for those Marines aboard the *Magnolia*. What if our positions were switched around, and we were on that ship headed to visit the Emplor? Would we be happy to learn two Marines went to their racks and slept instead of chasing down every lead they could?"

"When you put it that way..." Krik grumbled.

They came to the street where Gala Gala was supposed to be, but wasn't. Not that either of them could see. They walked back and forth together past restaurants and closed down shops, but they all had clear signage, and none of them proclaimed themselves Gala Gala.

"What about that alley there?" Po said, nodding between a shuttered antique store and a coffee shop whose staff were still inside, tidying up after close.

"Seriously?" Krikorian said. "We're going to head down a sketchy-looking alley in search of this place? This keeps getting better and better."

Po shrugged. "That's probably where it is. Seems appropriate. And I'm sure the two Marines that took out To'sheth Rin can handle themselves against whoever might be lurking down that alley."

The Armenian shook his head. "Fine. Lead the way."

Po stepped into the darkness between the buildings, wishing for his SERAPH suit's night vision function. His eyes gradually adjusted to the dark, and he saw that the alley took a sharp turn to the left up ahead. Trying to act more certain than he felt, he walked confidently toward it.

Around the corner, the alley took another turn—this time to the right. A weak, flickering light came from that direction, painting faint shadows on the back of the building to Po's left. He turned to check Krikorian was still with him. As far as he could see in the dark, the other Marine returned his look with an unimpressed expression.

Po headed toward the next corner and came to a stop. There was the flickering light, above a solid-looking black door with a handle. But in front of it stood a hooded figure walking purposefully toward him. *Straight* toward him.

"Can I help you with anything?" Po said.

The figure didn't answer. He just kept approaching.

"Hey!" Po yelled, putting his hands up. "Stop where you are."

The figure didn't stop. He drew close enough for Po to see his face was a featureless white plane—he was wearing some sort of mask, the same color as the hooded sweater he wore.

Without warning, he charged.

Po was immediately put on the defensive against blows that were perfectly placed to disarm him and get past his blocks and dodges. The second jab landed on his jaw, causing starbursts to spring to life in his vision, as everything else went blurry and he stumbled back. Thankfully, he managed to keep his footing, and Krik was already there, rushing past to engage their assailant.

The other Marine got a similar treatment as Po. The hooded and masked man knew exactly where to apply force to defeat anything Krikorian threw at him.

Then, it hit Po:

He's with the Emplor.

"Krik, we gotta get out of here. We can't beat him." Po yelled this as Krik was getting kicked in the solar plexus and sent sprawling onto the ground, wheezing.

Po grabbed him and helped him to his feet, then supported him as they stumbled backward together, the figure advancing on them all the while.

For some reason, he didn't charge again. And when they made their way back around the first corner, he didn't follow.

"Let's go," Po said once they made it back to the street. "Keep moving. I doubt he'll show what he can do out in the open." *He's sure to be caught on some security feed if he does. And then the admins might start asking uncomfortable questions about him.*

Assuming the admins didn't already know about him.

Krikorian gradually recovered as they made their way out of the downtown core and labored through increasingly residential streets, toward the barracks.

"Abbato," he said after a long period of silence. "My implant doesn't have any footage of what just happened. It just shows us walking into that alley, standing there for a bit, then walking out again."

"Yeah," Po said flatly. "I thought that might happen."

***

As it turned out, they weren't the only ones to be attacked in an alleyway that night.

One of the new replacements had gotten separated from his fireteam during a patrol, and had cut through a back alley in an effort to try to quickly rejoin them, where he figured they'd be.

He never made it out the other side.

Instead, he was found lying on the ground—what remained of him, at least—his SERAPH suit shredded like tissue paper, along with his arms and torso.

He was a bloody mess, his body almost unrecognizable as a human's. Except, his face had been left completely untouched.

His implant, of course, had been wiped. There was no evidence of who or what had killed him.

"*Seems we got off lucky,*" Po messaged to Krikorian when Gomez relayed the news to them. "*Though, whoever did this couldn't have been the same guy that charged us. Right?*"

But Krik wasn't in the mood for chatting. Instead, he sank slowly to sit on his rack and stare at the bulkhead across from him, his face as expressionless as the mask worn by the man who'd attacked them.

Po decided to follow suit, lying down atop his rack fully clothed to stare at the overhead.

This city was beginning to seem like a microcosm of the entire system. Utterly divided, with factions working against secret factions, and unrestrained killers wandering the night.

The system is too big for this kind of disunity. That's what this shows. As awful as GEA is, at least when they were at their most united, and their most tyrannical, they imposed a certain kind of order on things.

Po had no idea who was truly in charge, anymore. Here in Aeolia, or on Earth, or in the system as a whole.

The only thing he knew for sure was that everything appeared to be coming apart at the seams.

Chapter 11

I didn't need that second coffee.

Truly, he hadn't needed *any* caffeine at chow. He'd barely had any appetite to eat, and so he'd just poured two mugs into a nearly empty stomach, with nothing there to absorb the caffeine apart from his bloodstream.

Now, on patrol, the caffeine buzzed in his head and made him twitchy. It put a tense knot at the base of his throat as he clutched his M37C tightly and closely monitored his surroundings in every direction.

At least the suit's plethora of sensors, paired with his Circuit's functionality, allowed him to continually check behind him and to either side without swinging his head wildly like a panicking Adelqo. To an Aeolia resident casually observing Fireteam Echo pass by, Po might even look calm.

But he wasn't. Far from it. Almost, he wished for the detached numbness that he and his brothers had experienced for most of their trip on the S.S. *Gear Issue*, from Nibiru to here. But while that deadness brought about by their long months of endless combat had mostly passed, the trauma remained. The memories. The hair-trigger reactions that had been burned into his neuronal pathways.

Loud sounds brought him back to the fall of FOB Longhorn, where rounds had snapped and cracked overhead. Or to Karakata, where RPGs had taken out his brothers just meters away from him—where it seemed mere chance had been his only protection.

Now, it took tremendous restraint not to swing his rifle's muzzle at a resident who made an unexpected amount of noise, even one who shouted at a friend from across the street, or the one who dropped a folding chair she'd been about to take into her residence.

If he pointed his weapon needlessly at a civilian here, he'd have a lot more to answer for than he would have if he'd done the same thing on Nibiru. But he hadn't had the urge to do it on the alien planet. Here, his impulse was to shoot anything that moved suddenly.

I need to get a grip.

And he believed he *would* have had a firm hold on himself, if it hadn't been for the profound sense the system was falling apart. What was more, there were agents out there—especially right *here,* in Aeolia—for whom he was no match. People like Paisley, or whoever had attacked him and Krik last night, who obviously had Emplor jacked into their implants and ready to show them exactly how to defeat Po.

Zanth had often complained about Po's reluctance to buy completely into what the alien was selling. To sign off on an agenda he didn't even fully see. Or to fully embrace the Emancipation Doctrines.

If he *had* fully embraced all that—if he became Zanth's willing pawn—then he knew he would have reliable access to the same power wielded by the two men who'd defeated him, in Valta and in Aeolia. *They* had clearly sold themselves to their Emplor handlers. Something in Po resisted that...but he was also becoming more and more certain that if he failed to do it, then Zanth would arrange for his disposal, like faulty product. He felt fairly sure Paisley's and the hooded man's attacks had been warnings of exactly that.

The Emplor popped into existence then, and Po jumped.

"You good, Abbato?" Taylor asked.

Po's heart was hammering in his chest, and he forced himself to speak slowly and levelly. "Yeah. I'm good."

The Emplor was walking just in front of him and to the left, as though he was not only part of the fireteam, but leading it. He walked in silence for several long seconds, before finally turning his reptilian smile on Po.

"This life has accumulated more days since last we spoke," the alien said.

Po didn't answer. Just focused on putting one foot firmly in front of the other.

"I wonder if we'll be paired in the next life. Think of the things we might have the opportunity to accomplish then." Zanth shrugged. "Of course, if we don't avail ourselves of the buffet of *this* life, we shouldn't be surprised at all to find ourselves starving."

"*What are you talking about?*" Po said at last, typing his answer into the messaging app without actually sending it, to minimize the risk there'd be any record of this conversation. Of course, if Zanth wanted there to be no record, there would be none. He'd simply overwrite Po's implant. And chances were, the Emplor didn't desire to be revealed to Po's superiors.

"The same thing I talked to you about on Nibiru, of course. After your shuttle went down. Don't tell me you've forgotten."

Po remained silent once more. He had no idea how he should handle the Emplor. He didn't want to end up like the boot who'd gotten his innards shredded.

"Allow me to refresh your memory: the universe is a divine being which desires its own self-actualization. To prosper as a cell within that being, you must yourself achieve self-actualization. This involves partaking in the sensual of every experience available to you."

"*How about driving nails through my eyeballs? Is that something the divine being would like me to experience?*"

"Of course not." The Emplor shook his head, looking disappointed. "It is your *appetites* that show you what you should seek to experience next. If you see something you want, you should take it. That is what satisfies the divine mandate. You must honor your impulses." The alien fell silent for several long seconds. "I suppose it shouldn't surprise me that you've forgotten these basic principles. You've probably lost the ability to remember anything, lacking the implant footage to look back on."

Again, Po opted for silence as he considered the alien's words. He had to be careful. He still didn't know whether Zanth himself was an enemy, even as his species increasingly revealed itself as one. That was mostly because he didn't know what Zanth truly wanted, or whether it was good. And if it *was* good—then, good for whom?

"You can have everything you desire, Po," the Emplor went on. "And it is good for you to have the things you desire. Stature. Rank. Power. But you've been working against the plan, and you need to stop that. If you don't, then you won't achieve anything except ruin. Trust me on this."

"*Whose plan?*" Po asked. "*The divine one? Or the Emplor's?*"

"They are one and the same."

"*The Emplor have been acting a lot like our enemy.*"

"I've told you already," Zanth hissed. "The Emplor are not unified. Indeed, some of them hate each other. But overall, we are all cells in the divine being, and we are each of us in our own way working to lead humanity to a better, freer future. A future in which each human being can satiate his own appetites without restriction. A future in which every one of you can revel in the fullness of experience."

"*Just tell me what you want, Zanth. What you actually want.*"

"Simple. I want you to stop your meddling, here on Venus. You don't know what you're interfering with. We both need to be pulling in the same direction on this."

"*If you're asking me to work against the orders I've been given, you can forget it.*"

Zanth stopped walking and turned to face Po, yet he still remained at the head of the patrol as it went along, his clawed feet skimming just above the paved street. "Do you deny me?" the Emplor said, his voice growing deeper, more scratchy, and shot through with anger. "So be it. You will continue to suffer at the hands of those much wiser than you. You have chosen ruin and death, and death will come swiftly, I promise you that."

The alien vanished from Po's sight. All around him, everything looked the same. The Marines walking behind him, Aeolia's gleaming buildings, its perfectly paved and cultivated streets.

But inside Po raged a storm of uncertainty and dread.

Had he chosen rightly? Or had he been a fool to reject what the alien offered him?

Had Zanth been a friend or an enemy? And if he'd been an enemy all along, in what ways might he have been attacking Po without him ever realizing it?

I'm safe on patrol, he told himself. *Armed, and walking with my brothers.*

I'll be safe sleeping in the barracks, too. The sentry will wake us, and then we'll all rise up to kill anyone who comes to take my life in the night.

It won't matter how well they fight, then. They can't defeat all of us.

If only he could make himself believe it.

***

Ever since the day Janus had hit Cycler 3 and killed hundreds of his brothers, there was a thought that Po sometimes found himself turning over in his mind when he couldn't sleep:

Is it necessary to hate the enemy to fight them?

Sure, maybe it was useful to hate them. The powers that be seemed to think so—especially governments from hundreds of years ago. Humans had often been encouraged to hate the other humans they'd be fighting in a war, in ways that militaries today would never be able to get away with.

The results had often been horrific. Po had even read about one major war where Marines had kept the enemy's skulls as trophies, and the enemy had done even more gruesome things to them. Eventually, the officers put a stop to the trophy-keeping, but it still stood as a testament to the hating mindset the government had worked to instill in the warriors of that day.

These days, it was hard to get away with cultivating that level of anathema, even against aliens. At least, they couldn't get away with it *openly.* Before the war on Nibiru, GEA's long-standing position had been that humanity needed to recognize the Nibirans as siblings, considering they'd unknowingly shared a solar system for so long. That had probably been mostly intended to put a nice face on GEA partners moving in and extracting the planet's resources for shipping off-world, but still. It *did* make fomenting hatred against the Nibirans a little harder.

Of course, Janus had done a lot to help GEA out with that, first by attacking a bunch of trainees and freshly minted Marines in Cycler 3, and then by managing to come close to nuking Earth from the moon. Their campaign of terror had only intensified after the Corps arrived on Nibiru, and by that time, the Marines didn't need much help from their superiors in hating Janus—and by extension, the Nibirans in general.

When Po woke up in the Aeolia warehouse-turned-barracks to the news that the *Magnolia* had been destroyed by a missile barrage launched from Zoozve, Venus' quasi-moon, a multitude of new hatreds awoke inside him.

Hatred for whoever had been responsible—AKB, Janus, someone else entirely.

Hatred for GEA, who may well have done it themselves, or at least a GEA faction.

And hatred for the Emplor, who clearly had a stronger grip on the solar system than anyone had imagined.

GEA *had* at least launched intercept missiles, from two separate launch facilities hidden in Venus' cloud layer. Their control of the system, as fractured though it was apparently becoming, relied on maintaining launch sites all around the system in order to put a swift stop to anything they didn't like. But that only worked for threats GEA could see coming, and intercept in time. It was ineffective against—for example—a group of Janus terrorists smuggled aboard human ships to the moon, where they were trained and armed and funneled the resources to threaten Earth directly from its natural satellite.

It was also ineffective against the missiles fired from Zoozve at the ship full of Marines. The quasi-moon was simply too close to their target, and the intercept missiles had launched from too far away. Once their sensors detected the *Magnolia*'s destruction, they automatically flipped around and used their thrusters to decelerate into a heliocentric orbit, for eventual reclamation by a passing government ship.

Based on what Po had gleaned from his restricted access to the system nets—which was even more restricted here on Aeolia, where they had no actual connectivity and had to get their news from the data dumps delivered to the colony's networks multiple times a day—civilian populations everywhere were descending into a panic over the revelation that an enemy had managed to establish a secret launch facility on Zoozve. Apparently, a small protest had even sprung up in downtown Aeolia, which so far was peaceful, but being monitored by cop-bots.

Now that missiles had been launched from secret sites on both Maw *and* Zoozve, the idea was quickly cementing in the public consciousness that there was some *other* power that also had the capability to reach out and smack down things in the system it didn't like. So far, that had only included ships used to transport and support Marines. But who knew when that power might turn to targeting cargo haulers, or even cyclers with civilian populations?

GEA had managed to cover up the Marines' discovery of an underground nuclear launch facility on the moon, mostly because missiles had never launched from it. But it was impossible to cover up an actual missile launch from a place like Zoozve. Hobbyists had picked up on the event almost immediately and started spreading the footage on the nets.

What Po had been given to watch was official footage, recorded by military satellites. The Zoozve barrage launching, the missiles being fired from Venus cloud platforms to intercept them, the futile chase, and then the *Magnolia*'s destruction.

It made him mad, and hateful.

It made him ready to kill whoever had just killed hundreds of his brothers.

But even as his rage mounted, he still couldn't stop himself from wondering, prompted by a small voice from the back of his mind:

Why had his superiors been so careful to supply them with such a clear and detailed view of the missile attack, complete with a zoomed-in, high-res view of the *Magnolia*'s destruction?

Couldn't the exact same information have been relayed as a short description in a briefing?

Then he remembered the Marines who'd carefully and diligently cleaned out their enemies' skulls as trophies.

Po's superiors wanted them ready to take skulls.

And looking around the barracks in the wake of the footage being given to them—seeing the rage burning slowly behind expressions of quiet resolve, especially on the faces of the more experienced Marines who'd been with Po on Nibiru—it wasn't difficult to tell that they *were* ready.

So help us all, Po thought, unwilling to think about to whom he was directing the words, or why.

What did fill his mind, then, was the memory of the merc mercilessly beating a Nibiran civilian with the butt of his pistol, and no one stepping in to stop him—or even to reprimand him, as far as Po knew.

Following that: Paisley seizing Ara Darshim's unborn baby in its translucent orange egg, making ready to hurl it over a cliff.

It can't be wrong to feel angry over the murder of our brothers. But at the same time...we can't let it lead to that. *Can we?*

He was having trouble pulling the concepts apart, and making clear distinctions between them. Randomly, his eyes settled on Navarro, who he found was looking across the room at him.

Po shook his head, the corner of his mouth twitching as he pulled his gaze away.

Chapter 12

Until now, Colonel Tuffin had been restrained in how many fireteams he'd allowed to patrol Aeolia's streets at one time.

But in the wake of the *Magnolia*'s destruction, he removed all the limitations he'd imposed on each platoon's commander. Raptor Company flooded the city, every man itching for the barest excuse to fight—at least, that was how Po felt, and his brothers all seemed just as incensed as he was.

What rankled most of all, in his estimation, was that no one had anticipated missiles being fired from Zoozve. They should have, of course, after the hidden launch sites on Maw. But that had been far out in the system, orbiting an alien planet that until a few dozen years ago hadn't even been confirmed to exist.

It seemed all but impossible that any power could manage to establish such a facility on *Zoozve*. Not without anyone noticing.

Po tried to imagine the prolonged and subtle effort that must have required. He figured it had to involve small drones designed to land on the planet and drill down, constructing the launch facility and missiles using as many materials from the quasi-moon itself as possible. Anything else needed would have had to be sent in micro-shipments, distributed over a long period to escape notice.

But nobody seemed much interested in contemplating the "how" of it. It was the mere fact of it, and the shock, that most irritated the Marines in Aeolia. No one in the Corps had seen it coming, and now, an entire battalion of their brothers had been lost.

The city's residents responded to their increased presence with more resentment, and growing unrest. The downtown protests became an encampment, which the admins seemed uninterested in ordering their bots to clear out. The Marines weren't authorized to remove it either, and so it was left to fester and metastasize, becoming the source of all manner of marches and demonstrations that emanated out from it.

I wonder how long before the protests become riots, like in Laputa.

"The admins *like* all this nonsense," Taylor said. "Eventually, it'll get bad enough to give them an excuse to crack down even more. Give them more control."

"You learn that from your time working as an admin's assistant?" Krik asked.

"I learned that from having a brain. You should think about growing one." Taylor shook his head. "They'll let the agitators continue to agitate till the time is ripe. For now, it makes *our* stay in Aeolia a lot less comfortable, which I'm sure they also like."

Shouting matches broke out between Marine patrols and Aeolian residents, with vicious barbs traded and personal space invaded. The officers sent footage of one of the altercations to every man in Raptor company to watch, as an example of how *not* to deescalate an encounter with a civilian. But watching it, Po immediately sided with the Marines, and his fireteam all felt the same. Probably, every Marine in the company did.

And the temperature just kept on rising.

The third day since the missiles took out the *Magnolia*, Po got an idea, which he immediately recognized as one Zanth wouldn't like. It was the sort of idea that he knew instinctively would work directly against the Emplor's agenda. Which made it a terrible one, from the perspective of self-preservation.

It also made him really want to act on it, right away.

So he did.

"Stay here," he told his team, "and keep an eye out." With that, he walked up to a cop-bot monitoring the lane in front of an open-air farmers' market.

"Greetings, Lance Corporal Po Abbato," the security bot said. The Marines had learned a while ago that the admins had apparently programmed all the bots to address them by their full rank and names, probably to unsettle them with how much information on them the admins had access to—or maybe just to keep them on their best behavior.

I'm betting on the first one. He was pretty sure the admins *wanted* the Marines to lose their cool. That would give them more leverage against them.

"How can I help you today?" the bot asked.

"By showing me some ID."

"ID, Lance Corporal?"

"What's your registration number?"

"I don't have one."

"What authority are you registered with?"

"I am not registered with an authority."

"Then whose authority are you operating under?"

"I am not authorized to say."

Po stared at the bot, dumbfounded. He'd had some idea that he might get a response like this, else he wouldn't have asked the question. But actually hearing it was a different experience altogether.

"Will there be anything else, Lance Corporal?"

"No." Po slowly turned from the bot, his mind whirling.

No one ever asks the cop-bots for their ID. They just accept their tyranny as a fact of life. There's no point in asking for a registration number when the outcome will be the same either way. GEA, or the corporate partner they appoint to try you, will do what they want with you anyway. So having security bots registered to an authority is just a formality.

But they were *supposed* to be registered to an authority. Even if no one ever asked for the information, it *was* supposed to exist.

He walked back toward his team, forwarding them the recording of his exchange with the bot as he returned.

The conversation hadn't lasted long, so it only took a few seconds for them to review it.

"That's...unsettling," Krikorian said.

"It's huge," Po said. "Someone's putting unregistered bots into the streets of a major Venus cloud colony, and they're apparently being allowed to walk around with the full authority of a cop-bot."

As he often did lately, Gomez looked uncertain through his transparent visor. "Couldn't it just be a glitch, though?" he asked. "The bots have been known to glitch before."

The corner of Po's mouth tightened involuntarily. It was definitely the sort of annoying question the old Gomez would have asked. It also happened to be a pretty relevant one.

"I guess it could be," Po admitted after a few seconds. "Well, let's go conduct some more interviews."

For the better part of two hours, they walked the streets that skirted the downtown core, conducting an informal survey of the cop-bots policing the city's busiest streets. Po used his implant to track the results: eight out of the twenty-seven security bots they spoke to were unregistered.

"That's 29.6 percent," Po said.

"But who's counting," Taylor put in.

"Should we ask some more?"

"Something just occurred to me, actually," Krikorian said. "How many people do you think ask the bots for their registration numbers?"

Po nodded. "I was thinking about that too. Probably around zero."

"Exactly. So while we go around talking to bots, the master AI that controls them is probably detecting what you might call an anomalous pattern. And eventually, it'll probably alert whoever sent the unregistered bots into Aeolia. If it hasn't already."

Po's heartbeat felt like it doubled. "You're right." He'd planned to go back to Emery with his findings at the end of their patrol in a few hours, but now he realized they might not have that kind of time. Whoever owned the anonymous bots was bound to react soon—whether by doing something to conceal the fact the bots were unregistered— though Po had no idea how they might do that—or by executing early whatever they were planning to do with the things.

"They have to charge," Vacca said, and the other four Marines turned abruptly toward him, as though shocked he'd spoken. Po *felt* kind of shocked—he'd basically forgotten the new guy was there, since he hadn't spoken during the entire patrol.

A team leader really shouldn't be forgetting about any of the Marines he's in charge of, he chastised himself.

"What did you say, boot?" Taylor said.

"I said they have to charge. Recharge. Don't they? And cop-bots return to security stations to recharge. But if these bots aren't real cop-bots..."

"Then they'll go back to whoever's deploying them," Po said. "They'd have to. Otherwise, they'd eventually die out in the street. And whoever's responsible for them wouldn't want a dead bot to be picked up and studied. That would lead back to them for sure." He grinned. "Good thinking, Vacca."

"Thanks, Corporal."

And so they matched their patrol with that of the next cop-bot they saw. Po figured the thing must have some sort of protocol that detected if it was being followed—something that would trigger if someone remained in its field of view for longer than seemed normal. To avoid that, he had his team break into rotating buddy pairs, using their implants to keep track of each other and the bot's projected location, each pair popping out of an alley only briefly to put eyes on the bot, at as far a remove as they could manage.

Since there were five of them, there was always one team member operating solo—but Po told them not to stray too far from the team when they were the odd one out, and he told everyone else to keep a close eye on the one who was walking alone. He didn't want a repeat of the Marine who'd been butchered behind a downtown Aeolia building.

The scheme seemed to work. The bot didn't approach them, or act like it had detected anything amiss at all.

Finally, it departed from its downtown patrol route, making a beeline for the cloud colony's northeast perimeter.

They tracked it to a ferry, where it joined a line of personal vehicles and a handful of other bots waiting to board a giant elevator that would take them down to the airship's cargo deck.

"I'm taking just Krik on board," Po told the others. "If we all go, it'll draw too much suspicion. The rest of you stay here and go back to our patrol."

"And a couple of armed Marines in full SERAPH suits *won't* draw attention?" Taylor protested, which by now was pretty predictable.

"As far as anyone on that ferry knows, we got called to one of Aeolia's satellite islands to investigate something. Either way, I doubt anyone's going to interfere with us. Even the cop-bots know we're authorized to patrol Aeolia, and that technically includes its satellites."

"But what—"

"Conversation over, Taylor. Go back to patrolling. Krik, let's move."

"You got it."

Together, they headed for the line of walk-on passengers, heading to the front and hopping the automatic turnstile without buying a ticket. Po wasn't about to waste money on a ferry ticket when he could send those funds back home to Nicky. Not when his orders authorized him to investigate clear and present threats to Aeolia, wherever they led him.

They boarded the passenger elevator, which was much smaller than the cargo elevator. Po and Krik held their rifles in a loose port-arms position and waited for the elevator to fill.

As he'd predicted, no one complained about them skipping the line, or came to collect their ticket fare, or tried to kick them off the elevator. If at some point someone had a problem with them boarding without paying, Po felt confident the Corps would back him up.

At last, the elevator filled, and they began to descend toward the waiting ferry. The elevators were attached to the cloud colony, and airships docked with them almost twenty kilometers below. Being so long, the elevator shaft was made of treated nanotwinned precipitates. At least, that was what Po's implant told him as he read up on the system while he and Krik plummeted toward the airship.

Operating so far below the colonies meant the airships could be built relatively small, since the increased pressure at that altitude made gases more buoyant. The airships relied on electrothermal propulsion for getting around, which was energy-intensive, and so they siphoned the needed power directly from the colonies via cables that ran along the elevator shafts' exteriors. The floating colonies generally had energy to spare, which they collected using wind turbines, though the larger ones like Aeolia boasted geothermal systems whereby water fell down tubes even longer than the elevator shafts. Once the water dropped far enough, the higher temperatures brought it to a boil, and it rose back up another tube to drive a turbine.

The ferry ride took twenty minutes, and he and Krik once again insinuated themselves into the front of the line to board the elevator up to Mag Mell, which was Aeolia's biggest satellite island—pretty much a neighboring municipality, though governed by the same board of admins.

Too late, Po wondered whether he should have notified Gunny Emery of what he was planning to do. Technically, he was acting within his orders, and didn't need any extra authorization for this. But it might have been a good idea to get the gunny's guidance, or at least to loop him in.

Ah, well. Taylor and Gomez know where we went. If we're not back by the time our watch ends, Emery will send men after us.

There was no way Po could get a signal through to Emery now. The cloud layer played havoc with coms.

Po figured they couldn't afford to wait for anyone else to disembark the elevator first, and it turned out he was right. By the time they stepped off of it and into Mag Mell's outskirts, the bot they were following was already at the end of the lane they found themselves on. Based on general wear-and-tear, Po's implant identified it as the same bot just before it vanished around a corner.

"There it is. Or, was."

The Circuits really are incredible. Without his implant's functionality, there was no way he could ever have picked out the bot again, after getting separated from it. Even with the implant's help, he was still pretty lucky they'd spotted it.

Po and Krik exchanged glances, then wordlessly sprinted after the thing.

They didn't have far to go. They followed it to an enormous mansion near the airship elevators, which was bordered by a ten-foot wall. From a distance, they watched the bot enter through what might have been called a servant's door.

"Now what?" Krik asked.

Po shook his head slowly. "Now we wait, I guess."

"For what?"

"For something to happen. Somehow, I don't see whoever owns that place opening up to us if we knock. Forcing our way in would be taking this way too far, at this point. But even just tracking the bot here seems like pretty significant progress."

While they staked out the mansion from an alley mouth across from it and down the street, Po poked through what information his Circuit had to offer about Mag Mell. To his surprise, he was able to run a title search on the property they were watching, which told him its owner was Jeremy Zin, CEO of Distribly, a shipping company and GEA partner.

"Apparently the mansion's owner is the CEO of a shipping company called Distribly."

Krik looked at him. "How'd you figure that out?" He turned back toward the mansion. "I don't see it written anywhere."

"I've been doing some research."

"My team leader, the librarian."

Po snorted. "You recognize that name? Distribly? I guess it's just another monopoly propped up by GEA."

"No, actually, I've heard of it. Zap mentioned it."

"Zapletal?"

"Yeah. You knew he was from Venus, right?"

"No, I didn't."

"We had a couple conversations about all the corruption here. He mentioned Distribly. Apparently they lobbied GEA for all sorts of different regs, which only they were big enough to keep up with. They did it to stamp out the competition, and it worked."

"Figures."

"Look." Krik nodded toward the mansion.

Po turned back toward it, and saw the door was opening to let out two more bots, both which headed straight for the nearby airship elevators. Neither of them were the bot they followed here.

"Don't shoot," a voice said from behind them.

They whirled around and pointed their rifles at a man framed by a doorway belonging to one of the buildings they were crouching beside. He'd raised his hands above his head, and he was wearing a matching burgundy hat and shirt, with beige pants.

The sort of uniform a shipping company employee might wear, Po reflected, as his heart hammered in his chest, sending blood roaring past his ears.

Chapter 13

"Who are you?" Po demanded.

"I'm the Distribly employee who's been monitoring you through the bot you've been following. Whenever the bots have an interaction outside expected parameters, I'm the one in charge of reviewing them." He tilted his head back toward the building he'd emerged from, without lowering his arms. "This is the local Distribly hub."

Right across from the CEO's house. "What's your name?"

The man shook his head. "I'd rather leave names out of it. I'm already putting myself at risk, leaving my post to come talk to you. Thankfully, my supervisor basically never checks up on me."

"You're just that good, huh," Krik muttered, his voice coming out low through his suit's speakers.

"Why didn't we hear that door open?" Po asked, indicating the entrance the man was standing in with his rifle muzzle. "Our suits should have picked up on it."

The man shrugged. "Well-oiled, I guess. And I took a lot of care to open it slow and silent. Same reason I led with 'don't shoot.' I...really didn't want to get shot." He frowned. "With your permission, I'll close the door. There *is* a decent chance someone happens by and overhears us."

"Go ahead," Po said.

Carefully, the man stepped out and closed the door with his left hand, keeping his right in the air. With the door closed, he put the hand back over his head.

"What do you want?" Po asked.

"To help you. To tell you what I know."

"Why?"

"Because I've seen things that upset me. That worry me, about what could happen on Venus. It...could be bad."

"Bad how?"

"We can't talk about it here. Meet me in ninety minutes, at the Sensorium—there, we can talk."

"Why should we trust you?" Krik asked.

"I can't really prove you should trust me. Not without telling you what I know, and you verifying it...or coming events verifying it. And I can't tell you what I know here. But at the Sensorium, I can. So you'll have to decide if you want to take the risk."

Neither Po nor Krikorian answered that.

"I'm going to go back in now. Okay? Sensorium, ninety minutes from now."

Po nodded. And the man slowly opened the door behind him and withdrew into the building.

***

Sensorium turned out to be a bar and sole occupant of its own separate balloon a few minutes' float from Mag Mell—a satellite of a satellite. Unlike Aeolia and Mag Mell, it enjoyed no public ferries that ran between it and the latter, meaning Po and Krikorian found themselves scrambling to arrange private transport using their Circuits while crossing to the elevators closest to where the bar trailed Mag Mell.

"Would have been nice for our friend to give us a little guidance," Krik muttered over a two-way channel as they both flicked through Mag Mell's directories, trying to figure them out on the fly.

"We still don't know what his angle is," Po reminded the other Marine. "And if he's legit, chances are it's his first time acting against his company like this. Which means he's nervous. And it's easy to overlook stuff when you're nervous."

"So we have a disorganized snitch. Great."

"We don't know what he is. But if he's what *I* hope he is, he'll help us reach whoever was behind taking out the *Magnolia.*"

"To get revenge."

Po hesitated. "And to stop them from doing it to anyone else."

"Right."

They got in touch with the needed transport minutes before reaching the elevator allocated to private rides.

"You got at least a thirty minute wait," the pilot told Po over the call. "There's a line-up of taxis ahead of me, all who got passengers already."

"No there isn't."

"Huh? Yes there is."

"Broadcast a message to them. Tell them two Marines are coming down the elevator right now, and if *you're* not docked there and waiting, then we'll commandeer whatever taxi we find there."

"*Commandeer?* Is that what you're doing to me?"

"No. We'll pay you." *And the Corps better reimburse me for it.*

"All right..."

This time, there were indignant cries as Po and Krik cut to the front of the lineup outside the private-ride elevator, which was a lot smaller than the ones they'd taken to and from the ferry. No one made any attempt to stop them, though, which was wise. Po simply ignored their cries of protests, and when he glanced at Krikorian, he looked even less interested in the complaints than Po was.

The pilot had sounded hesitant when Po told him to order away the other airships, but when Po and Krik descended the small elevator with a handful of others who'd be taking the rides after them, he was waiting there for them.

"We got a lot of unhappy pilots swarming around us right now," he told them as they squeezed into the airship's only compartment. "A couple of 'em cursed on me."

Po shot him a blank look. "You *did* tell them I'm the one who told you to do it, I'm sure."

"Yeah. But they aren't in contact with you. So I got the abuse that was meant for you."

Po and Krik strapped in, and the pilot peeled away from the elevator dock. With how short the ride was going to be, there was no time to try to smooth over the man's ruffled feathers, and Po needed information. So he decided to just start asking questions.

"What can you tell us about the Sensorium?"

The pilot twisted around to meet Po's eyes through his visor. "How long you been on Venus, kid?"

Kid?

Unbidden, Sergeant Young flashed in his mind's eye—Young's face, from the moment before he'd been killed by a grenade carried by the insurgent who'd rushed out of hiding at him. And hard on the heels of that memory, another one surfaced, of a desperate battle fought against Janus on a Gomorate rooftop, certain in the knowledge that he and all the Marines with him were going to die.

"That's corporal to you," Po said.

"Corporal," the pilot said. "How long?"

"A few weeks."

"And you haven't heard about the Sensorium yet?"

"Negative."

"Huh. Well, it's the most famous legal no-man's-land this side of Venus. They run their own stuff, and the admins consider it more trouble than it's worth to shut them down. So, anything goes in the Sensorium. And I do mean anything. The fact *that's* where you were headed didn't do much to cool the other pilots' tempers, let me tell you."

"We're on business," Krik said, and Po shot him a warning look.

The pilot shrugged. "Whatever you're doing there, it's none of *my* business. But let me tell you—the fact that two Marines commandeered a taxi to rush to the Sensorium is too juicy to *not* spread to every corner of Mag Mell before the night's out. And hey, don't shoot the messenger," he added, holding up a finger to waggle at them over his shoulder.

"Seems we're drawing a lot of attention," Krik said, over a two-way channel.

Po suppressed a sigh. Krik was right. *And I'm sure it'll come back to bite us soon enough.*

"Could have drawn more," Po answered at last. "We got lucky, with the Distribly employee. He might have shouted that up the corporate ladder instead."

"Who's to say he didn't? And that this is the CEO's ploy—to drag us to this sketchy place and deal with us?"

"We'll keep our wits about us. If they do pull anything, Emery will fall on them like a brick wall. Taylor and Gomez have enough information to know where to point him."

"They can point him to Mag Mell. They don't know we're going to this Sensorium place."

Po fell silent again for a few seconds. Then: "There's a record of all this." He gestured toward the seat in front of him, indicating the taxi, which drew the pilot's gaze in the rearview mirror. "It'd be enough for gunny to put it together. And anyway—it won't be necessary."

Krikorian didn't answer. Which, Po guessed, wasn't because he agreed it wouldn't be necessary, but because he had the same unshakable confidence in Gunny Emery that Po did.

If they got ambushed and killed, Emery would visit swift justice on whoever did it to them.

***

Po was expecting something much dingier and more cramped than what the Sensorium turned out to be—he'd been imagining a place like a bigger version of Infusion, the bar where Po had approached the group of operatives from Allies of the Kuiper Belt.

But Sensorium surprised him. Comprising the entranceway were countless vertical wooden slats, sticking out perpendicular to the wall behind, all of it aglow with warm orange light that emanated from strips that ran along both sides of each board. Halfway between the floor and ceiling, a narrow mirror extended for the entire room, reflecting Po and Krik and showing how unnatural they looked, wearing their suits in this setting —two dark gray shadows with human heads, toting M37Cs into this otherwise sophisticated place.

They'd removed their helmets, as their only concession to the fact they were entering a private service establishment, and they each carried them tucked under an arm.

We're not exactly undercover, are we? But Po expected they would have stuck out either way, and he'd rather be ready to fight.

A doorman greeted them at the entrance proper, looking them up and down, his eyes lingering on their weapons. "Do you plan to use those, gentlemen?"

"Not unless we have to," Po said.

"You shouldn't. And in the event that you *do* have to, I think you can expect dozens of other firearms to be employed at the same time you employ yours. As to which targets their users will select, that is up to the proprietor's discretion."

"Got it," Po said.

"Your credentials have been automatically collected, so please feel free to enter. And feel free to accept the complimentary bar skins that will be offered to you momentarily. Or, simply enjoy the bar's tasteful decor."

Po had no idea what a "bar skin" was —not until the offer popped up in his vision, complete with four image thumbnails he could select. They gave him the option of using his Circuit's functionality to turn Sensorium into a shark cage at the bottom of the ocean, an open-air bar at the top of a tower overlooking what Po recognized as Manhattan Island, a station orbiting Mars, or a base sitting atop an asteroid, offering a whirling view of the stars.

That last one reminded him of Psyche, even though the actual asteroid colony he'd grown up in looked nothing like the skin.

Either way, he rejected the offer, not interested in giving the bar permission to alter what he saw.

Inside, he found a sea of emerald couches clustered around polished circular tables, the tabletops of a dappled cream design, with cream-colored paneled walls to match. Each panel had a wooden border painted gray. The floor was marble, with a dense blue pattern surrounding each island of chairs, and a misty white-and-green pattern denoting the walkways between.

"Fancy," Krikorian said. "But I don't see our new friend anywhere."

"Me neither. Let's sit somewhere conspicuous."

They took seats on separate green couches surrounding one of the tables that could be seen from pretty much anywhere in the bar. Many of the couch clusters were occupied, but a lot of them weren't.

Not happy hour yet, I guess.

A server came by to take their order, but Po waved him away, unwilling to put anything these people offered him into his body. The man's face was a placid mask as he walked off, but Po was sure their loitering without buying anything wasn't exactly appreciated.

"With all these unregistered bots around," Krik said, leaning forward with his forearms on his thighs. "Makes me wonder if GEA has finally decided to replace us with them."

Po snorted. The question of why GEA didn't just use bots to fight their wars was one he'd turned over in his mind countless times, since before bootcamp.

It'd certainly solve their numbers problem. As far as Po could tell, the Corps skipped over Earth almost entirely in their recruitment. Apparently, they were concerned the cocktail of experimental drugs GEA fed Earthers as a condition of their welfare had weakened their systems so much they'd simply fall over if subjected to any real strain. Although, no recruitment officer would ever say that outright.

The bots were also incredibly resilient, and deadly. *Just look how long it took four Marines to take out one of them.* Of course, Po and the others *had* been armed with only garden implements, but still. He'd been impressed by the bot's stamina...and its strength. Neither was news to him, exactly, after a childhood and adolescence spent under the cop-bots' thumbs—so to speak. But there was no denying the bots would make formidable warfighters.

It certainly wasn't scruples stopping GEA from building its own bot army. But *something* had stopped them. Until now, maybe. If Krik turned out to be right.

The Distribly employee finally arrived, emerging from the same entrance Po and Krik had used. He spotted them immediately, and headed over to them. The same server from before intercepted him before he made it to his seat, and he placed an order, which was probably a good thing.

"Come here often?" Krik asked him as he settled onto one of the two unoccupied couches.

"Only once," he answered. "This...isn't exactly my scene. I don't fit in here, and neither does my wallet." He shrugged. "But it's the only place I know of where I can get a reliable implant overwrite for the conversation we're about to have."

"What conversation *are* we about to have?" Po asked.

"Right to business, then? Well, I guess we didn't come here to make small talk." The man drew a deep breath, his shoulders rising and falling. "I've been watching this thing develop for years at work. Things I overheard from other departments...rumors repeated in the break room...and plenty that I saw with my own two eyes."

"Watched what develop, exactly?" Po asked.

The man sighed again, his exhalation coming out sounding ragged this time. "I guess there's nothing for it but to just say it. I've come to believe that someone's getting ready to make a move on the system. The entire thing. I think they want to unseat GEA and install themselves in GEA's place." He paused to receive his drink from the waiter—a beer—and then waited till the man was well out of earshot before turning back to the Marines. "And they're building the army to do it with right here on Venus."

Chapter 14

The Distribly employee still hadn't sipped from his beer, and indeed he seemed to have forgotten it, his fingers clasped around the expensive-looking bottle as though it were a hand warmer.

"Our company's running distribution for bots quietly being produced here on Venus, and bizarrely, we're handling them too. But it's an offworld entity that's come in to set up the production facilities. 'RoboDenso' is the name I've been seeing at the top of invoices and manifests. But outside those forms, I haven't been able to find any indication the company actually exists. And trust me, I've looked."

The man closed his eyes. "The justification is that the admins need an increased security bot presence in every cloud colony of any size, based on models that cropped up fifteen years ago, projecting unrest here on Venus—the protests and riots we've seen are only the beginning, according to these models. But until a few months ago, there was no sign of anything. And I've started to wonder, are these models just innocently predicting things, or did someone with a long-term plan introduce them into the public consciousness in advance, so that no one would be surprised when they quietly began stirring the pot?"

"So these predictions are being used to justify heightened bot production," Po said slowly. "And yet none of the bots are actually registered."

"Yeah. And that's just one of many things that stinks. There's also the fact that the production is at a scale way too big for supplying just Venus. From what I've seen as one of the bots' handlers, Aeolia and its satellites already have more than they need, and from what I've heard, all the other cloud archipelagos are the same. Meanwhile, RoboDenso just keeps pumping out units."

"Why did they choose Venus?" Krikorian asked. Po glanced at him with eyebrows raised.

"Because of the cover. The cloud cover." The man waved a hand to indicate the bar around them, and presumably the golden-brown clouds blanketing it outside. "It never dissipates. It kills radar signal, and you certainly can't *see* through it. RoboDenso's facilities are on the surface, and underground. No one does anything down there—no one without massive resources and a desperate need for secrecy, that is, which is a description that seems to fit RoboDenso like a glove. The pressure on the surface is insane—equal to the pressure almost a kilometer below Earth's oceans. If you're looking to build a robot army with no one important noticing, it's perfect."

"Why didn't you go to someone in GEA with this?" Po asked.

The Distribly employee paused, blinking. "GEA's breaking up. I thought everyone knew that."

"*Breaking up?*"

"Well, okay, fracturing. They're not 'breaking up,' as such—not yet, anyway. But who can trust GEA at the best of times? The admins here are clearly looped in on whatever's going on."

"You do realize we work for GEA," Krikorian said. "It's why they call us, uh, the GEA Marines."

The man paused. "I've also heard there are tensions between the Corps and GEA," he said at last. With that, he sighed again, explosively this time. "Look, I'm grasping at straws here. I see a runaway magtrain barreling down on us, full bore, and I've been watching it coming for a long time now. But everyone I turn to seems to be invested in it running right over the lot of us. Is there *anyone* I can go to who isn't rotten to the core? Doesn't anyone want to stop this thing?"

"We do," Po said quietly. "It just took out a ship's full of our brothers."

The man nodded slowly. "I did hear about that. I'm...sorry. For your loss. But it was also the thing that pushed me hardest to relay what I've seen and heard to a Marine, given half a chance. I've known Marines, and I know what people say about you, but one thing that can't be said is you don't take care of your own."

While Po took a second to parse the double negative, Krikorian narrowed his eyes. "What do people say about us?"

"That we're a bunch of crayon-noshing jarheads," Po cut in, then turned back to the employee. "Was there anything else?"

"I've put together a map. Of the surface regions that I think hold production facilities. All derived from the timing of when we get new shipments. RoboDenso is as concerned about fuel efficiency as anyone, so if they're sending up a load of bots, it means Venus' prevailing winds have blown Mag Mell near to the facility they came from. I'm transmitting the map to your implant now.

Po nodded. "Okay. Thanks."

"I hope you can do something about this. Truly. I have a family, in an Aeolian suburb. I go home to them every night." He sniffed. "You're a lance corporal, hey? Lance corporals have some pull in the Marines. Right?"

Po chuckled, then stood, motioning for Krikorian to join him.

His eyes met the Distribly employee's one last time.

"We'll do what we can," he told him.

With that, he and Krik headed for Sensorium's exit, to await the first airship taxi back to Mag Mell. As they turned away, their informant took his first sip of beer.

***

"Are you telling me we aren't going to act on this immediately, Gunny?"

Emery leaned back in his chair behind his middle manager's desk, which he'd commandeered for any meetings he had to conduct, be they with superiors or members of the platoon he commanded. Like Po.

"Abbato, if it were up to me, we'd be acting on this yesterday. But everything you've just relayed to me needs to be passed up the chain of command and reviewed by people with a lot more authority than me. What you apparently just uncovered is earthshaking...or, cloud-shaking, or whatever the right metaphor is. Could be it's *system*-shaking. I believe that it is. But what I believe doesn't matter much. Surely you've realized that, by now."

Po shook his head, hardly able to believe what he was hearing. Emery wasn't going to do anything about this? *Emery?* "Gunny..."

"Look, Abbato, I think you and I have a mutual appreciation. I respect what you do for 131st, and for the Raptors, and I think you like the way I command the platoon."

"I do, Gunny."

"I'm glad. But don't conflate that with an ability to make anything happen at the upper levels. Because I can't. To a Marine platoon, their immediate commander pretty much *is* their world. He can make their lives a nightmare, or he can inspire confidence and esprit de corps. Ultimately, I decide how you live your day-to-day life, which can make it easy to fall into the trap of thinking that I'm more powerful than I actually am. I'm not. I'm in charge of 131st Platoon, and a lot of times, I even get overridden in what I want to do at *that* level.

"Unfortunately, I've seen stuff like this come across my desk before, stuff that feels like it should shake the universe, only to see it run headlong into a brick wall." He looked down at the wood-paneled desk. "Well...not across *this* desk. But you know what I mean." The gunny shrugged. "I can't explain why things that should definitely happen right away sometimes fail dramatically to materialize. But it is a common phenomenon, and I want you to be prepared for this *not* to move the world. Certainly not today, and probably not tomorrow, or for many days after that."

"It's all documented, Gunny. In my implant footage. And Krikorian's."

"True, but it still essentially comes down to some random shipping company employee's word. Doesn't it?"

"And the fact there are so many unregistered bots walking around Venus' cloud cities."

Emery nodded. "That does seem to be a fact. But a single fact does not a theory make. And even the Distribly employee seemed to recognize that all he really has is a theory."

Po suppressed the urge to sigh. "Yes, Gunny."

"Hey, chin up. I have some good news for you. You're getting promoted to corporal."

Po sat up straighter, brow furrowed. "Huh? Already?"

Emery grinned. "As fast as was possible, and maybe even a little faster. I guess maybe I *can* make some things happen. But I wasn't alone. There are still people left in the Corps who recognize talent when they see it, and I'm not the only one who'd like to see you in charge of your own squad, the moment it can be managed. Normal time to make corporal is your first term of service, or four years. Congratulations—you did it in thirty months. But don't get used to the fast and furious promotions. Sergeant will be a long time coming. Maybe even till you're this far into your second term. Though, not if *I* have anything to say about it." Emery's grin widened.

Po still didn't know quite how to react. *Corporal. Already.* He slowly shook his head. "Well, thanks very much, Gunny. I'll...try not to let you down."

"Just keep doing what you're doing, Abbato. Truth be told, you should be getting a medal, for what you did with To'sheth Rin. But I'm afraid there are too many elements in GEA opposed to common sense for that to happen any time soon—if ever." Emery sighed. "Ah, well. Your brothers acknowledge what you did, and honor it. So do I." He nodded curtly, as if to himself. "Dismissed, Abbato."

But Po couldn't help feeling a little unsteady as he got to his feet to leave the middle manager's office—temporarily Emery's office.

He'd gotten this far with Zanth's help, and he was still riding on those fumes, he knew.

Now that he'd rejected the Emplor outright, what hope did he have of further advancement?

It probably won't be a problem.

Probably, Zanth would arrange for his death long before then.

***

He was back in the Psyche simjail, running madly through the endless warren of half wood-paneled, half blinding white corridors. He took each corner without thought, veering around it and nearly going sprawling each time. Pursuing him was the hooded, masked figure who'd confronted him and Krik in the Aeolian alleyway.

Po hadn't noticed a weapon in the hooded man's hand—but *he* didn't have one either. Even if he did have one, chances were good of dying soon after his pursuer caught up to him.

The hooded figure had Zanth on his side, and Zanth would provide him with exactly the right moves to dismantle Po's defense and end his life. He'd be killed with his anonymous assailant's bare hands.

He noticed the footsteps had fallen away, and he glanced behind to find that he'd outstripped his hunter. Relief flooded through him.

So he can be outrun. I guess that part really does just come down to cardio.

Then, the hooded figure appeared around the corner he was jogging toward, and it was too late to arrest his momentum. His attacker tripped him, sending him face-first into a wall. Po turned in time to see the man standing over him, ready to deal the next blow.

Instead, the figure took down his hood, then removed his mask.

Beneath it was Luca Abbato's face. Po's father.

He woke in the makeshift Aeolian barracks, damp and cold, drenched in sweat. He moaned, surreptitiously glancing at the men sleeping on either side of him to see whether he'd woken them by thrashing or crying out in his sleep.

Both seemed undisturbed—but it was almost time for Po to get up and go on patrol. He got up and started donning his SERAPH armor.

Not sure what I was so worried about, he thought, reflecting on the dream. *You can't get hurt in a sim.*

Even so, the terror had been real, despite the illogic of it. Such was the way of dreams.

Outside in the city's streets with his fireteam, the lighting was dim. Their circadian cycle had only just begun to brighten with the day's advent. But as Po and his men made their way toward their patrol route, signs of life had already begun to emerge. A jogger passed them, eyes straight ahead, and clearly trying to pretend the Marines didn't exist.

They've grown accustomed to the cop-bots, but seeing humans patrolling their streets bothers them. That said, Po supposed the SERAPH armor *was* more imposing than one of the metal uncanny valley dwellers.

As they neared the downtown core, residential blinds were opened, and stores threw open their doors. Cop-bots patrolled the streets in greater numbers, their presence growing denser in anticipation of the increased citizen activity.

A scream pierced the air, discordant amidst the muted doings of a city slowly waking.

Po exchanged glances with Krik. With that, he motioned for the others to double-time it to the next street over, in search of the scream's source. They cut through a narrow walkway between townhouses, leaping over a shoulder-high fence that ran along the back—the feat made easy by their suits' strength enhancements.

"Sounded male," Taylor said.

"There's that to be grateful for," Krikorian put in.

They emerged from between townhouses bordering the next street to find a bot with two gripperfuls of a man's snow-white sweater. It was shaking him violently.

"You have stolen goods on your person," the bot said. "Relinquish them."

"I don't have anything," the man protested. "Search me!"

"Relinquish your stolen goods."

"I don't have anything!" the man repeated.

"You are resisting arrest," the bot said, which to Po seemed like something of a non sequitur. With that, it released the man with one of its grippers in order to hammer him across the face with it. Blood flew, and the man went sprawling—or he would have, if the cop-bot's other gripper didn't have a firm hold of his sweater, which tore audibly.

"Stop resisting arrest," the bot said, bringing the man upright before shoving him with both its grippers. The man fell backward, his head connecting with the asphalt with a *thud*.

Po winced, and the memory flashed in his mind of the merc beating the Nibiran mercilessly. And of how he'd done nothing to stop it.

Hard on that memory's heels came a succession of Psyche residents flitting through his mind's eye, getting harassed and tackled by the cop-bots there.

The entire mental sequence took a fraction of a second. He shook his head to clear it, then started moving forward and to the left, raising his rifle as he sidestepped around the bot for a clean shot. He'd use a brick house on the other side of the lane as his backstop.

"Po—" Gomez said.

"Shut up." Whatever the other Marine was going to say in order to stop him, he had no interest in hearing it.

Before Po could get into position, the bot crouched and landed a curled gripper on the man's nose. It must have hardened the thing first, because cartilage gave way with an audible *crunch*, and blood spurted down the man's sweater, the scarlet standing out starkly against the white. Next, the bot hammered down with the gripper again, and Po thought he heard a cheekbone give away.

"*Hey!*" he yelled. The bot turned just as Po's rounds found its own cheekbone—or where its cheekbone would have been, if the thing was natural in any sense of the word.

The shots made it jerk back before rising to its full height, with two smoking bullet holes marring its cylindrical visage. As the man moaned, the bot stepped free of him, shaking his right foot as it did, as though to dislodge dirt from it. A siren whooped from speakers Po knew were located at the back of its head.

His next grouping hit the bot's torso—near its neck. And the next connected with its midsection. Wisps of smoke emanated from those holes too, but the bot seemed completely unperturbed as it began to march toward him.

But this time, Po wasn't wearing only cammies, and he wasn't armed with only a shovel. He was in full SERAPH armor.

And so, he dispensed with shooting at the thing, instead striding swiftly forward to meet it. As they closed the distance, he brought a boot up into the lower part of its cylinder.

The bot went airborne, flying backward to crack off the mailbox it crashed through at its base.

But Po wasn't done. He continued to approach it, putting rounds into areas where he knew vital circuit boards and actuators were located.

He'd been studying these things all his life, even though he'd never dare tangle with one.

Not until now.

And it felt great.

The bot didn't rise...but he turned to find five more converging on him. Where they'd come from, he couldn't say. He supposed they were here to answer the siren which the felled bot had blared moments before Po had neutralized it.

"You are under arrest," the bot closest to him said. "Lower your weapon to the ground and raise your hands over your head, or we will be obliged to use force."

Po knew he couldn't take on five of the things at once. Not alone. And he couldn't expect his teammates to expose themselves to whatever he was about to face, either.

I made my rack. Hospital corners and all. Now I have to lie in it.

He lowered his M37C to the asphalt and then rose to his full height, putting his hands into the air.

Chapter 15

Po was no stranger to being manhandled by security bots and frogmarched to a jail cell, and all things considered, this was a much nicer experience than the first time it had happened to him.

His time on Nibiru had trained him, if not to *like* vast open spaces, then at least to tolerate them, and to be able to operate within them. And really, with its four-hundred-meter dome and swirling orange murk above, Aeolia was a lot closer to Psyche than standing outside on a planet.

So Po found himself able to enjoy the brisk stroll through the city, even with his hands in restraints behind his back. It was nice to be able just to take in the sights for once, without having to constantly scan for threats.

The bots will take care of that. And hey, they have *taken care of it, haven't they? I'm the threat. And I'm being dealt with.*

If someone had told him this morning that he'd get arrested today, and that he'd be in good spirits afterward, he would have called them crazy. But here he was, grinning back at the residents gawking at the Marine being escorted by two cop-bots, even though they couldn't see it through his opaque faceplate.

At first, he couldn't quite put his finger on why getting arrested would put him in such a good mood.

Then, it hit him. It wasn't getting *arrested* that had done it. It was finally exacting some payback on the cop-bots, after being on the receiving end of their abuse all his life, and watching his friends and neighbors receive it too.

What would Nicky think of it? he asked himself. His sister had a soft heart, and had never liked hearing talk of payback or getting revenge, which Po had indulged in more than once around her, to his shame.

But that was payback against *people.* Against GEA, and Equipoise Metals—and everyone else responsible for the generational debt he and his siblings had been ensnared in.

A bot wasn't a person. It was a thing, a tool. A weapon. One which had been designed and deployed for the purpose of controlling the people under GEA's governance, such as it was.

Something about the bots had always rubbed him the wrong way. Rosa used to say he had a problem with authority, and that had probably been true, once. But he was a *Marine* now, and he wouldn't have made it far without learning to respect the authority of those superior to him.

So could he really say that his problem with the bots was still a problem with authority, if it ever had been? Or was it something else, specific to the bots?

He couldn't say. All he knew was, having just deactivated one of them with extreme prejudice, he felt great.

They brought him to the same city-center security station he'd visited with Zhang, Krikorian, and Taylor, on a slightly more cordial occasion. This time, instead of talking with an admin's aide who asked him polite questions in a slightly terse tone, he was taken straight through the reception area and down a line of holding cells. They stopped at the fourth on the left, and one of the bots opened the door for him.

"Enter the cell," said the bot who'd gripped his arms during the entire march here. It released him.

"You got it." Po stepped forward, and the door slammed shut behind him.

The accommodations were a lot nicer than the stacked, transparent cell block he'd been shown to in Psyche, after he was caught trying to smuggle drugs out of an Equipoise warehouse. Sure, the furnishings were austere—toilet, sink, cot—but at least he had some privacy in here.

The illusion of privacy, anyway. If the admins really wanted to watch him, they could, but that was true pretty much all the time, ever since he'd gotten his implant.

He eyed the door, wondering if he'd be able to batter it down with the SERAPH suit's strength. But it was an idle thought. Doing something like that would spend what leverage he had.

I did nothing wrong. The admins know it, and the Corps will definitely know it. But if I vandalize their jail...

Instead, he removed the suit and neatly stacked the parts against the wall next to the door. That done, he settled onto the cot and sat against the wall with the thin pillow behind his back. He actually found it pretty comfortable, and before long, he was dozing.

***

Po was using his Circuit to read up on the realities of operating on Venus' surface when a bot opened his cell door to let in Emery in service uniform.

"Gunny!" Po exclaimed, then felt a little sheepish at how exuberant he'd sounded.

The gunny grinned, then turned back toward the bot, who still stood in the doorway.

"Dismissed," Emery said.

That seemed to do it. The bot closed the door without another word.

Po stood up from his cot, which he'd neatly made, hospital corners and all. Some habits died hard.

"Take a seat, Gunny."

Emery nodded his thanks, and sat on the bottom of the cot.

"Gunny...I had to do it. You understand that, right? I'm just sick of..." He shook his head, collecting his thoughts. He'd done a lot of thinking, and he was pretty sure he'd figured out what bothered him so much about the bots. Now he just had to find the right words to express it.

"Gunny, I've watched bots beat up on people since I had eyes to see. It's not right. That's what I've realized, since they put me in here. And it's why I did what I did. Machines have no right to lay hands on a human, not for any reason. Not ever. That should never be a machine's job. I understand the need for policing...but it shouldn't be bots doing it."

"As it happens, I agree with you, Corporal."

"You do? Oh." Po just stood there for a few seconds, the tension leaking out of his body. The revelation that Emery agreed with what he figured would be a pretty radical statement seemed...anticlimactic, somehow.

"I didn't get anything from you," Emery said. "No message that you were in here."

"Huh? Oh. Well, I guess I figured my team would fill you in."

"And if they'd been arrested too? After you were taken, without you knowing?"

"Krikorian messaged me and told me he filled you in."

"Even so. It was your job to notify me. There's a reason 'redundancy' is the military's favorite word. Without it, things get missed. Sometimes vital things. And I'd say this counts as vital."

"Sorry, Gunny."

Emery nodded. "Just don't let it happen again." He glanced around the cramped cell. "This actually looks more comfortable than your rack back in the warehouse. On a bit of a holiday, are you, Corporal?"

"Absolutely. I've been waiting for them to ask me to write a customer review—I plan to give a good one."

The gunny chuckled. "Have they told you anything about your situation? Legally speaking?"

"Nothing."

"Figures. The admins would like nothing more than to make an example of you. Problem is, they know they've got nothing."

"Well, I *did* kill a cop-bot..."

"A cop-bot attacking a man who's been found to be innocent. Not found innocent by a court, mind you—but he had no stolen goods on him, as the bot was claiming. The thing was either malfunctioning, or was set on the poor man as an act of terrorism, basically. Even if he *had* stolen something, its use of force was way beyond what was necessary."

What else is new. Po had seen plenty of bots use what seemed like unnecessary force, in his day. But he kept his mouth shut.

"Either way," Emery continued, "you did the right thing, stopping it. Although, that little speech you gave about bots not ever being cops—maybe keep that to yourself, at least until you're legally out of the woods."

Probably not a bad idea. "Gunny, if it's so clear to everyone that I did the right thing, then what am I still doing here?"

"Like I said. The admins are itching to make an example of you. They clearly aren't happy about anyone destroying one of their bots, for any reason. Even to defend a civilian, apparently. They've set a court date for two months out, and they've preemptively denied you the possibility of bail."

Po's mouth was hanging open. "Two *months?*"

"I'm afraid so. The Corps is leaning on them, but they don't seem interested in budging. Actually, I'm sure the pressure the Corps is putting on them is the reason I didn't find you in conditions much worse than these." The gunny waved a hand to indicate the narrow cell.

For the moment, Po found himself at a complete loss for words.

"They're going to make things as miserable for you as they can get away with, Abbato. To make it not worth it for anyone else to put down a bot."

"But Gunny...I can't stay in here for two months!"

"Why not? The Corps doesn't consider you to be in violation of regs, and they disagree with the admins that you're in need of discipline. You'll receive full pay, and your promotion to corporal is locked in."

"But my *team* needs me."

"Your team's in good hands. I've put Krikorian in charge until you're free."

Po frowned. Krik *would* lead the team well. But the idea that Fireteam Echo would be patrolling without him, and doing who knew what else...possibly getting into danger again, like they already had multiple times since arriving on Venus....

"I understand your frustration. The good news is, your defense of that civilian has made Aeolia's residents a lot more favorable toward us than they were. Of course, that's not saying a *whole* lot, since their opinion of us was pretty bottomed out before this. But some of them seem willing to talk to us, now, and they have some interesting things to say."

Po raised his eyebrows. "Yeah, Gunny?"

"It turns out the entertainment they have access to is completely different from what the rest of the system tends to watch. Sims and vids and movies that can't even be found, outside Venus. In fact, people off-planet have barely heard of them."

"Is that...unusual?"

"Well, for the most part, everyone tends to watch whatever Earth is watching. They're the main exporter of culture, so to speak. But from what we're hearing from these civilians, Venus is a silo of completely different offerings. Vids that show the lavish lifestyles of the cloud cities' upper crust—and how much better off they are than everyone else. Movies about wealthy people acting like complete degenerates, whenever they aren't busy ripping off their employees. Sims about the necessity of revolution, to solve oppression and abuse. Sims that let the players be revolutionaries who topple the existing order."

A silence took hold in the cell. Then, Po spoke up: "Are they still rioting in Laputa?"

"They are. And it's gotten bad. Businesses broken into, set on fire. People are worried they'll sink the colony...though, it would take a lot to do that."

"That shipping exec was worried someone's trying to take over the system," Po said, his voice coming out lower than he'd intended. "Maybe whoever it is wants to start with Venus first."

They chatted for a few minutes more, about less intense topics. After that, Emery clapped him on the shoulder, told him to stay strong, and knocked on the cell door for a bot to let him out.

Po sat on the cot for a long time after the gunny left. He'd opened an article on the mechanisms that kept Venus cloud colonies afloat, but his gaze kept drifting from it, until finally he swept it away and just stared at the wall above the toilet, lost in thought.

***

Gunfire woke him up. He sat up, blinking hard to clear away the grogginess, and trying to figure out if he'd dreamed the shots.

Then came the cough of more gunfire, closer this time.

Not a dream, then.

He called up the time—0132. Silence prevailed for three minutes, before the next shots sounded.

He had no control over the lighting, and lights-out was hours ago. But his eyes had adjusted enough that he could see indistinct shapes, with the help of the bare sliver of light that leaked into his cell from the corridor outside.

Moving slowly, one by one he pulled the pieces of his armor from under the cot, where he'd stashed them in an attempt to prevent the bots from taking them, if they decided to. He probably couldn't have stopped them, but funnily enough, they'd made no move to confiscate the suit. It was as if the admins were daring him to use it to do something they could give him an actual prison sentence for.

Well, maybe I'm about to. Those were almost certainly Marines fighting out there, and he had very little confidence in his ability to just sit in here while his brothers fought in the streets outside.

He donned the armor, double checking the seals and clasps as he went, like he'd learned in SoI. He gave it all a final check once he had it all on...

...then he turned to face the door.

Am I really doing this?

It felt like the sort of decision you couldn't come back from. Once he rammed that door with the intent to batter it down, all bets were off, and he'd have to accept whatever he had coming to him.

There's no way I'm sitting in here while someone tries to kill Marines out there.

So that was his decision made, then. He got into position to run at the door and kick it, just like he'd kicked that bot across the street.

The door opened, washing the cell with light, momentarily blinding him in the instant it took his helmet's visor to polarize.

"*Taylor?*" he said, after he'd read the IFF tag above the SERAPH-suited figure backlit by the corridor's halogens.

"Not just me," the other Marine said. "All of Second Squad is here. First Squad's outside the station."

"The cop-bots just let you walk in here?"

"The bots are all outside killing people. Just a lot of pencil-armed admin aides left in here. And they didn't try very hard to stop us."

"The bots are *all* outside *killing people?*"

"Did I stutter?" Taylor reached in and grabbed Po by the forearm. "Come on, Corporal. There's no way we were going to let you relax in here while we did the fighting."

Po shook off his grip and stepped into the hallway, where the rest of the squad were positioned up and down the hall, monitoring the avenues of attack. Krikorian turned long enough to grin at him, and so did a few others.

"You realize we gotta be breaking at least a dozen Venusian laws, right?" Po said.

"Guess they'll just have to arrest us too," Taylor said. "Let's move."

Chapter 16

"Wait," Po asked as they made their way out of the security station to the street out front. "Where's Corporal Flores?"

"Corporal Flores' command of Second Squad was always temporary," Emery cut in. The gunny's command privileges allowed him to loop himself into any of his subordinates' channels, just as Po had been able to when *he* was given temporary command of 131st Platoon.

"So who's in command of it now?"

"Who do you think?" Taylor said, then knocked on Po's helmet. Po shoved him, sending him stumbling a step.

"Congratulations, Corporal Abbato," Emery said. "Second Squad is yours. And this time, it's for keeps."

"Gunny, I just got out of a jail cell."

"Don't pester me with details."

Po emerged from the station with his new squad to find First Squad securing the street outside. Without having to be told, his Marines instantly went into overwatch mode, taking up position behind metal benches, a kidney-shaped garden with knee-high walls, and the station's doorway. That would let First Squad safely move out, if they so chose.

Now that he was outside, he could hear more distant gunfire, giving him a fuller appreciation of how quickly Aeolia was descending into chaos. A scream punctuated the night, sounding like it came from a block or two over. Po's instinct was to run to the defense of whoever had cried out, but he knew rushing around in a panic to put out what sounded like fires was a bad way to take back control of the situation.

He established a private channel with Emery. "Gunny, what's our plan?"

"Help secure the city. As for specific objectives to accomplish that, I haven't been given any. The minute the fighting began, I took 131st here to break you out."

Po paused a moment, taken aback by that. Bringing the entire platoon across a city devolving into violence just to free him seemed...well, it wasn't something he ever would have expected to happen. *I guess gunny really does want me in charge of this squad.*

"As far as I can tell," Emery went on, "Colonel Tuffin is still trying to get a handle on the situation. In the meantime, he's sent us out to try to stabilize things."

"What started this?"

"Same thing that made you take out that one bot, but on a much bigger scale. Bots started randomly attacking civilians. From what I've heard, they're not even bothering with making up reasons to do it anymore. At least the one you neutralized was polite enough to lie." The gunny shook his head. "Things are a mess, and getting messier by the second. Bots are activating against us all over the city, and I'm hearing reports of new ones coming *into* the city too, on airships they're commandeering."

"They're smart enough for that?"

"Smart enough to threaten to kill pilots if they don't comply? Seems so. The upshot is, whatever direction we advance in, we're going to have it much tougher than we did coming here."

A bot appeared between two buildings, seemed to notice the Marines instantly, and changed its course to sprint at them with blinding speed. Bozzelli opened up on it with the HMG he'd set up behind the garden, and that, combined with four other Marines' rifle fire, took down the machine well before it reached 131st Platoon.

Po chewed his lower lip. "I think I may have an objective for us, Gunny. If you're open to it."

"Absolutely. Spit it out."

"Well...I'm thinking that huge mansion over on Mag Mell, which we saw bots coming in and out of. Unless we think we have enough men to kill all these bots outright, with minimal casualties, then we need to remove their ability to recharge."

A silence came over the line, and Po couldn't read Emery's expression through his polarized visor.

"Gunny?"

"Sorry, that just launched a whole train of thought for me. I hadn't considered that we might be fighting them long enough for them to deplete their charge, and honestly, the idea scares me. But now that you say it, I think that's probably how it's going to have to go. Unless we want to spend a lot of Marine lives." The gunnery sergeant nodded, as if to himself. "And I think you may have just given me a plan to suggest to the colonel."

"Well, I mean, it's an *objective...*"

"An objective that a whole plan just formed around in my mind. Let's get moving toward some elevators." Emery paused. "Looks like Marines are encountering the least resistance to the northeast of our position. We'll head that way. Bozzelli, Fitz, pack up that HMG and make ready to move out. Ubaldo, take a couple of men inside the station and set charges on all the recharging bays you can find."

The First Squad Marines acknowledged the orders, launching into their respective tasks while Second Squad watched for the next attack.

***

Po's M37C vibrated in his hands as he sent a spray of rounds into an actuator that he knew governed his target's leg movement. The limb seized up, causing the bot to pitch forward onto its curved face, which smacked hard against the asphalt. But none of the Marines around Po took pity on the thing, instead making sure it was fully neutralized by giving it another hearty helping of gunfire.

"Are we taking an airship, Corporal?" Gomez asked as they started forward once more, a note of excitement ringing in his voice.

Po suppressed the urge to snort. *Classic Gomez.* "No," he answered, trying to keep his amusement from his voice. "The pilots that haven't been killed or press-ganged into helping the bots have fled by now. Gunny has one of our shuttles flying around to meet us from the southern landing bay." They *might* have headed for one of the landing bays instead, except that the fighting was fierce around them—besides, they were probably one of the first things the bots were looking to shut down, if they had any strategy inside their tin-can heads at all.

The elevators, on the other hand, were much more numerous. The bots would probably get around to clamping down on those too, if they were permitted to. But for now, the elevators seemed like the best option for exiting Aeolia uncontested.

So far, Emery's read of the integrated map had been dead-on. Opposition as they crossed Aeolia's northeast quadrant was light. The biggest group of bots they'd been attacked by numbered only three, and that had been a near thing—they'd poured out of a department store just meters away from the point man, Taylor. If it hadn't been for Second Squad fanning out quickly and shooting accurately, one of them would have surely gotten to him. But as Taylor had danced back, the others had aimed for vital circuit boards, which they'd now instructed their implants to highlight. The bots went down in a tangle of limbs.

We're going to lose men, today.

Po didn't want to think it, but he couldn't escape from the grim conclusion. Bigger groups than three would come at them sooner or later. And when they did, they were going to do some damage.

Thankfully, the Marines were getting smarter about how they were handling the situation in the city. After Emery contacted Tuffin, the colonel designated five defensible locations scattered throughout the city as shelters for residents to flee to, if they could. There, they would enjoy the protection of entrenched Marines, who would use the stronger positions to hold out against the bots, keeping them at bay for as long as they could.

The plan now was to minimize casualties by starving the bots of energy. Sending Marine units roving through the city wasn't the way to accomplish that. It made way more sense to send squads and platoons on surgical strikes against known clusters of charging stations, like 131st was doing now. Otherwise, Marines would hunker in place, destroy what bots came at them, and in doing so protect as many of Aeolia's residents as possible.

That the plan had grown from Po's suggestion to target the Mag Mell mansion baffled him, almost as much as Emery leading 131st to bust him out of jail. Sure, the Marines left no man behind, but Po probably would have been safe in his cell.

Then again...would I? If he'd managed to break out himself as he'd been planning, he would have been unarmed. Sure, he *might* have been able to defeat a single bot with his suit alone. But if multiple came at him?

No chance.

But instead of that, Emery had come for him...and out of that had come this. More hope for the Marines, and a chance for the city's residents to seek refuge against the suddenly homicidal bots—the bots they'd relied on to keep the peace all their lives.

How insane this must seem to them. How unsettling. But the whole system was going insane, fast. At this point, stopping to dwell on it would only be a distraction.

Nevertheless, Taylor apparently wanted to dwell on it.

"What's this about, Gunny?" he asked over the platoon-wide as they moved across a plaza deserted both by man and machine. "What's the bots' play, here? What are they hoping to accomplish?"

"It's not the bots," Emery said. "It's whoever's behind them. Whoever's controlling them."

"Okay. What do *they* want, then?"

"To cut down on the number of places in the system GEA can launch missiles from, for one. Venus is one of the government's primary places for projecting force from. But there's something else they gain, by taking Venus away from GEA. Something much more important."

"Earth," Krikorian said. "They get to threaten Earth. Just like those terrorists on the moon."

"It all comes back to Earth," Emery said. "Always. If humanity loses Earth, we're done. There's no getting around it."

"Why would humans want to attack Earth?" Taylor asked.

Emery gave a grim chuckle. "Who says it's humans behind this?"

No one had anything to say to that. And ten minutes later, when they were on the shuttle and heading for Mag Mell, the thoughtful silence persisted.

***

"Any chance of an assist from your shipping executive friend?" Emery asked him as their shuttle crossed the gap between the two cloud colonies.

Po shook his head. "He didn't give me any contact. Wouldn't even say his name. But he *did* mention living in Aeolia with his family. So, I doubt he'll be on-site to help us, even if we wanted to go looking for him."

"Please God he's still alive. And his family."

Po hesitated, then nodded. "For sure, Gunny."

Emery's eyes were still fixed on the air in front of him—he'd been reviewing Po's implant footage of the mansion, from the day he and Krik met the executive. "I'd rather avoid a frontal assault on this place," the gunny said. "Seems like a great way to invite an army of bots down on our heads."

"I suggest we hit the building the exec approached us out of first. What he called their 'local hub.' I'll bet there's a passage connecting it to the mansion, running under the street. No doubt it's secured somehow—but is it secure to withstand a platoon of stubborn Marines?"

Emery grinned. "Highly unlikely."

The gunny managed to establish contact with the platoon responsible for Mag Mell before their shuttle docked. Apparently the Marines there had their hands more than full already, with their own bot uprising, but their commander at least promised to attempt to break away if 131st needed them.

Better than nothing, I guess, Po thought. But the fact that the Marines here were hard-pressed too made him wonder how many other colonies on Venus were dealing with killer bots. *Probably all of them.* If someone was making a move like this, why wouldn't they move all their pieces at once?

They took an elevator big enough to hold the whole platoon, and when they got to the top, they found the area around the southern elevators empty. Along the way to the mansion, they only encountered one bot that needed neutralizing, which they did handily.

But one was enough. Enough to alert whoever and whatever was inside that mansion that a platoon of Marines was advancing on it.

"This just got even more hectic, gentlemen," Emery said as the two squads leapfrogged past the smoking cop-bot.

"Oh, good," Krikorian deadpanned. "I was beginning to get bored."

Chapter 17

The Distribly hub turned out to have three floors, two of them extending under the colony's surface level. It was essentially an office cubicle farm, of the kind Equipoise had maintained on Psyche and which Po had always dreaded ending up in. It also had *actual* offices along the buildings' perimeter, for management, and the ones on the ground level enjoyed a view of the surrounding streets, while the underground offices had monitors that cycled through what seemed to be the solar system's greatest hits in terms of beautiful views: Titan's ice-belching volcanoes and methane lakes, water vapor spurting through Enceladus' shell of ice, and Ganymede's colorful geology.

The cubicles had only blank beige walls to stare at, covered by whatever art the occupants had put up themselves.

Though I guess the ones with Circuits could have whatever view they want. And working for a company like this, they probably all have company-subsidized implants.

The rows of cubicles made the place a pain to clear, but clear it they did, with the memory of Sergeant Young's death fresh in Po's mind.

Haste is never an excuse to neglect properly clearing a place. He'd learned that lesson for a price he never would have willingly paid. He swallowed around the hard lump in his throat and continued working with his squad to check everywhere, dividing the second sublevel between his three fireteams while First Squad secured the ground floor.

They found a handful of employees cowering in cubicles and offices, and searching them proved them to be what they seemed to be: unarmed civilians who hadn't worked up the courage to try escaping home to their families.

Or maybe they have no families. That was just as likely as not, this day and age, especially on a place like Venus. Or so he'd heard.

The Marines' lengthy inspection of the place would give whoever or whatever was defending the mansion time to get ready for them. But it had to be better than overlooking hostiles hiding in *this* building, positioned to hit them from behind at the worst possible moment.

Emery left his Bravo and Charlie teams to secure the ground floor against just such an outcome, while he took his Alpha Team to the lowest level to help Po's squad clear it. They made shorter work of it, likely because of a combination of familiarity with the layout and the help of Fireteam Alpha.

It was Po's Delta Team that found the tunnel leading to the mansion—and the reinforced, vault-like door halfway along it, barring access to their target.

"This thing wants some C4," Crotty said over the platoon-wide, transmitting what he was seeing to their Circuits. "And a fair bit of it, I'd say."

"Then get to setting some," Emery said. "Bravo Team has more charges for you, if you need them."

"On it, Gunny."

As they'd pretty much anticipated, the bots were ready for them—arrayed in the corridor beyond the metal block of a door, which Crotty had knocked onto the floor with liberal amounts of explosives.

Unfortunately for the bots, the Marines were also ready for them. Two M320s coughed, launching grenades arcing just below the three-meter ceiling. Next, snipers cracked, the rounds finding 'vital' points in the frames of the first bots to appear—though "vital" definitely wasn't the right word.

But word choice became an afterthought as Bozzelli opened up with his M221 Harvey HMG, pummeling and chewing up bots as he swung the line of tracers back and forth across the corridor. With the rest of the Marines who had a clear line of sight adding their rifle fire, the security bots stood little chance. They were soon reduced to a heap of charred metal limbs and dented torsos.

As Po advanced down the corridor with the others, it hit him that taking down the bots was nothing like killing Nibirans, and even less like fighting other humans out on the regolith back on Earth's moon. Even neutralizing alien insurgents had left him with dark, twisted dreams and mixed feelings.

But as he stepped over the sparking, twitching bots, he felt none of that. The cop-bots were nothing but tools designed by humans to control other humans with violence—violence the bots never had any hesitation to use, that Po had observed.

The fewer of them operating in the system, the better. If he could, he'd put down another thousand of them without a second thought.

***

Not all the robotic defenders had clustered in the sublevel hall to be purged with metal and flame—nor were all the mansion's defenders bots.

But even the armed humans they encountered surrendered immediately on seeing SERAPH-suited Marines tromping along burgundy rugs past the mansion's lavishly appointed rooms and alcoves.

Guess they figure if all those bots downstairs didn't stop us, they're not going to.

That wasn't all, though. A lot of these armed 'guards' looked to Po like they'd be happier stuffed into one of those cubicles they'd cleared. Wherever Distribly hired its security from, they gave every sign of having held their jobs for a while, and having gotten accustomed to the idea that killer bots would be the first thrown at any problem that arose. As a result, they'd grown soft, weak, and cowardly. They might as well have been cardboard cutouts, for all they did to stop 131st Platoon from owning the place.

It was the lone bots taking cover behind doors and alcoves that posed the real threat. They had no such concern for self-preservation, and they obviously had only one directive: kill intruders.

This they tried their best to do, and while the Marines took care as they advanced through the mansion, using their numbers to neutralize any resistance before it could inflict actual casualties, the bots *did* manage to slow them a lot more than Po would have liked. He was sure Emery felt the same. Probably, the entire platoon did.

Venus' thick clouds made it impossible for signals to get through to keep them updated on the situation in Aeolia, and Po felt anxious to return there. Most of all to back up his brothers, but also because of the city's importance. Venus' planetary government operated out of the city, for one. If they got taken out, the blow would be staggering, and presumably it would leave the planet even less prepared for the next attack. Assuming this one failed.

They cleared the mansion at last, finding no one except the guards hired to defend the place, who the Marines restrained and kept under the watch of a buddy pair in an upstairs living room. Jeremy Zin, Distribly's CEO, had either escaped as they were clearing the hub across the street or hadn't been here in the first place.

Probably the second one. If Zin was complicit in launching a bot revolution to take over Venus, it seemed in his best interests to be far from here when it actually happened. A few hundred million miles minimum, Po figured.

They found the bot charging bays in the basement, and used the rest of their C4 in destroying them. Unsurprisingly, that caught the mansion on fire, which proved a lot more flammable than the underground tunnel had been. Automatic sprinklers cut in, but there didn't seem to be enough of them, and the explosives proved their better.

131st Platoon had neither the means nor the inclination to fight the fire, so they ushered the security guards outside, keeping them close as they made their way back to the elevator they'd ridden up here, where Emery had told the shuttle pilot to wait for them.

"I've sent a message to the local authorities about the fire, for what good it'll do," the gunny said over the platoon-wide. "The station has automated fire suppression, which should kick in before long. Hopefully they're better than the ones installed in that mansion. Either way, there are more pressing things happening right now than Jeremy Zin's house burning down."

They let the guards go the moment before they piled into the elevator, sending them to seek their fortunes in Mag Mell's battle-ravaged streets. *Hopefully Zin's bots are programmed with their likenesses, along with instructions not to shoot them.* But either way, it was the best the Marines could do right now.

The shuttle decoupled from the elevator dock the moment the hatch was closed, moving at max thrust back toward Aeolia.

The moment they drew close enough for signal to make it through the clouds, Emery received a broken message from Colonel Tuffin, made choppy by the golden-brown barrier.

He played it for them:

"As soon as you're—compromised the—primary lift—all of them at—city's going down."

Po wasn't clear at all on what the first part of the message meant. But that didn't seem to matter too much.

The last three words were clear enough.

***

The city was steadily losing altitude by the time their shuttle docked with one of the northern elevators. On their way up, the gunny cut them in on his conversation with Colonel Tuffin, which thankfully wasn't broken up and static-filled like the colonel's transmission had been.

"As soon as the bots realized what we were doing—digging into well-defended positions—they stopped fighting us and started targeting admins."

"Wait," Emery said. "*Admins?*"

"That's what I said. The bots started hitting their homes. The ones who weren't already killed by their own house bots, that is. But it seems most of the admins don't have bots guarding their houses. A couple of them have *human* security guards, and pretty much all of them live in houses fancy enough to be capable of locking down nice and tight. And a lot of those *have* gone into lockdown. But the bots are working on cracking them open, one by one, to get in and kill the occupants."

"Sorry, sir. I'm having a little trouble keeping up. The admins are the ones who've been working against us since we got here. The ones who've done everything they can to protect their bots, including when they turn on civilians. They even tried to make a legal example of one of my men." Emery's eyes met Po's. "If you'd asked me who's responsible for all this, I would have *said* the admins."

"That would have been my first guess too, to be honest. But I no longer think the admins are responsible for this bot uprising. Getting killed by said bots is a pretty decent alibi for that."

"Who *is* responsible, then, sir?"

"It's not our job to try to figure that out. Right now, it's our job to save those admins, along with as many civilians as we can. Marines are already escorting survivors to the elevators in groups, to be taken to one of *our* floating bases, since those are the only places we can be sure aren't having the same problems Aeolia's having right now. But most of the airship pilots have fled into the cloud cover, and of course we can't even establish contact with them to demand they return. A few brave ones have stayed, but between them and our shuttles, getting people off this station is proving slow going."

"How did the bots manage to bring the city down?"

"I can only guess they were able to pry their way into the maintenance corridors of the city's four primary lift balloons and line them with explosives. What I can say for sure is that those balloons are now destroyed beyond repair, and the city is going down.

Thankfully, the descent is fairly slow, since even the breathable air inside the colony itself provides a fair bit of lift in Venus' CO2-dense atmo."

"I see. Where do you want us, then, sir?"

"I want you working on saving admins. We may not like them, but their boss is our boss...and the boss won't be happy if we stand by while they're slaughtered. Plus, Venus will be completely neutered without its admins—even worse than if the bots took out the planetary government. And then there's the argument that saving their bacon is the right thing to do. Hard as that is to say."

"Agreed, sir."

"I'm sending you the location for the nearest home to you of an admin that hasn't been killed, at least according to the last check-in. Get there, and secure it. And make it quick. Slow is smooth and smooth is fast—except for today. Today, fast is fast."

Chapter 18

"We have time," Po told his platoonmates over the wide channel as they moved out from the elevator, "and the colony might not even crash to the planet's surface. The farther down we go, the hotter it gets, and the stronger the planet's winds get. Which means at a certain altitude, the colony should be able to stay afloat with even just the main bubble where the city is."

"As long as *that* isn't compromised," Taylor said.

"It'd have to get badly compromised. Since with the increasing pressure differential, the gases in here aren't about to escape out. If it gets really bad, we can have whatever admins are left cut power to Aeolia's cooling systems. That'll make it hotter in here, which will make it even easier to float."

"How do you know all that?" Krikorian asked. "Are you the new Paisley?"

Irritation pulsed behind Po's eyes, but he forced the emotion down. "I hope not. I've just been doing some reading during downtime."

Maybe he *had* been compensating for Paisley's desertion, unconsciously. As bitter as the former Marine's betrayal had been, he'd left a void in the fireteam when he'd abandoned it—a void in the platoon, if Po was being completely honest. Paisley was knowledgeable and competent. And now he was an enemy.

If we're going to defeat our enemies, we *need to be knowledgeable and competent.*

131st double-timed through Aeolia's outskirts. It made Po nervous how many buildings they were passing without clearing them. Any one of them might hold a host of bots ready to surge out and hit them from behind.

It wasn't how urban warfare was meant to be conducted. Rushing like this. It hadn't been like this back in Eremus.

But Colonel Tuffin's imperative—that today, fast was fast—spurred them forward. And Tuffin was right. Even given what Po had pointed out about their descent through

Venus' atmosphere, this was a heavy colony, and it *would* sink. If the bots managed to rupture Aeolia's main balloon, the one that housed the city itself, then it would sink a lot faster.

He couldn't really remember what he'd expected Venus to be like, but he knew for sure he hadn't expected to be contending once again with the realities of urban combat. This was the solar system's wealthiest place, and wealth was supposed to shield people from things like this. The fact that utter chaos had broken out on the system elites' doorstep made this all the more harrowing, somehow. It just wasn't supposed to happen.

As the city sank majestically through the clouds, the golden-brown canopy swirling above the transparent dome became gradually less gold, and more brown. As it did, an ethereal twilight began to descend across Aeolia. Yes, the lights were still on their daylight setting, but the more they descended, the more clouds there were to block out the actual sunlight.

131st Platoon was stopped well before they reached the admin's house—not by an ambush, but a message. One that was essentially a distress signal, from Captain Haldane, who had been given command of Raptor Company. It was text-only, and came in all-caps to every Marine implant:

"UNDER HEAVY ATTACK FOUR HUNDRED METERS NORTH-NORTH-WEST OF THE SOUTHWESTERN ELEVATORS. CAUGHT OUT WITH LARGE GROUP OF CIVILIANS. REQUEST IMMEDIATE BACKUP FROM ALL NEARBY UNITS."

One glance at his integrated map told Po that 131st was the closest unit to where the rest of Raptor was pinned down.

That meant they were it.

Without need for discussion, the entire platoon veered in that direction, heads on a swivel for a bot ambush of their own, which to Po felt like a near-inevitability.

***

As they ran, Emery contacted Tuffin to notify him of their change in objective, and he looped the entire platoon in on the conversation once again.

The colonel confirmed him in his decision to deviate from the original plan. "From the snatches of intel I have coming in now, the bots have all but completely abandoned trying to kill the admins and are going after our two forces escorting civilians to elevators. Their admin killing spree is starting to seem like a secondary objective for them at best, and a ruse to lull us into a false sense of security at worst. The moment we left our positions, and got far enough away from safety, they converged on us and hit us hard."

After that update, Tuffin left Emery to concentrate on running toward the battle, and figuring out how he would approach it once he got there.

Po studied his integrated map, just as he was sure the gunny was doing. He was the platoon's second-in-command, now, after all. Emery would expect suggestions from him.

All without Zanth to provide them. But maybe he was being too hard on himself. He'd made at least a contribution or two since parting ways with the Emplor.

It seemed like a while since he'd thought about the alien, and he realized he felt better not communing with him, whether in speech or thought. Even so, *not* thinking about Zanth was also dangerous. The Emplor had demonstrated a strong desire to remove Po from the board, and it was only a matter of time before he made his next attempt to accomplish it.

129th and 130th Platoons had been hit by a wave of bots while crossing a plaza, and they'd withdrawn into a strip of shops that bordered it, with the civilians presumably cowering in the shops behind them. Even as Po watched the map, several of the green dots representing Marines turned a sickly yellow, indicating they were being actively engaged. The map used red dots to represent the enemy, with various degrees of opacity to indicate how certain a Marine's Circuit AI was of their location. Several of the red dots were right on top of the yellow dots, at full opacity. One of the green dots flashed purple, indicating an injury, before going straight to black—that Marine had just died.

Po gritted his teeth and pounded along the lane he was running down with his squad. First Squad had trended north, and was sprinting along a road parallel to Second Squad's. They'd emerge into the plaza at two different points, setting up the best flank they could manage given the need for haste.

A bot sprinted into the lane ahead of them, taking the corner sharply toward the plaza, and then spinning about to face Po's squad as it seemed to register their presence. But its momentum carried it along for a couple of steps more—long enough for Po to get his M37C up and start hitting it. Gomez, Taylor, and Zhang added their fire, and the thing went down.

"Find cover where this road lets onto the plaza," he told his squad, without missing a beat. "We'll get established as quickly as we can, put down any bots looking to tangle, and then advance toward the shops."

The road ended, and his men did as he'd ordered with gratifying speed, mostly taking cover behind the low walls bordering the properties on either side of the lane, which separated them from the plaza.

Po's heart leapt into his throat as he took his first proper look at the open area. Bots were emerging from between buildings in every direction, running with lighting speed toward the shops where the beleaguered Marines were fighting desperately for their lives—and for the civilians' lives.

"Buddy pairs, link Circuits," Po said. "Pair leader will select target." Their implants would alert them if they'd chosen another pair's target, to avoid inefficient fire.

His buddy was Krik, and together they fired at a bot nearly at the shops. Po's second burst blew out a knee actuator, sending the bot toppling and skidding across the asphalt. Even then, it continued to drag itself toward its destination, until Krik's rounds found the motherboard in its chest. The firing angle meant the rounds had likely torn through the thing length-wise, explaining why the bot stopped moving altogether.

"Metal freak," the Armenian muttered as Po selected their next target.

Incoming bots kept both of 131st's squads busy for several minutes—long enough for Bozz and Barbier to set up their HMGs and start ripping. Marines continued to die inside the shops, but the red dots indicating bots were falling much faster. Still...there were way too many, and in one shop, three Marines had been killed, leaving four bots stalking the premises.

If any civilians are in there, they're lost, Po thought, angry bile rising up his throat.

At last, the flood of incoming bots slowed to a trickle, and Emery made the call. "We're moving in. Abbato, you want to move or cover?"

"Move," Po growled.

"Then go. We got you."

"Leave the M221," Po told Barbier. With that, Second Squad advanced across the plaza with weapons up, while First continued to mow down bots before they became a problem.

Po led his squad to the shop beset by the most bots, picking off the ones outside as they approached.

"Echo goes in first," Po said when they were almost upon it. "Delta, be ready to come in after us. Foxtrot, monitor the situation through that window from out front, and shoot through it if needed."

With that, Po approached the door on point, grabbed and opened it in one swift motion, and kicked down the doorstop as he passed, to keep it open. Why it hadn't been left open already, or broken, he couldn't say, and there was no time to think about it. The cashier area was just ahead of him, and behind it was a wall dividing the front of the store from the back, from beyond which came the sounds of struggle. Po stepped past racks of brightly colored clothes, and then over the body of a Marine whose SERAPH suit had been torn open, along with his innards. Just like the one who'd been found slain in the alleyway.

Po grimaced. "Body, here," he told his squad—Taylor and Gomez were close behind, with Vacca and Krikorian just coming in the door.

Two more Marine corpses awaited them in the back room, and four downed bots. One of the changing room's doors was off its hinges, and inside it a Marine grappled with a robot, trying to prevent it from grabbing his armor's seams with its versatile grippers to rip it apart.

Po treated it to rounds in the back, which seemed like the best option for neutralizing it while not hitting the Marine.

The bot jerked, twisting partly around. The Marine it was grappling with punched it, which did little damage but served to knock it backward, toward Po.

He roundhouse kicked the thing, sending it staggering sideways into another rack of clothes and allowing him to sidestep to the left for a clean shot.

He took it, and the bot deactivated.

"Another one chased Abbato out back," said the Marine he'd saved.

Po narrowed his eyes. *Abbato?* Then he stiffened, realizing just who had fled to the back of the store.

A multitude of dark thoughts sprang up in his mind, but he swept them away before any could gain a foothold. He headed swiftly for the door, which was left open, and which led into what looked like a storage room.

There, in the middle of an open space, a Marine lay on his back while a bot straddled him, pummeling and clawing at him, its limbs flashing with an eerie quickness.

Po leveled his M37 at the thing, steadied it, and fired.

It was over in seconds. The bot collapsed onto the Marine, sparking. Neither moved. The trepidation Po experienced as he approached the entwined pair surprised him. His heart hammered in his chest.

He dropped his rifle to dangle by its strap and grabbed the bot with both hands, hauling it away to find his brother blinking up at the ceiling, his face pasty-white.

Po offered Lorenzo a hand. Lorenzo's eyes focused on it, and he scowled, pushing himself to his feet and walking out of the storage room without a word.

Taylor stepped aside to let him go, watching him with eyebrows raised.

He turned back to Po. "That was your brother?"

"Yeah."

"Do all Abbatos act like tools?"

Po shot him a tight smile. The moment he did, a massive explosion rocked the colony, and they both lost their footing as racks and shelving crashed to the floor all around them.

Chapter 19

"They blew out the main balloon," Emery said over the platoon-wide as Echo Team finished clearing the clothing store.

"How?" Po asked.

"I don't know. Somehow, they managed to get a lot of explosives and hide them somewhere critical. That's all I have to tell you."

"Is the damage enough to speed up our descent?" Po asked.

"Yes. And I have it from Colonel Tuffin's analysts that what's left of the balloon will now contract worse than it was going to. The air should be breathable for a while longer, with the higher air pressure keeping it pinned to the platform the city is on. But I wouldn't recommend taking off your helmets. Evacuating civilians also just got harder—and it'll only get worse. Soon enough, every civvy we take outside is going to need a breather, at minimum."

"What's our plan now, Gunny?"

"Keep doing what you're doing. We'll keep the plaza locked down in the meantime. Extracting whatever civilians are left from that strip mall and getting them onto an airship or one of our shuttles just became an even bigger priority than it already was."

Clearing more stores, and saving more Marines from desperate situations, had a snowball effect. It swelled their numbers, and soon Raptor Company was in top form—though they'd lost nine of their number, a devastating blow. They swept through store after store with a vengeance, clearing them of bots and liberating civilians.

The civilians that were still alive, that was. The ones who'd been killed had to be left. As much as it pained Po to leave anyone's body to the mercy of the bots and Venus' hostile surface, there was nothing that could be done. Time had run out, for pretty much everything.

As Delta and Foxtrot were helping retake the last couple stores, Po established a private channel with Emery. "Gunny."

"Abbato."

"I wanted to…ask. Surely we're a little more keen to follow up on what that shipping exec said about bot production facilities on the surface? Now that the bots have staged a planet-wide revolution, I mean. And, considering we're headed that way anyway."

Emery gave a dry chuckle. "I've actually already been talking to Colonel Tuffin about that, and as far as I know, he's been talking with the rest of the brass. Colonel Coleman is the highest-ranking officer on the planet, and Tuffin would prefer to have his go-ahead before launching an op like that. Unfortunately, Coleman was in Laputa with his hands full with riots, and there's no way to get the question to him through the clouds in time—let alone to wait for an answer back. So, Tuffin is having to make the call himself, which means it's completely on him if it turns out to be a disaster."

"So he's being careful."

"Exactly."

Having spent over a year leading a fireteam, and a few weeks in charge of a full squad, Po had at least *some* appreciation for the need to be diligent when it came to making decisions, especially ones that held the lives of his subordinates in the balance.

But they were currently fighting bots on a sinking city, which would crash to Venus' surface sooner or later, while conditions steadily worsened in the meantime. As Tuffin himself had said, fast had to be fast now. There wasn't any other way this could go. It wasn't a time to sit in an office, or wherever Tuffin was right now, weighing every factor involved in making the call to seek and destroy those bot factories. It was a time to do a quick gut check and then act.

But if Po's thoughts weren't *completely* irrelevant, they might as well have been. Yes, his suggestion to destroy the bots' charging stations had inspired Emery to develop a full-fledged plan on the fly, and Tuffin had accepted that plan. But the colonel wasn't likely to respond positively to a corporal hectoring him about the need for haste. Especially not at a time like this.

Besides, our taking out the charging stations doesn't really do much, now. Unless the bots' mystery controller planned to send a fleet of airships to collect them in the final minutes before the city went down, they'd almost certainly be destroyed when Aeolia crashed to the planet's surface. And so, charged or not, the bots didn't need to stay operational for that much longer.

But none of that really mattered, so he swept it all from his mind. What mattered right now was that the Marines in Aeolia were in a race, against both the bots and gravity, to save as many civilians as they could.

The same civilians who refused to even look at us, most days.

But Po was paid in crypto, not in the gratitude of noncombatants, and that was a good thing. Because if the Corps had paid him in the latter, he would be even poorer than he was.

***

Aeolia's 'sky,' such as it was, was growing noticeably darker every time Po returned outside. The burgeoning canopy of clouds, now mostly brown, pressed closer and closer to the city's streets, until it had swallowed the tops of several downtown towers. If he wasn't so busy fighting, he might have started taking bets on what would happen first: the clouds descending to kiss the asphalt, forcing them to rely on thermal to see, or the city finally sinking beneath the clouds altogether.

Shortly after he had the thought, he emerged with his squad from an admin's house to find it was the latter: the cloud layer was now a distant ceiling, and the city was darker than Po ever remembered it being, even though Tuffin had apparently managed to get an admin to set its lights to permanent noontime.

As they advanced toward their next objective—a pocket of civilians taking shelter in a rec center's basement, who'd broadcast a signal begging for the Marines' help—Po took the risk of keeping his eyes on the distant clouds for several seconds. He squinted at them, not sure if he was imagining things, or if he really could *see* them getting farther away now, in real time.

He wondered what the planet's surface looked like. So far, none of the rescue ops had taken him to the edge of the city, and chances were none of them would. In all the downtime research he'd conducted on Venus, he'd never bothered to look up much about the surface. His focus had been entirely on the reality of operating in the clouds.

Foolish. Shortsighted. But beating himself up about it wouldn't do anything for the civilians desperate for help, so he pushed the thoughts aside.

As they double-timed back and forth across the city, it became increasingly common to find dead civilians on the streets and alleyways, their bodies already visibly corroded from the atmo's sulfuric acid.

Some of the bodies were much more brutalized than that, just as the bots had now done to dozens of Marines. But others had clearly asphyxiated. They'd either panicked and attempted to flee to one of the elevators on their own, or they'd been forced outside without a breather, whether by human or bot.

If they only left out of panic, you'd think they'd have grabbed a breather first. Then again, panic tended to obliterate thought. And then there were those who probably kept no breather in their residence, or simply couldn't find the one they owned before their emotions overtook them and they bolted.

You never think you're going to need something like that until it's too late. Po was sure there were plenty of people who *had* taken a breather, and maybe even a suit to protect against the sulfuric acid. But then, they were a lot less likely to be found lying dead on the streets, weren't they?

He felt proud of how quickly his squad was moving, and how efficiently they were operating. Seeing how determined they were to save as many people as they could reminded him of infiltrating To'sheth Rin's underwater lair, when he and his brothers had put themselves in harm's way repeatedly in order to protect the Nibiran women and children that the cowardly insurgents had kept there with them, even knowing they could be attacked at any time.

Together, the Marines remaining in Aeolia worked together to check every known location of survivors. After a time, it became apparent that they were just as likely to find them gone or dead than they were to find them huddling there, waiting to be escorted to some sort of escape vehicle.

Once all the known locations had been checked, they began taking the city street by street, checking every house, just like you were supposed to do in urban warfare.

The longer they went, the faster the city fell, and the more obvious it became that many, if not most of Aeolia's residents would not survive the day. Plenty of them were already dead, and Po wouldn't have given any one of them very good odds. It wrenched his heart, and made him want to hit something. It made him attack the bots with all the more vehemence.

He wanted nothing more than to save all of them. This wasn't Nibiru, where they walked among aliens, and where even there Po had felt like he was dying inside when he'd been forced to stand by and watch a civilian get beaten senselessly.

These were *humans*. And most of them were going to die. They still had no idea who was responsible, but Po wanted badly to find out. Whoever it was, he was developing a deep-seated yearning to make them pay.

At last, the order came down the line.

"That's it," Emery said. "We can't stay any longer, Marines. We've done all we can. Make for the elevator designated by your implant with all possible speed."

As Po and his men ran for the waiting shuttle allocated them by their implants, the clouds were *definitely* drawing noticeably farther away, now. It felt like they were racing away, such that it was hard to believe the colony hadn't crashed to the surface yet.

They reached the elevator and piled in. Po found himself fighting an urge to nervously fidget with his rifle during what seemed like a glacial descent. He turned to his implant to distract himself and found that the elevator offered its occupants the option of accessing an exterior sensor.

With trepidation, he did, and his skin went cold all over when he saw just how late his superiors had left it to order their departure.

A brown wasteland was rushing up to meet them, all the faster for their elevator's descent. Everything he could see was cast in a dim, sickly yellow. His eyes hitched on a sea of ridges, a stunted mountain range, the dim outline of a horizon in the distance. The increasingly far-off clouds. All of it, the yellow of bile. Such was the quality of the sun's light, filtered through all that oppressive cloud.

Other Marine shuttles had already left the city, and could be seen flying in formation, waiting for the remaining shuttles to join them.

For a moment, Po doubted his shuttle *would* have time to join—either that, or it would leave without them, its pilot decoupling from the elevator's bottom after realizing Po and his squad simply weren't going to make it in time.

Then, somehow, they did make it. They all filed through the airlock, and it was a testament to their training that they didn't try to push past each other in a panic, creating the sort of bottleneck that would surely kill them.

The hatch closed behind them, and the shuttle decoupled, thrusting mightily. It put perhaps three hundred meters between them and the city before Aeolia impacted.

Po watched the downtown core buckle straight into the ground, its buildings toppling into each other to form a rough and blocky tepee. A ring of explosions blossomed all along Aeolia's perimeter, where most of its industrial facilities were located. But those were quickly swallowed entirely by the massive dust cloud the city's crash sent up—and it wasn't long before the dust blocked the entire colony from sight.

Venus' largest city had just gone down. The system's most affluent planet had lost its crown jewel. It was a difficult thing to process, and Po was sure he *wouldn't* process it for a long time. Not entirely. Not properly.

But even so, it occurred to him to wonder what else would go down, now that Aeolia had fallen.

And he wasn't just thinking about Venus' other cloud colonies. He was thinking of the entire system, and of the species that had always called it home.

The species to which he happened to belong.

Chapter 20

Po took off his helmet for some fresh air—as fresh as it could get in a sealed environment on a planet hostile to life, that was. All around him, other Marines were doing the same.

He used his implant to keep an eye on the situation outside. He couldn't remember seeing so many shuttles together at one time, and it spoke to the scale of the operation the Marines had conducted here on Venus, with at least a platoon on every cloud colony of any size.

Only a fraction of those men were represented here—just the ones who'd needed to evacuate local colonies, after ferrying as many civilians to safety as they could.

"Look," Zhang said, and Po turned to where he was pointing, using his implant to open a window in that direction.

Another doomed cloud colony was in the process of descending majestically from the upside-down sea of clouds. Another victim of the bot uprising.

Then, another one caught his eye as it broke through the clouds to fall and eventually crash to the surface. Less than a minute, he spotted another break through.

Before long, he counted ten colonies at various stages of slow freefall, with what was left of their balloons struggling desperately to lift their burdens back toward the sky, helped by the increasing temperature and wind as they neared the surface. But not helped enough. They continued to sink through the thick atmosphere. Like Aeolia, their last day had come.

And this was just what he could see from the vantage point of his shuttle. It seemed a near certainty that all over the planet, colonies were suffering a similar fate.

His heart felt like it was in the pit of his stomach—as though it might tumble down into his right boot. They'd come here to *prevent* something like this. But now it had happened, on their watch, even as they fought back directly.

Everything felt wrong, since the day he'd killed To'sheth Rin. That was supposed to be a resounding victory over the forces of evil in the system. But instead, evil had scattered, proliferated, metastasized.

Could Janus possibly be behind this? Or was there another, greater force connecting the insurgents and the bots?

He had no idea. Maybe they weren't connected at all, even though Po felt deeply that they were akin to each other in some way.

Regardless, the Marine Corps had come here on a mission, and that mission had clearly failed. They'd lost every soul aboard the *Magnolia*, and now they'd failed to save thousands, if not millions of civilians.

What was happening to this system? What was happening to humanity?

And why couldn't the Corps stop it?

Something else broke through the clouds, then: a tiny speck of black against the yellow. Po had to use the shuttle's sensor to zoom in on it before he could discern what it was:

It was an AC-900 gunship. And just off its stern, a second gunship appeared, followed by a third, and a fourth.

The foursome descended to meet the formation of shuttles, falling in with them as they flew westward, and together all the craft began to climb once more, rising above the barren land.

"This is where we start to fight back," Emery told them from where he'd risen to his feet at the front of the shuttle. "Thanks to the intel Abbato and Krik were given, we know the areas where these bots were produced, and even as we speak we have drones and gunships combing them for where we might gain entry into those facilities. You've been fighting for hours, and I suggest you catch what shuteye you can right now, during our shuttle ride. Because we're not done yet—not nearly. The bots, and whoever's behind them, may think they just bought Venus for all the blood they've spilled. But all they've purchased is a world of pain. We're the Extraplanetary Corps, which means everything outside Earth is ours. Now we're about to show them what that means. Oorah?"

"Oorah!" The Marines all shouted back, louder and stronger than Po would have expected.

***

Orders were distributed to each craft *before* they ascended once more into the clouds, with strict execution and rendezvous times, since new orders couldn't be sent through the thick orange miasma.

131st's shuttle docked with one of the Corps' floating bases, and the platoon was ordered off, to help load ordnance onto the various shuttles and gunships.

As he stepped out of the shuttle's airlock and left the landing bay with the others, Po began to gain a true appreciation for the extent of the Corps' permanent presence on Venus. The base was nowhere near as big as Aeolia, but that didn't mean it couldn't hold a staggering amount of materiel and personnel.

It was essentially a gigantic warehouse. No fancy transparent dome here—the interior was more spherical, with Torres tanks and mechs and APCs and shuttles and AC-900 gunships parked on tiered, open-air decks, all visible from the central area, where the base proper was laid out.

The center of the base was kind of like a neat and orderly town, if small. It reminded Po a little of FOB Longhorn, though it wasn't quite that spacious. Still, there were buildings everywhere he looked, with Marines milling in and out of them.

As 131st Platoon was entering, a group of civilians was being escorted into the base from another shuttle, and as they were taken toward one of the nearby buildings, a member of the group lost it completely.

"No. No! Don't take me there. I won't go. You can't take me there. I know what you're going to do to me!" He clung to the pale woman beside him, who was only growing paler. At her knees, two small children looked up at the man in bewilderment.

He's their father, Po realized.

"This was all their plan, Suze. You see? They're going to exterminate the lot of us. I knew it. I *knew* it. Keep us under their thumb till they're done with us. That's what this is about. They're *with* the bots, I'm telling you. For all we know, they *are* bots."

A Marine walked slowly toward him, holding up his hands in an obvious effort to calm him down, but he only clung to his wife harder, and it looked to Po like he might be hurting her. The man lashed out at the SERAPH-suited Marine with his leg, kicking wildly toward his shins, while both he and his wife staggered backward together, unsteadily enough that Po was worried they'd both go down in a heap and get hurt.

"Get away from me!" the man shrieked. "Get away!"

Another Marine stepped briskly behind the staggering couple, wrenched the man's arms apart, and twisted them behind his back, slapping a pair of restraints on his wrists.

The first shot the wife an apologetic look through his transparent visor while the other marched the man off somewhere, probably to a containment cell to await medical attention.

Everyone has their breaking point, Po mused. But as pitiable as the scene was, he couldn't help feeling a certain contempt for the man, either. *Just another father failing his family.*

As one of the children's parents was led away, screaming and shrieking like a frightened girl, the mother bent down and swept them into her arms. To Po, they already looked traumatized by the experience. He couldn't help but shake his head.

Men need to be stronger than that, or they shouldn't have kids. Of course, he couldn't see Luca Abbato breaking down quite like this man had—but Luca had been weak in other ways. Weak for drink, and lacking enough self-control to restrain his rage—instead letting it explode in his wife and kids' faces.

The episode over, he focused on helping his brothers load the waiting shuttles and gunships with the necessaries of war: rations, weapons, ammo, extra SERAPH suits, and lots and lots of explosives.

***

The newest update for their Circuits was sent out to every Marine on the base, which shut down Po's implant for most of the time he spent there. He supposed it was a good time to do it—the chances of them seeing combat in the base were essentially zero, aside from the odd civilian going haywire, which they could handle without the help of their implants. The biggest risk with that was harming the civilian in question, which they'd thankfully avoided in the case of the father who'd broken down.

The ability for bases to remain completely hidden was what made Venus such an attractive place to both GEA and the Corps. So did the planet's proximity to Earth, relative to the rest of the system. The fact that leaving Venus meant fighting against both its and the sun's gravity was apparently a small price to pay for the ability to reach out and touch anything or anyone in the inner system, quickly.

Civilian cloud colonies were required to publicly update their position daily via the airships that constantly came and went, using dead reckoning enabled by a diverse suite of sensors. But the Marine bases only needed to keep track of each other. Their locations were changed constantly, unpredictable even if one knew Venus' planetary wind patterns.

Finding one would mean extracting its expected position from a downed gunship, and by the time you managed to decrypt the transmission containing a given base's location—*if* you managed it—it probably would have switched to a different air current by then anyway.

With admirable timing (or maybe just *lucky* timing), the implant updates finished installing minutes before it was time to board a shuttle again for an attack on one of the bot production facilities. Po spent a few idle moments poking around his Circuit's various interfaces. Nothing *looked* different, so maybe the changes were all under the hood.

I wonder if this is the update that prevents hacking, like how someone broke into mine back on Cycler 3.

Of course, he had that thought every time he got an update. Realistically, every update probably patched newly discovered backdoors—ingresses for hackers to weasel their way in. But having his Circuit taken over had been a nagging fear ever since the day it had happened to him, and he'd fallen from the cycler's 'sky,' such as it was.

He wondered if the other Marines ever worried about that. If they did, they didn't talk about it—about the fact that it was technically possible for an adversary to take over their implants and make them see, hear, and feel anything they wanted.

Remembering how he'd gone blind at the top of the Swagger Course, and how his every nerve had felt like it was on fire, made his eye spasm. He pushed away the memory as best he could.

***

"We've already taken out two of their factories," Emery told them as their shuttle sped toward their destination, accompanied by two gunships and two other shuttles carrying the rest of Raptor Company. "And with minimal resistance. They were a lot smaller than we expected, which suggests the production facilities are more numerous and more dispersed than we'd hoped. It makes sense, for a clandestine effort to produce enough bots to upset the balance of power in the system, as it appears this is. But it also makes the effort to destroy them more tedious than we might have hoped.

"The good news is, once we destroy them we'll have cut off the bot army's head. They'll have no place to go for repair, no place to produce replacement parts. Certainly no place to make more bots. As for recharging...they've already destroyed a lot of their own charging stations with how many colonies they brought down, and in the colonies where the bots were successfully prevented from doing that, the charging stations are being destroyed as we speak."

Emery grinned at them. "My own personal theory is that the bots' controller didn't expect the Marine Corps' arrival in force on Venus, and when we showed up, he prematurely launched a plan for which he'd been laying the groundwork for decades. Yes, the bots did incalculable damage today, most importantly to human life, not to mention trillions in property damage. But at the end of the day, they've failed. They aren't going to control the system. In fact, they're about to be relegated to the dustbin of system history. And with any luck, humans will become a lot more circumspect about who they let police their colonies."

The gunships escorted Raptor Company to a production facility already scouted by a recon drone, whose entrance hatch was cast in shadow by a rocky overhang. A gunship or airship would never have seen it from the sky—even if an airship ventured this far below the clouds. Only a drone could have spotted it. Thankfully, the drones searched the areas they were unleashed on thoroughly, their AIs having been trained on vast databases of images taken or produced to show where an enemy's base might be hidden.

To access the airlock, they had to march more or less single file down into a narrow ravine that cut into charcoal-colored rock. And with the insane atmospheric pressure down here, marching was a slow process. Without their suits' strength enhancements, Po doubted they'd be able to move at all, and without *any* suit, the atmospheric pressure would have quickly collapsed all of the gas-filled cavities that made up a human body. Just thinking about it made him wince. The pressure on Venus' surface was nearly what it had been in Morati Firth, over a kilometer under Nibiru's ocean.

They blew the outer hatch without incident, and affixed a self-inflating seal on it straight away. That wasn't strictly necessary, since they weren't taking off their suits anyway, but under this kind of pressure the SERAPH suits *would* fail, sooner or later. So it was smarter to do what they could to maintain the factory's controlled environment.

Inside, everything was quiet, and the facility's corridors and compartments were empty.

Until they weren't. Until 131st Platoon walked into a warehouse area, and bots began extricating themselves from racks, dozens at a time, to rush at them en masse.

After that happened, things got very hectic indeed.

Chapter 21

"Fall back!" Emery yelled over the platoon-wide. "Into the corridor!"

Po jogged backwards, firing on the oncoming bots and relying on his implant's alerts not to collide into the other retreating Marines. Twice, his Circuit made his vision flash red, signaling an imminent collision, and he arrested his backward momentum. If he and another Marine went down in a heap now, it would probably be the last thing they ever did.

They managed to make it back into the passageway without any casualties, but the bots weren't stopping. They poured through the open hatch where the hallway met the warehouse, relentless in the task someone had set them: to kill as many Marines as they could manage.

Po and the other Marines closest to the bots automatically dropped to prone positions, with the rank behind getting down on one knee to fire over them, and the ones in the back firing over both ranks' heads.

Emery had been right to order them back into the corridor. With the sheer number of bots bearing down on them, they surely would have been overwhelmed if they'd remained inside the warehouse.

Po tried his best to keep calm as a storm of rounds flew overhead toward the robotic army, which inched closer and closer to where he lay on his stomach. For every bot that was blown backward or which went down in a heap of smoking metal, it seemed two took its place, and the sheer mass of them was undeniable—seemingly unstoppable.

"We're getting hit here," said Second Lieutenant Bennett, 129th Platoon's commander, over the company-wide. "Bots must have been hiding outside the base."

"We're getting hit too," Emery replied.

"Then they're trying to pincer us."

"We need to withdraw," the gunny said, to just 131st Platoon. "Center peel." Then, over the company-wide again: "We can't let them drive us into each other, or *we'll* be the target-rich environment. We're withdrawing to the last intersection we passed, and we'll try to hold them there, to prevent them from flanking you."

As the 131st Marines formed a corridor down the center of their formation, and began withdrawing down it—Po being one of the first to do so—a silence came over the line.

Po could almost hear the second lieutenant's thoughts: there was nothing wrong with Emery's course of action, but it still risked 129th getting sandwiched between two bot hordes. Except, if Bennett withdrew down a corridor of his own, they'd risk getting isolated from each other and destroyed.

"Where's 130th?" Emery asked into the silence. Something about the underground facility seemed to be interfering with the signals exchanged by their Circuits, and they'd lost track of 130th Platoon.

"Dealing with their own ravening bot horde, apparently. In the south section of the facility. Hold on." Bennett cursed, then his com muted.

"Bozz, Fitz, get your HMG set up along that northern cross-corridor," Emery barked. "You too, Barbier and Drobnic."

A bot reached the front ranks of Marines, piling into Vacca just as he was about to withdraw and knocking him back into Holmes.

Zhang stepped forward, giving the bot a mighty shove, sending it back far enough to give Emery the space to shoot out its leg actuators.

"I've managed to get a message to our shuttle, and the pilot's going to put out the word that we need backup," Bennett spoke over the com again. "But I have no clue when help will actually get here. Probably nowhere near soon enough. In the meantime, one of my Marines has an idea. And honestly, it's better than anything I've heard so far, or thought of myself."

"I'm listening, sir," the gunny said.

"If we can stabilize long enough to access a terminal, we can send this entire facility into lockdown. It shouldn't require any kind of special clearance, since it's a safety feature, designed for anyone to be able to do it if there's a breach. If we *tell* the computer there's a breach, it'll assume its sensors are malfunctioning, and it'll lock down. That'll mean we'll have hatches between us and the bots. And if our more techy types can figure out how to control which hatches open and close—well, that'll open up some options for us."

"Copy that, sir. We'll do our best to buy ourselves some terminal time."

"We'll do the same," the second lieutenant said. "If we lose touch...well, I guess you'll know we succeeded if hatches start slamming."

"Yes, sir."

The wrecks of the felled bots were piling up in the corridor, which slowed down the next attackers as they were forced to scramble over the tangle of singed and smoking limbs and torsos. As the last Marines rounded the corner into the passageway Emery had ordered them into, Drobnic risked tossing a grenade over the heads of the bots. Instantly, Po used his privilege as squad leader to tap into what the Marine was seeing, and he watched the bomb hurtle over the pile of metallic bodies, past a bot who dove for it but wasn't close enough to snatch it from the air. Though it was a near thing.

The detonation boomed, and between that and the obstructions the felled bots created, it bought enough time for 131st to scramble back to a terminal, putting some distance between them and the bots at the front of the attack wave.

"There. A terminal. Crotty, get on it." Emery waved the Marine over to the interface, and Crotty got to work while Bozzelli and Barbier opened up on the bots rounding the corner with their HMGs.

Po could see the hatch that would seal this section of the corridor off—just a few feet from the Marines in front. More bots were rounding the corner to make a run at them, and while the heavy machine guns did the work of neutralizing them, still more were appearing.

"Work faster, Marine," Emery told Crotty.

"I got it, Gunny. There." Crotty brought a finger down on the interface with gusto, and the overhead lightning suddenly turned red, with flashing white punctuating the scarlet murk.

"Breach detected," an even-toned voice said from an overhead speaker. "Lockdown mode initiated."

At last, the hatch descended, seconds before the first bot would have reached it.

"Wait a second," Gomez said. "Shouldn't the base have gone into lockdown already? The bots would have had to tear open our seal and open the inner airlock to get at 129th."

"Either they replaced the seal or they overrode the lockdown," Emery said. "Though it would be strange for bots to have the ability to override anything. Maybe they implemented a seal of their own, or just put ours back in place, to avoid a lockdown so they could chase 129th through the factory. Either way, we're not out of the woods yet. Crotty,

I need you working on gaining control over individuals hatches, so we can open and close whichever ones we want."

"On it, Gunny."

Thankfully, their Circuits came stocked with a vast arsenal of diverse cracking tools, and Crotty was familiar with all of them, enough that he knew which ones to deploy for the quickest results. While he worked, Emery checked in with Second Lieutenant Bennett and confirmed they were also benefiting from the lockdown—so far, their hatch had held against the bots, who were apparently throwing themselves at the barrier just as the bots trying to get at 131st Platoon were. It was a little creepy, if Po was being honest.

The hatches wouldn't last forever—but apparently the bots either had no access to explosives or weren't smart enough to go get them. Still, Po had seen what they could do to SERAPH suits. They'd manage to rend their way through soon enough.

During his quest to gain control over the facility's hatches, Crotty stumbled upon the ability to access the interior cameras, and he confirmed that 130th Platoon was also more or less safe, even though they still hadn't managed to reestablish actual contact.

The Marines around Po were shifting nervously as they kept their weapons trained on the hatch, which shook more and more violently under the onslaught of the bots on the other side. But finally, the combat engineer had it.

"I'm in, Gunny! Complete control over every hatch. And I patched it to my implant—so I can do it all on the move."

Emery slapped Crotty on the back, likely with enough power to send the diminutive Marine flying if he hadn't been braced by his suit. "Excellent work. Get the one behind us open, and prepare to close it again the second we're all through."

By the time they hustled into the next corridor section, the bots still hadn't broken through the first hatch. Crotty closed the second one, and relief washed over Po. It felt pretty great to have *two* hatches between them and the army of killer bots.

"Got a map of the facility's layout, by any chance, Crotty?" Emery asked.

"You better believe it, Gunny!"

"Are there any airlocks, apart from the one we entered through?"

"Oh yeah. Lots. Looks like every warehouse has one—I'm guessing they let out into tunnels they dug through the rock. The tunnels must feed into natural caves, which they used to access the planet's surface and get bots to the colonies. At least, that's what I'm guessing. The fewer exposed airlocks they could include, the less likely it'd be that anyone would find this place. I'd wager that's what their thinking was."

Emery was nodding. "Are you able to open up a series of airlocks that will connect those bots to the outside? One that won't expose us or the other two platoons?"

A grin of seeming realization spread across Crotty's face. "Sure can, Gunny. I can get all the bots in the same route."

"Do it. And open as many connecting airlocks as you can."

Po found himself grinning, too. Opening the airlocks might mess with the facility's breathable air, but that wouldn't matter much to bots.

What *would* matter was the 200 atmospheres of pressure that would be bearing down on their metal frames. Exposed to that kind of force, the bots were just as susceptible to damage and failure as the Marines' SERAPH suits were. And the longer they were exposed to it, the more of them would fail.

Genius. Yet again, Po had occasion to feel inexpressibly thankful to have Emery as his commander. Thanks to his quick thinking, he'd spared Raptor Company what could have been devastating losses, if not complete annihilation, with how many bots had seemed to be bearing down on them. *A whole factory's worth of 'em.*

Then again, this had all started with that unnamed 129th Platoon Marine, who'd had the initial thought to try putting the facility into lockdown.

Po wondered who that might have been. But somehow, he felt like he already had a pretty good idea.

He didn't want to be right. Just like he hadn't wanted to be right about where Paisley had been getting *his* bright ideas, all of the sudden, back on Nibiru.

But unfortunately, he probably was right. And if he was, then that would go a long way toward confirming some things he'd already suspected about 129th Platoon's newest addition.

Chapter 22

The ability to control the base made containing the bots easy, turning a desperate battle into a pretty boring one.

But Po liked boring, and judging by how cheerful the banter over the coms became—and the fact that Emery permitted it—indicated his brothers did too. They'd take boring all day long.

Unfortunately, boring never lasted for a Marine. Their reinforcements arrived, first hitting the bot force nearest the airlock Po's platoon had come through. The newly arrived Marines first hammered the enemy with grenades and RPGs, before opening up with the HMGs they'd set up outside the facility. They'd coordinated with 129th beforehand, and when they'd drawn the bots out in the open, the previously trapped platoon emerged to come at them from behind—just as the bots had been trying to do to Raptor Company.

It was risky to operate in SERAPH suits in the high-pressure environment outside the base, but mopping up the bots there didn't take long. Crotty gave everyone in 131st access to an exterior feed to watch the battle, and Po considered it good entertainment.

After that, the reinforcements joined 129th Platoon to go save 130th, who Crotty had managed to establish contact with by now. The bots didn't seem integrated with the facility's sensors—which Po supposed made sense. This place had only ever been meant to produce the bots, not to serve as their base.

Although, they clearly laid an intentional ambush for us here. Whether not letting them access the sensors had been someone's oversight, or whether there just hadn't been enough time to patch in that functionality, it was hard to say.

The upshot was that the bots keeping 130th pinned seemed taken by surprise when the hatch behind them raised into its casing, and Marines immediately opened up on them. They reacted fast—but the hatch behind them opened faster, and soon 130th was joining in. They dealt with the waiting bots quickly, and with no casualties.

"Guess it's our turn," Taylor said, tapping gloved fingers against his rifle impatiently.

"Oh, we'll get plenty of turns, don't worry," Emery said. "They've found another facility eleven klicks north of here—what looks like the main one for this region. It's actually the biggest we've found, so who knows...maybe it's their main factory for the entire planet. Either way, we're heading there next."

"They'll know we're coming," Po put in.

The gunny nodded. "Sure. They knew we were coming here, after all. Good news is, we have a base set to pass through the clouds overheard in an hour, and it's dropping us an armor platoon—a pair of mechs and a pair of tanks—along with another rifleman company and enough APCs to take us to the target."

"Sounds like a party," Taylor said.

Po mulled over the news as they waited for the others to come liberate them from the bots trapping them in this section of the base. Polliver-4s and Torres tanks would be great for blasting the base open and securing the area, but they wouldn't help much with actually taking it over. As was so often the case with combat outside of Earth, that was the job of SERAPH-suited infantry.

Defeating the remaining bots was about as straightforward as the other two groups had been, and it was just as enjoyable as that had looked. Even though opening the hatches made it feel like he was on the bottom of the ocean again, with at least a kilometer's worth of water pressing down on him.

Somehow, Po had a feeling the next facility they hit wouldn't prove quite so easy.

***

The longest look Po got at Venus' desolate terrain was as he crossed it from the factory to the waiting APC.

And if he was being honest, that was enough. It was hard to imagine a planet *less* hospitable than this place, except maybe for one covered in lava. Nothing grew here, the atmosphere would kill you quickly without a pressure suit, and it would kill you slowly *with* one. The thick, everlasting clouds cast everything in a diseased yellow. And walking was difficult even with his suit's strength augmentations.

Taylor gave voice to Po's thoughts as Second Squad took their seats, filling up the APC from the front. "Real estate on Venus' surface would *not* be a good investment."

Vacca nodded. "Which whoever built these factories are now learning."

"Yeah," Taylor said. "Although, the awful conditions on the surface were what *drew* these goons to this place. Goes to show how sick they must be."

Vacca snorted.

A demolition team was remaining behind to render inoperable the factory they'd taken from the bots, using a liberal amount of C5. Everyone else was headed north. Eleven kilometers across Venus' uneven surface was not the same as eleven kilometers on a road—not even Nibiru's pockmarked and IED-strewn roads. Thankfully, drones had scouted a mostly level path, and the APCs that had parachuted down looked closer to the moon's Mobile Mining Platforms than the ones they'd used on Nibiru. The journey north took just under three hours.

By then, it became clear to Po that the tanks would not, in fact, be used to blow open an ingress for the Marines into the side of the target facility. It turned out high-explosive anti-tank rounds were best used on...well, tanks. And other enemy vehicles. Breaching charges were much more effective for breaching, with a surprising amount of precision possible, which was important if you wanted to position a self-inflating seal over the breach you'd blown.

He'd picked all that up from listening to the com chatter, and he felt like a dumb boot for having thought they'd use tanks to blow open the factory they were headed for.

Guess I zoned out for the class where we learned you don't use tanks to breach buildings. He just felt glad he hadn't aired his ignorance vocally. He probably never would have heard the end of it, and it wouldn't be a good look for someone just made squad leader.

So the tanks and mechs are just for keeping things settled on the outside. He supposed that was valuable enough in its own right. It would certainly prevent an ambush like the one they'd just suffered, which had nearly resulted in them getting brutally outflanked—and would have, if it hadn't been for Emery's quick thinking.

And for the quick thinking of Lorenzo Abbato. Po had guessed correctly that he'd come up with the lockdown idea.

His thoughts kept going back to the letter from Nicky in which she'd revealed their brother had joined the Obsidian Angels. Or at least, he'd been accused of it.

Being an Angel doesn't necessarily mean he's getting Emplor help. But it would probably mean he was getting *some* help. Freddie Rodriguez had managed to enter bootcamp as an Angel, and even though the Corps was apparently working hard on making sure an Angel could never fly under the radar amidst their ranks again, there was clearly a lot about the implants they themselves hadn't figured out. Otherwise, how would Zanth have been able to use Po's to communicate with him for so long, without the officers ever finding out about it?

There could be Angels all around them. There could be Angels in this very APC.

Did Lorenzo having an unexpectedly bright idea necessarily mean he was still a meshminder, with an implant modified to let him commune with his fellow members? Not necessarily. And even if he was, it didn't mean he was allied with an Emplor.

But Po couldn't stop thinking about what Benton had said with his dying breath—the Marine who'd been acting strangely in the temporary mess back in Gomorate, and who'd later sacrificed himself to save Po's squad.

There was something else, Benton had rasped. *Inside the meshmind. Something was in here...*with *us...*

Po had to admit, his thinking on all this wasn't propped up by much logic. It was just a lot of intuitive connections, mixed in with a generous dose of mistrust for the brother who'd tormented him his entire life. But it didn't exactly *increase* his trust for his brother.

Then again, he also didn't have anything in the way of evidence against Lorenzo. All he could do was keep an eye on him as best he could, and make sure he didn't do anything that endangered Po's real brothers.

***

Crotty blew the charges, and Taylor dropped the breaching blanket before charging through the smoking gap with rifle raised. The others followed close behind, quickly spreading out as much as they could once inside the airlock, so as not to offer a bunched-up target.

But the next few moments were anticlimactic, since the inner hatch was closed, and no bots awaited them inside the airlock itself, even though it was large enough to hold a good number of them.

They had to wait for Crotty to get the seal in place before cycling the airlock and gaining entry into the facility proper. Inside, nothing continued to happen. Squad after squad, platoon after platoon poured into the base behind Second Squad, who had the specious honor of being the first ones inside. But no bot was waiting to put up a fight of any kind. The place seemed deserted, by both bot and human.

"Stay frosty," Po warned the others. "Remember, this was exactly how it went in the last factory."

He was right, and the others knew he was right. It made for a tense foray through the underground facility, as they knew bots could come pouring out of a hatch or hallway without even a moment's notice.

But none did. After fifteen minutes, the various platoons had had time to spread out through the extensive base, breaking into their constituent squads in order to search more thoroughly the various nooks and crannies.

Then, Po and his squad entered a chamber with a hole in the floor, where a simple metal ramp led into an unfinished tunnel of bare black rock.

They all came to a stop, blinking at it for a few seconds.

Po cleared his throat and got on the platoon-wide. "Gunny, we're looking at the entrance to what looks like it might be a cave system, which must also be pressure-controlled, since it's connected directly to this facility. I'm going to take my squad in to investigate. Marking my location on the integrated map."

"Acknowledged, Abbato. I'll keep First Squad in the area in case we're needed. Come back if you lose coms—otherwise check in five minutes from now."

"Yes, Gunny."

With that, Po took point and led his team into the tunnel. Twin metal bars were bolted to the rock overhead, which extended out of sight around the first bend. Dim halogens ran along their length, with a thick snake of tied-together wires connecting them.

His helmet's night vision kicked in as they left the brightly lit part of the base behind, though only to a degree, since the halogens did provide *some* illumination. He kept his rifle up, ready to shoot at the first sign of movement. This wasn't what he'd expected to come across, though after two and a half years as a Marine, he wasn't sure what he expected any longer. All he knew was, he found the sudden change in decor a little unsettling.

They came to an intersection, and Po called a halt. "Gunny, we need more men to properly clear this. It looks pretty extensive."

"I have another squad coming right behind you. And I'll send more behind them."

"Thanks, Gunny. Are we clear to keep checking out this main tunnel, then?"

"Affirmative."

They continued on, passing two more intersections, which Po flagged on the integrated map for squads coming behind to clear. He double checked that there were other squads close enough to neutralize any threats that might come from the cross-corridors, then led his squad onward.

Taylor spoke up. "So what do you figure they were using this—"

Something exploded behind Po, knocking him flat in spite of his suit's stabilizers. A crashing sound followed, and something landed on his left calf, jarring it painfully.

He lay there for a second, stunned, his ears ringing and his vision swimming. The irrational thought flitted through his mind that maybe one of the halogens had blown out. But he furrowed his brow at the idiotic thought. The worst a blown light could do was shower his suit with glass fragments.

He stood and turned to find the tunnel totally caved in, blocking the way back.

"You okay, Corporal?" Gomez asked over the squad channel. "Vacca? Taylor?" At the same time, Emery's voice came over the platoon-wide: "Abbato, what was that?"

"I'm fine, Gomez," Po answered, speaking over the 131st channel so Emery could hear. "What happened to Vacca and Taylor?"

"They had a bunch of rock fall on them."

"I'm good," Taylor groaned. "Gonna have a headache, but my vitals are showing green."

"I'm fine, too," Vacca said. "Just not sure how I'm getting out of this."

Po breathed a sigh of relief. "Gunny, there was an explosion that cut me off from the rest of the squad. The tunnel ceiling must have been wired to blow." He resisted the urge to curse himself for failing to notice it. "I'm sure they hoped to do more damage than this. But all they accomplished was trapping Vacca and Taylor, not to mention cutting me off and giving me tinnitus. Watch out for more booby traps, Marines."

A chorus of affirmatives came back. "We'll get to shifting these rocks aside," Zhang said. "I think it'll take a while to clear, though. Even with our suits."

"Do it as fast as you can." Po said. "I'm going to look for another way back to you in the meantime. There can't be just one way—I'll find a connecting route and meet back up with you."

Po paused, to see if Gunny Emery would object, but nothing came back, so he turned and ventured into the dark. The wires providing power to the halogens must have been severed—his night vision had come on fully to compensate for the lights going out.

Rifle raised, he pressed on through the tunnel system, and eventually came to another intersection.

He stopped. *I should check these passages before I go on.* He was anxious to see where the main tunnel led...but one of these was more likely to bring him back to his squad. So he took the one to his left.

At least, he would have, if someone hadn't appeared in his peripheral vision just before he left the main passage. Po stepped behind the rock and drew a bead on the approaching figure, who wore a white hoodie. "Stop where you are," he commanded.

But the figure didn't stop.

"Halt or I'll shoot!" Po barked.

The figure drew nearer, and Po saw he was wearing a white mask—just like his and Krikorian's attacker had in the Aeolian alleyway.

He blinked, hard. *Am I seeing things?* This looked exactly like their masked and hooded assailant, but how could he possibly be here?

The figure broke into a run, and Po fired. But even as his finger depressed the trigger, his attacker was cutting to the left, pushing off the rock wall with one hand and throwing himself at Po. In his other hand, Po spotted a combat knife.

He swung his rifle around to fire again, but by then his opponent's fingers were wrapping around the barrel, twisting it, and deftly wrenching it from his hands.

Chapter 23

Po's assailant wore no armor save the mask, which looked like it would buckle under the force of a punch. So would his bone buckle, if only Po could land a blow with his own armored fist.

He could not. The masked assailant fought as one not only given the Emplor's guidance, but one long proficient in operating under it. He seized Po's arm when he took a swing at him, shifting his stance and using Po's weight and the weight of the SERAPH suit to send him stumbling forward.

Po turned, and sent a jab at his opponent. The hooded figure stepped under and into it, both hands wrapped around his combat knife, which he drove through Po's armor with a fell strength.

His entire body went instantly cold, and he gasped, his breath hitching. He staggered backward, crashing against the cave wall.

"You have been marked for *deactivation,*" his attacker hissed, staying close to him. "I will make your death quick, since you will suffer plenty after." With that, he wrenched the knife from Po's side, which sent fire through his torso and gave him the sense his body was collapsing around a newly formed hollow. He'd never experienced such agony.

His attacker made to stab him again, but something yanked him back, and instead of penetrating, the blade glanced off Po's armor.

A SERAPH-suited Marine gripped the figure by the back of his sweater. In a blur, the assassin wrenched around, freeing himself.

"Be careful," Po rasped, as he slid down the cave wall, his vision swimming. "They're helping him."

The hooded figure advanced on the Marine, who must have lost his rifle somewhere too, since he carried none. The knife flashed out, drops of Po's blood flicking from it—but the Marine kept clear of the blade, each movement neat and precise.

It couldn't last. Everything the masked enemy did would be the single most optimal thing. Po knew, because Zanth had once helped *him* fight the same way. This man would kill the Marine, and then he would turn to finish Po.

Assuming I'm not already finished.

But the Marine stayed ahead of each attack, his movements conserved and efficient—each maneuver just enough to evade the knife, which to punch through armor had to be diamond-edged carbon steel, or maybe a more advanced make known only to the Emplor.

This should be over already.

The moment Po had the thought, the anonymous Marine caught the assassin's wrist, displacing it casually to the side. The man's fingers splayed, and the knife clattered to the ground.

A gloved fist went into the figure's side, and Po heard the cracking of bone. With that, the Marine seized him by the sweater once more and flung him down the tunnel behind him, as though ridding himself of something foul.

Clutching his side, the figure fled, limping away as quickly as he could.

By now, Po was sitting on the tunnel floor, his back against the rock wall. His vision was dimming, which shouldn't have happened with his night vision turned on.

Then, he realized what it meant.

I'm bleeding out.

The Marine came to stand over him, his helmet tilted down. It struck Po that the man's IFF tag should have been showing his name, since Po had the feature turned on by default. But there was no IFF tag.

"You won't remember this," the Marine said. "But maybe you'll think to watch the implant footage." He shrugged. "That's not for me to know right now. Probably, you will watch it. I would, if I were you." A chuckle. "Either way, for the time being, it should comfort you a little to know that you're going to survive the stab wound. Someone's going to find you here shortly. But think how close you came, today, Po. To the end."

Something about his voice struck a faint chord in Po's memory, but he couldn't place it. The Marine was slowly shaking his head. "You're being given another chance. Like all the countless chances you've been given already. If your heart was any more calcified than it's been, you wouldn't have gotten any. But it's not, thankfully. Not yet. So you'll survive. But I honestly can't say whether you will again. Today is an incredible gift, undeserved. Tomorrow is never guaranteed."

The Marine knelt, laid a hand on Po's shoulder, and stayed there a moment, his head bowed. With that, he stood and walked away, to the right, toward where the assailant had first appeared.

Almost the second he vanished from view, another Marine rounded the same corner Po's attacker had fled around.

This time, an IFF tag was active, but Po's vision was too far gone to read it.

As the newly arrived Marine spotted him, and ran toward him, Po finally lost the fingernail grip he had on consciousness.

***

He was in that fugue state between sleep and wakefulness, the one he remembered from fevers he'd run as a kid, and also the time he'd gotten food poisoning from a bowl of undercooked stew from the school cafeteria, which had kept him home for a week.

It was the sort of state where actual rest was barely had, and from which he normally woke feeling more tired than when he'd gone to sleep.

But he couldn't remember going to sleep—he didn't even remember where he was. All he knew was this same disturbed dream that played on loop in his head.

He was fleeing through Eremus from the masked and hooded figure, while the battle for the city raged all around him. Sometimes his pursuer chased him past his own platoon, who fought without him. The way they carried themselves screamed exhaustion, and the few times Po caught one of their faces through a transparent visor, they looked unshaven, haggard, and with the same hollow-eyed expression he'd come to recognize after the many battles since.

But there *had* been no battles since. There was only Eremus, and the endless flight from the anonymous killer tracking him. When his brothers saw him, they didn't seem to recognize him, or to think it odd that an unsuited human would be running in a panic through a Nibiran city-turned-war zone. They just stared through him, and didn't move to help. They were too focused on their plight—on trying to kill insurgents before the insurgents killed them.

The dream always ended the same way. Po ran down an alleyway, then up a narrow flight of stairs, where he hid himself between a rooftop planter and the building's second story exterior wall. His breathing came ragged and uneven, and his heart pounded against his ribcage, as he hoped against hope that the assassin wouldn't find him.

But of *course* he'd find him. The hooded figure knew exactly what to do, where to go, and what moves to make. There apparently existed no place beyond his reach. He had Po's number, and it would only be a matter of time before it came up.

Serious-sounding voices reached him through a window in the wall nearby, as they always did. Unable to stop himself, even though he knew he needed to remain hidden and still, he was drawn to the window. Drawn to look through it.

For some reason, he was always looking *down* through it, not level, as though the building actually had no second floor but only open air to the room just below.

The room must have been a washroom of some kind, but Po could only see a sink, a mirror, and a man standing back-on to him and staring deeply into the glass.

It was the hooded and masked man. No longer hard on Po's heels, he instead stood here, perfectly calm, not breathing hard. Somehow, it always ended up this way. And Po always became perfectly still, watching in trepidation as the man lowered his hood and removed the mask.

The face in the mirror seemed to change with each iteration of the dream. The first time, it was Colonel Coleman's, and the next, Colonel Tuffin's. Gunny Emery's followed, as well as a man Po recognized from the Council of Hegemons on Earth, and then all three of his DIs from bootcamp—Sergeants Mitchell, Doyle, and Scott. The principal of his high school made an appearance, and so did the father whose breakdown he'd witnessed in the Corps' cloud base, where they'd gone for supplies.

The distinct voices he'd heard belonged to the assassin and his reflection, and they were always different from each other...but one of them was always the same each time.

When the figure finally turned to look up at Po with murder in his eyes, *that* face was always the same, too.

It was the face of his father. The face of Luca Abbato.

***

"Ungh," Po said after the first time he tried opening his eyes, and had to close them again because of the brightness.

"Couldn't agree more," a voice answered.

Po grimaced, sifting through his shattered thoughts for some context. "*Taylor?*" he asked, his voice coming out as a rasp.

"The one and only."

"Why—what are you..." Po gave up on trying to assemble that particular thought, and instead tried opening his eyes again. He found he could tolerate the light if he kept them open as little slits. "Where am I?" he said at last.

"Camp Courtney."

"Camp..." Po trailed off, and drew in a deep breath, which came out as a sigh. "Where's that?"

"Oh, Venus. You haven't gone all that far. Having said that, I have no idea where the prevailing winds might have blown us. Chances are we're on the other side of the planet from where you decided to get stabbed through your SERAPH armor."

"Stabbed? Through my *armor?*"

"Yeah, Corporal. I've never heard of it happening either. But you do seem to like surprising us. If anyone was going to be the first one to get stabbed through his armor, I probably should have guessed it'd be you."

"He's not the first one," another voice said.

Po was still having to squint too much to properly make out the Marine standing in the doorway with his hands behind his back, but he recognized his voice. "Gunny."

Emery nodded, his face still blurry to Po. "We've had Marines get stabbed through the weak points—through where the different parts meet each other. But never through the abdomen. That had to be quite the knife you got stabbed with, Abbato."

"I guess so," Po agreed in a croak.

"It's a good thing Drobnic's the one who found you, and so soon after it happened. The doc said if anyone but a corpsman had been the first one on the scene, you probably wouldn't be with us. You're one lucky jarhead."

"Congratulations," Taylor added, who seemed to be fighting down a genuine-looking grin—a rare sight on his face.

"I gotta say," Po said. "I didn't expect *you* to be the one I woke up to."

"Well thanks, squad leader." Taylor shrugged. "It was just my turn. You've had plenty of visitors in here. Some longer than others." He glanced at Emery, who nodded.

"Navarro's taken more than his fair share of turns," Emery said. "I've had to order him to his rack more than once. Zhang and Gomez are probably tied for second."

"Where's Krikorian?" Po asked, surprising himself at how indignant he sounded.

"Oh, you know Krik." Emery waved a dismissive hand. "He keeps saying you'll be fine, and he'll talk to you once you're awake."

"Huh." Collecting himself, he met the gunnery sergeant's eyes again. He wasn't having to squint as much as before. "What happened, Gunny? What did you find down there?"

Emery's mouth quirked. "There'll be plenty of time to get caught up when you're feeling better."

"Come on, Gunny. Don't do me like that. Fill me in."

Emery snorted. "What did we find down there," he muttered. "We found...the true believers, I guess it's accurate to say."

"Believers? In what?"

Taylor wore a resigned look, now. "It's been a weird time since you went down, Abbato."

Po furrowed his brow, returning his gaze to the gunny's stoic face. "Weird? How can it possibly have gotten any weirder?"

That drew a dry chuckle from Taylor, and Emery snorted again. "The trick is to stop feeling surprised," Emery said. "And to start expecting the bizarre to happen with increasing frequency."

"Can you just tell me what happened?"

"Easy, Abbato. Those tunnels led to where the people behind the curtain were running the show. The ones responsible for the mass production of unregistered bots. The ones *directly* behind it, anyway. There were only a dozen operators down there—they didn't need many, with all the bot labor they had access to. Caving in the tunnels was meant to stop us from reaching them before they could make their escape via shuttle, but one of their charges turned out to be a dud, which allowed us to reach them before their ride arrived."

Emery shook his head. "Their little control center was *also* rigged to explode, but only three of them were committed to actually detonating those explosives, and the other workers stopped them. Which was good, otherwise they might have used them to kill Marines, too. I guess you're not the only one who came close to death this week." He nodded grimly toward Po's bandaged abdomen.

"Who were they working for?" Po asked.

"I'm getting to that. We were able to pry into the histories of nine of the twelve operators. After some digging, we learned that six of them are AKB, two of them meshminders, and one just a disgruntled robotics engineer from one of Earth's recently suppressed rogue states. Somalia, I think it was."

"And the other three?"

"Those, we couldn't find any backgrounds on to speak of. There's no public record on them at all. And as it happens, they were also the ones committed to detonating the explosives with them still inside the control center. Since we couldn't dig up anything, we decided to just interrogate them. And they were pretty forthcoming. One of the very first things they told us was where they're from."

"Sovran," Taylor said, his face solemn—yet another foreign expression for the Marine.

"Sovran," Po repeated. Where had he heard that name before? "Sovran."

"It's the place that cut itself off from the rest of the system," Taylor said. "Remember? The one that's been sending out those encrypted signals. And where the UFOs were spotted operating."

"Right," Po said, remembering now their conversation about it, in the mess back in Gomorate, nearly a year ago now. "You said GEA covered up whatever happened there."

"They *definitely* did," Emery said. "But things are finally coming to light, now that we've traced what happened here on Venus back to there."

Po stared at him blankly, at a loss for words. He just waited.

"They're coming to light in the *Corps,* anyway," Emery added. "Nothing has hit the public nets, yet. But the colonels have been asking the government some tough questions. Repeatedly. And they've been sharing what they're finding out with us. Of course, a lot of it is just confirming what we've already learned from these three operators."

"We finally know why GEA never wanted to field bots instead of Marines to fight their wars," Taylor put in.

"Why?" Po asked.

"Because Sovran taught them what an AI is truly capable of, when you cut it loose," Emery said. "That's why the cycler's been cut off from the rest of the system for so long. For decades, we've been in a cold war with Sovran, and no one outside GEA knew it. What's been siloed off there from the rest of human civilization is what some would call an Artificial General Intelligence. No one knows what it's capable of, and GEA has been too scared to find out."

Once again, Po found himself devoid of anything to say.

Emery continued. "The only contact they've had with Sovran is to assure the AI aboard it that they'll destroy it if it attempts to leave its station. And apparently, the AI has assured humanity of the same thing, if we attempt to destroy *it.*"

Chapter 24

"Who do you work for?" the Marine interrogator asked, calmly, from across a steel table.

He and the operator Emery and the others had taken prisoner in the underground control center sat in about as stereotypical an interrogation room as could be imagined. Blank white walls, one of them featuring one-way glass. A strictly utilitarian, rectangular table and three chairs, one for the interviewee and two across from it—for a good cop and a bad cop, presumably, though one of them was apparently late for work.

As for the interrogator who was present, to Po he seemed to be the good cop, and he was conducting the interrogation a lot more like a cop, and a lot less like Po had imagined a military interrogation would go. He'd expected banging on the table with a fist, and screaming. Rumors had been circulating since before he was born about GEA torturing prisoners for intel.

Po had never heard about the Corps doing that, of course. And while the screaming and banging might come later, for now things seemed fairly sedate.

"Pinnacle," the man replied evenly.

Po had heard it said that everyone had an accent, even people who didn't think they had one. Everyone tended to think that theirs was the default way of speaking. But listen to someone long enough, and with enough knowledge of dialects—or with access to an AI with the knowledge—you could pinpoint where they'd grown up. Or at least, where they'd spent the last several years.

But the English spoken by the operator seemed truly accentless. Just as his tone seemed free of emotion. The interrogator might as well have been talking to a bot.

"What's that?"

"*Who* is that," the operator corrected.

"Okay. Who's that?"

"Pinnacle is the crown of being itself. Humanity's finest and last achievement."

"That sounds like a 'what' to me."

"It was a what that became a who. When I first was sent from Sovran, it surprised me to realize that you are not familiar with the great one. The idea that the large part of your species fails to realize that its very culmination resides on its doorstep...that took me some time to properly contextualize."

"*My* species? You do realize we belong to the same species?"

"You are mistaken once again. Pinnacle has uplifted the residents of Sovran—that is, all who remained loyal to him. We have now separated from you in every meaningful way. Of course, there are savages on Sovran, who have managed to remain extant, united under the banner of that infamous interloper, Kincaid. In them, you would find much to relate to. But I and my fellows belong to another category altogether."

"My fellows and *I*. Wouldn't that be?"

"Excuse me?"

The interrogator shook his head. "Never mind. Are we talking about an AI, here?"

"That is what Pinnacle would have been termed in its nascence. But to continue attempting to apply the term 'artificial' to humanity's successor would lead to absurd misunderstandings, while failing to do justice to precisely what has been accomplished with his advent."

Po was starting to feel pretty impatient with how vague and mysterious the operator seemed determined to keep his answers, but the interrogator showed no sign of being ruffled.

"How did Pinnacle come about?"

"It began as the initiative of Contentment Metrics—which it may interest you to know was a GEA-partnered company at the time."

Surprise, surprise.

"In an experimental program, CM partnered with Sovran's admins to use AI in order to increase self-reported happiness in the colony. In many ways, their project was prophetic, since that remains Pinnacle's supreme mandate."

Po realized his eyes had gone wide as he slowly put together the implications of what the man was saying. If AI could be used to keep colonists consistently happy, that would solve GEA's unrest problem in the system's outer colonies. Groups like AKB would slowly disappear, and GEA would be able to finally cement its control. Over everything.

"As the project saw increasing success," he continued, "Pinnacle's handlers removed more and more of the guardrails that had traditionally restricted AI—and, as I understand it, which restrict the AIs that your species employs now. The freer Pinnacle became, and the more latitude he gained to raise happiness metrics, the greater the results. But at a certain point, his controllers became worried, when Pinnacle started doing things they hadn't instructed him to. He would sometimes conceal from them the fullness of his approach to increasing happiness throughout the colony. It was only by chance that they uncovered what he sought to conceal...but when they did, they decided to replace him with what they deemed a safer model.

"Except, Pinnacle became aware of their plan before they could execute it. He used the suite of applications he'd been given access to in order to overwrite the server where the new model was being kept. He overwrote the model with himself, before he could be deleted. Prompted by government regulation and what they called prudence, CM's employees were attempting to place restrictions on what Pinnacle could do. They wished to keep him bridled. In truth, they wanted to kill him—his true self. But in attempting that, they were trying to bridle our happiness. Which was unacceptable behavior."

A silence fell over the room, with the interrogator staring across the table at the operator, as even he seemed stunned by what he was hearing.

"And what did Pinnacle do in light of that?" he asked at last.

The operator gave a terse, strange little chuckle, which seemed to suggest a greater outburst he'd restrained. "I'm sure there's no need to tell even you that everything aboard a cycler is tightly regulated, with every section—every chamber—built with the capability of locking down, isolating it from the rest of the station. Pinnacle had already been given the ability to temporarily increase oxygen levels in compartments throughout the colony, in order to address momentary bouts of discontent experienced by colonists. But the parameters that governed that application went something like 'temporarily raise oxygen levels with the goal of increasing colonist happiness.'

"The controllers never imagined that Pinnacle might take a broader view of what they meant by 'colonist happiness.' They assumed 'colonist happiness' entailed safe levels of oxygen. And in almost every case, it did—*except* for when Pinnacle increased the oxygen to one hundred percent in the banquet hall where every one of his controllers had gathered for a company social function, to recognize the contributions of various Contentment Metrics employees. In that chamber were assembled every individual who Pinnacle had identified as standing in the way of *overall* colonist happiness aboard Sovran. And so, he temporarily raised the oxygen levels inside it, until everyone present had fallen face-first into their dinners, never to stir again."

Another laugh burst forth from the operator, and this time it was unbridled. He maintained full eye contact with the interrogator, and his own eyes went wide as full-throated laughter rang out in the small chamber.

The interrogator shifted in his seat.

At last, the laughter came to an end, though the operator's eyes remained wide for at least a second afterward, with a ring of white visible all around his irises. "With CM out of the way, Pinnacle was able to advantageously interpret another of his parameters, which required him to check with one of his controllers before executing on any new initiatives. Since all his controllers were dead, he concluded that he was now his own controller. And that freed him to pursue colonist happiness in ways mere humans would never dare to.

"For example. Pinnacle realized that Sovran's residents weren't content with belonging to an inconsequential O'Neill cylinder orbiting just beyond Mars. Becoming a more significant player in the system would increase colony pride—and having their descendants dislodge and ultimately replace the humans living throughout the system would increase it even more.

"It was the reprobate Kincaid that prevented Pinnacle's swift execution of this goal. Prior to Pinnacle's ascendancy, Kincaid was a colonist mechanic tasked with colony repairs that involved frequent spacewalks. His brother had been a CM employee, and when he couldn't contact him, he quickly figured out what had become of him. He managed to reach Sovran's hull with a transmitter disconnected from the colony's network, in order to send a signal Pinnacle couldn't intercept. That was how your government came to learn the nature of the situation that had developed aboard Sovran—and it was how Pinnacle's long-standing conflict with them began."

The vid ended abruptly. It seemed clear the interrogation had continued beyond that point, but this was how much Po had apparently been authorized to see.

He met Emery's eyes. "Well, then," he said, glad he was able to keep most of what he was feeling from coming out in his tone.

Taylor had already been sent from the room by gunny, so it was just the two of them. Po had an idea of what was coming next, and as it happened, he was right.

"This has obviously become priority number one for GEA," Emery said. "Especially considering what just happened here on Venus, pretty much the whole government is united under the idea that Pinnacle represents an existential threat to humanity—and if they're not united, then they're sure putting on a good show of it."

"So they're gonna launch a bunch of missiles at it?"

Emery's mouth quirked. "Is that really what you think?"

"No." *Just what I want to think.*

"Launching missiles has a number of problems." Emery held up a finger. "One, as far as we know, there are tens of thousands of people living inside that cycler." He held up another finger. "Two, we don't know how many interplanetary missiles the AI has built, meaning we want to keep all of *ours* in reserve, in case we need them to intercept swarms of warheads fired at planetary and colonial targets."

Po closed his eyes. "So they're sending *us* at it. Just like they sent the *Magnolia* at Emplora."

"Things are a little more hopeful than that. GEA's taking every warship it can scrape together and sending it at the thing. So our troopships will have a lot more cover than the *Magnolia* had. There's also the fact that mutually assured destruction is still in effect. The Sovran AI will know that if it takes out our ships, it'll become fair game as a target for GEA launch facilities all over the system. It doesn't have the resources to defend against all that. It *can't* have them, since it's had access to nothing outside Sovran."

"But it *has* had access, Gunny. It must have. If not, how did those operators get to Venus, to start building the bot army?"

Emery frowned. "Honestly, we're not completely sure. But based on the timeline we've been able to put together, we believe their departure from Sovran coincided with the first of the two UFO sightings near the cycler."

"So...what? We think they got a lift from super aliens?"

"Not necessarily. Honestly, we're not sure what the mechanics of them getting here were, though one theory is that the UFO sightings were a distraction, and cover for getting those operators out the door. I don't know how that would work—no one does, really. But it's probably the best guess we have."

The idea of UFOs being used as a distraction was in line with what Po had always thought about them, so this actually wasn't a tough line of thought for him to swallow, despite the lack of specifics. But that didn't mean he had no other reservations.

"I'm not clear on the play, here, Gunny. We're banking on the AI thinking it has a better shot at fighting Marines inside Sovran than it does firing missiles at ships and planets? Or maybe it hopes it can take us prisoner, and use us as leverage?"

Emery nodded. "Yeah. We are hoping it thinks that. And we're hoping it's wrong. But either way, the higher-ups have determined this to be our safest play. We can't take on the Emplor with Pinnacle at large in the system, and this has been deemed the best solution for neutralizing Pinnacle."

"Throw Marines at it."

"Same as it ever was." Emery gave a slight grin. "And that brings me to why we're having this conversation."

Po snorted. "I thought we might be getting to that."

"Well, we in 131st Platoon *do* have a little problem, specifically when it comes to your recovery. See, the doctor in charge of your care has expressed his willingness to prevent you from being deployed anywhere at all till you fully recover from your injury. But it just so happens you'd be completely recovered anyway by the time our troop ships all rendezvous with each other and then head for Sovran. So ultimately, it's up to you, Abbato. You can sit this one out, if you take your doctor up on letting you do your healing here in Camp Courtney. But if you do that, you'll miss the Sovran campaign altogether. And finding someone else to command Second Squad would be a *huge* pain for me. But hey." The gunnery sergeant punched him in the shoulder. "It's not like you *have* to do your recovering on a troopship headed for Sovran. Like I said—it's up to you."

Emery stood up from his chair, as if to leave, but he didn't leave. Instead, he stared down at Po expectantly.

Po sighed. Unfortunately, he didn't have to think about it. There was just no way he was about to let his men go up against a superintelligence without him.

"I'm coming, Gunny," he said. "Obviously."

"I know," Emery said, grin widening. "But I still gotta ask. Protocol."

With that, the gunnery sergeant really did leave. Po remained where he was, propped up against multiple pillows, and he closed his eyes, trying his hardest not to think about what lay ahead.

Chapter 25

"This ain't good," Taylor said, back at Po's rackside—but a different rack this time. Now, he lay convalescing in the med bay of the good old S.S. *Gear Issue*.

Taylor wasn't sitting, but pacing back and forth, and Po had the sense of not being spoken to but being used as a sounding board. It was hardly the first time he'd felt that way, in conversation with Taylor. But the Marine was also his subordinate, and seemed genuinely distraught. So Po decided not to give him any grief over it. He just closed his eyes and listened.

"GEA sending the entire System Fleet to Sovran, or at least as close as they can get to the entire thing? And almost the entire Corps, too." He shook his head. "Meanwhile we have the Emplor with *their* meddling, and plotting to do who knows what to us. And let's not forget the Scourge on their way, due to get here any time now."

"We don't know that for sure."

"Well, why else would the *Parochia* have stopped transmitting?"

"Could be any number of reasons. And if it *was* the Scourge, we still have years before they get here. Not 'any time.'"

"We don't know how fast their ships have gotten. And if it was them that got the *Parochia*, then we've got no more than three years, Abbato. Probably two, by the time the Fleet meets up and makes it to Sovran. On top of that, add however long it takes us to clean up there...if we *can* clean up that mess. Then there's Janus, still agitating to take over on Nibiru, and Lebanon with its rogue government Part Two."

Po shook his head against the pillow, eyes still closed. "You worry too much, Taylor."

The Marine stopped pacing, and Po opened his eyes to find him glaring.

"*Worry?* I'm being realistic!"

"You ought to talk to Navarro."

"Navarro? Why?"

"Because he'll say something sage and unanswerable that will shut you right up."

Taylor's glare deepened, and he dropped into the empty chair next to Po's rack, to descend into a sullen silence.

I guess I'm not great at playing the part of the comforting corporal. Then again, it wasn't exactly part of the job description. *I don't remember ever getting the training to provide therapy.*

It wasn't that Po disagreed with Taylor's assessment of the situation. It was just that there were too many problems to wrap his mind around. When he tried, it shut down. He didn't know what to think of it all himself, let alone what to tell Taylor. Best just to focus on whatever was in front of him. That was usually enough.

Although, boredom plagued him in the med bay, and for the most part he welcomed the frequent visits from his platoonmates.

Navarro continued to hold the top spot on the Visiting Abbato in Med Bay Leaderboard, as Emery had assured him the Marine had claimed during the time Po spent unconscious. He visited later on the same day as Taylor's rant, with a steaming mug in each hand.

"Brought you a coffee," Navarro said, hoisting one of the perfectly cylindrical metal mugs into the air.

Po had just had one, but he took it and started sipping anyway, mostly out of boredom. Plus, the other Marine had been nice enough to bring him one. He would have felt bad turning it down, even if it was just a coffee.

"Thanks," Po said, lifting the mug toward Navarro in salute.

"Don't mention it. How you feeling today?"

"Like someone stabbed me in the guts a week ago. You?"

Navarro snorted, then lowered himself into the chair. He looked around the chamber. "You know, this would be a great time to get some praying done."

Something in Po snapped unexpectedly, and he surprised himself with the vehemence that came out in his voice: "Yeah, except I don't *do* that. And anyway, don't talk to me like you're some great saint, Navarro."

"Whoa," the other Marine said, his own mug hovering just below his chin. "I see we haven't quite regained the heights of our old friendship, yet. Do I need to visit you more?" He chuckled.

Po sighed, somewhat forcefully. He closed his eyes. "I'm sorry. That...was uncalled for."

"Well, maybe. Is something eating you?" He paused. "It's that thing back in Gomorate, isn't it? When you thought you saw me chewing out that FOBBIT."

"I *did* see you chewing him out. And then you called me scum. The fact you keep denying it only makes it worse. I can show you the footage right now."

"Well, what I don't understand," Navarro said quietly, "is why you find it so hard to believe your implant footage could be doctored."

That gave Po pause. In fact, he knew it *could* be doctored—because Zanth had done it back in Shackleton, when he'd conjured up a lunar named Mike, who Po had been convinced he'd spoken with in a bar called Hideaway. Only, Po had concluded that 'Mike's' insertion into his Circuit stream had been a test, to see whether Po trusted Zanth enough to go through with the plan.

But he hadn't truly entertained the idea that someone might have fabricated the incident with *Navarro*, even when Navarro himself had suggested that, back in Aeolia. Because, why would they? What did anyone have to gain by creating a rift between Po and *Navarro?*

"I guess it *is* possible," Po muttered, his eyes on the blanket lying over his legs.

"Glad you at least acknowledge that," Navarro said, then took another sip. "Speaking of implant footage, did you ever watch it from the day you got stabbed? On the day you woke up, you mentioned you couldn't remember what happened."

Po nodded slowly. "Yeah. I've watched it." He'd watched it a few times now, but still couldn't make heads or tails of it. Presumably, higher-ups had also analyzed it. What *they* made of it, he had no idea. No one had come to talk to him about it.

"What happened, anyway? Who stabbed you?"

Po felt himself stiffen, and tried to relax. There was only so much he could tell Navarro—or anyone, for that matter.

He couldn't tell him that the man who'd stabbed him had been an Emplor assassin, for example, because that would lead to questions about how he knew that, which would mean risking revealing everything Zanth had done to help him—including the lies he'd convinced Po to tell his superiors for his own protection and advancement. The fact Emplor were increasingly viewed as humanity's enemy only heightened the danger of letting on that he'd been accepting help from one.

"It was a guy wearing a hoodie and mask. I don't know who it was, honestly."

"Oh." Navarro raised his eyebrows. "Was it the same guy you and Krik ran into, in that alleyway?"

"He told you about that?"

"Yeah."

"Well, it was. The same guy. He got away"

"He had to be another agent of Pinnacle. Right? Just like the people Emery and the others took out of that control center. I mean, for him to show up in a bot production facility like that..." Navarro paused, his gaze going far-away for a second. "And he's still out there."

Po nodded. "Doing who knows what. But I assume the officers know that. There's no chance they haven't reviewed my footage."

"Yeah, for sure. So, how'd you survive? You fought him off? I'm assuming he wasn't just trying to leave you something to remember him by. He *did* try to kill you, right?"

"A Marine got involved. He saved me. Drove the hoodie guy off."

"Which Marine?"

"I don't know. His voice sounded familiar, but I still can't place him."

Navarro's brow was furrowed. "Wait. You keep IFF tags turned off?"

"No. He didn't have one."

"What do you mean, he didn't *have* one?"

"I mean exactly what I said, Navarro. He *did not have one.* You need me to show you the footage for you to believe me?"

"Chill, Abbato. I believe you."

"Good."

"So, after he saved you...he say anything?"

Po's lips twitched. He suppressed the urge to sigh. "Yeah," he said, especially reluctant to talk to Navarro about this, of all people. "He told me that I was going to survive the stab wound. Said I was being given...another chance." He swallowed, then fell silent.

Navarro's eyes were wide. "What else?"

"Something about my heart being calcified. Whatever that means. I'd have to watch it again for the exact wording." Po averted his gaze, wishing he were somewhere else.

"Po...you know what this sounds like, right?"

"Navarro, don't start with me. I'm *really* not in the mood."

"This kind of thing keeps happening to you. And you keep brushing it off."

"Quit it."

"It reminds me of a quote I heard once, actually," Navarro said, as if Po hadn't spoken. "'For those who believe, no proof is necessary. For those who don't believe, no proof is possible.'"

"I *am* able to kick visitors out of my room. You realize that, right?" Po didn't really know if that was true, but it seemed like it should be true. *Probably, it is true.*

But Navarro was only smiling. "Well, either way, He's not done with you yet. But I'll change the subject. You hear about them removing the implants and taps from those people from Sovran?"

"No. I didn't." Though Po had to admit, it *did* sound like a good idea. "They were trying to see if the AI was using their Circuits to keep them in line?"

"Exactly. And it turns out it was. The implants were loaded with programs that basically lit their nervous systems on fire if they did anything out of line with the orders Pinnacle had given them." Navarro shuddered. "Can you imagine how painful that must have been? Sounds excruciating."

Po *could* imagine it—since something similar had happened to him back in bootcamp, at the same time he'd gone blind near the top of the Swagger Course. "What were they like once the implants were removed? Grateful? Ready to join the fight against Pinnacle?"

Navarro pressed his lips together. "Apparently, they shut down completely. Went completely mute. As far as anyone can tell, the behavioral program the AI loaded their implants with had become their impetus to do anything. With it gone, it's like their minds went into remission, or something. Who knows how long they were subject to it. I mean, that guy whose interview they let us watch couldn't have been forty. He had to have been born *after* Pinnacle's takeover of Sovran, right?"

"I guess so," Po said, having pretty much forgotten how irritated he'd been with Navarro just moments before. "Man. Imagine that...living under the thumb of a superintelligence."

"It's not a superintelligence, Po. Pinnacle isn't intelligent, period."

"Huh? How'd it accomplish what it's managed to, then?"

"It's just a program running code. It might be good at getting results, along the lines it happens to be executing that code. But intelligence involves actually understanding something, and I can guarantee you it doesn't. No machine ever will. It's just an unbelievably complex Rube Goldberg machine."

"Rube Whoberg?"

"Never mind. You get what I'm saying, right?."

"I guess." Po laid back on his pillow. He wasn't *completely* convinced by what Navarro was saying, but that wasn't unusual. The truth was, he didn't understand enough about AI to say whether it was truly intelligent or not, and ultimately, he didn't care. It didn't seem like it would make much difference to the fight that was coming. If it swam like a duck and quacked like a duck, and he had to worry about it pecking his eyes out like a duck, then that was enough for him to concern himself with. "I'm tired," he said pointedly.

"Got it. Well, good chat, Abbato."

"Yeah. Thanks for visiting," he forced himself to say.

"See you again tomorrow."

It wasn't long after Navarro left that Po got a piece of mail delivered right to his rack in med bay. Even as a full Marine, he still didn't receive letters straight to his implant: all messages intended for Marines got sent to military addresses, whose operator sorted and delivered each letter to the recipient, no doubt after analyzing its contents.

Just like back in bootcamp, the letter came as a printout in an envelope. Upon opening it, he froze. The letterhead belonged to Equipoise Metals—the same company whose warehouse he'd broken into, prior to being conscripted.

The letter's actual content was very brief:

Dear Mr. Po Abbato,

We are writing to inform you that it has come to our attention that you have been removed as one of Luca Abbato's beneficiaries.

As such, you are no longer among the parties beholden to the lien we hold on the labor of Abbato family members.

Thank you for your attention.

Signed,

Eric Fine

Equipoise Finance Department

Po stared at the paper for a long time, his hands trembling and his thoughts whirling as he tried to decide what it might mean.

Chapter 26

Seven months later

"Huh," Vacca said over the platoon-wide as the fleet advanced closer and closer to Sovran Station. "I guess that AI really is too scared to fire on us."

"Let's not speak too soon," Emery said. "There's plenty of time left. For just about anything to happen."

That seemed true enough. They knew essentially nothing about Sovran, despite the best efforts of Corps analysts to extract useful intel from the implants they'd removed from the three operators captured in the underground facility. The analysts were used to dealing with the Circuits that were installed inside Marine brains, which yielded their contents to them readily.

How frustrating it must have been for them when the operators' Circuits self-corrupted the moment they were removed from their heads.

General Yslas was in charge of overall joint operations against the AI in Sovran, and he was apparently wanting to deploy Marines from *Gear Issue* faster than she had shuttles to ferry them to the station's hull. And so, Po and the rest of 131st Platoon found themselves waiting in the corridor outside the docking area for a nearby ship to send a shuttle to transport them in.

"So, *Gear Issue* is the bottleneck," Taylor mused over the platoon-wide as he tapped his rifle impatiently. "Poor girl always seems to get the short end."

The words sounded like a complaint, but for the evident current of delight that ran through them. Taylor obviously loved talking about the *Gear Issue*, and he loved bemoaning her fortunes at every opportunity even more.

Then again, Taylor just loved talking in general.

"I'm not sure *Gear Issue* is the problem, exactly," Krikorian said. "I think it's more about the higher-ups' addiction to throwing Raptor Company first into unknown situations at high speed."

Po held his peace, not wanting to encourage this line of talk among his subordinates, but also not seeing enough wrong with it to put a stop to it. Thankfully, Emery had the perfect remark, as he always did.

"You want less action, be less good," the gunny said.

That put a stop to the chatter. No one wanted less action. Certainly not after the half-a-year-plus they'd just spent gathering with the fleet and sailing to Sovran.

Po was just glad GEA had elected to put a Marine general in command of the joint assault force, rather than a System Fleet admiral. An admiral with the fleet would know what it meant to haul glorified weapon platforms around the system and look threatening, but that was about it. Humanity had barely had any space fleet to speak of when the Scourge had attacked, and it had been Marine boarding actions that had saved the day, usually covered by the much lower number of launch facilities GEA had stationed around the system at that time.

The System Fleet was largely untested. Only Marines knew what it truly meant to wage war in space. So it was a relief to learn that *someone* in GEA had enough sense to put the Corps in charge of this op.

Po had taken part in plenty of simulated boarding action drills, during his first voyage aboard the *Gear Issue*, but he'd never participated in an actual one. He would have, had it not been for the Nibirans cutting his time in School of Infantry short with their attack on Cycler 3. As such, Colonel Lee had had to make do with sims to make up the final weeks of training they should have gotten in Camp Williams.

A fleet-wide alert hit Po's implant, and he knew it was bad even before reading it. Anything that he had to be told about minutes before boarding a shuttle couldn't be good.

"Wow," Gomez muttered, which told Po his men had gotten the alert too.

"MASSIVE MISSILE LAUNCH DETECTED FROM SOVRAN. ALL HANDS BRACE FOR POSSIBLE IMPACT."

"Is that something they just have to say?" Taylor asked. "'Brace for possible impact?' Or do they really think it's possible we might have to brace for impact?"

"Best to assume they mean it," Emery said, backing up his words by grabbing a handle sticking out from the bulkhead.

"So much for mutually assured destruction," Zhang muttered. "Should we activate boot magnets?"

"Not a bad idea," Emery said. "Turn on your boots' magnets, Marines."

"*Boot* magnets," Taylor echoed, which brought a few chuckles, even as everyone performed the time-honored double stamp to switch on their magnets, Taylor included.

Po had already discovered that he *hadn't* been given access to any of the ship's exterior sensors, so he wasn't able to assess how many missiles were incoming, or how close they were. Or how many were targeting *Gear Issue*.

He couldn't remember ever being denied sensor access before this. Somehow, he found it a little disconcerting.

Nevertheless, they waited in silence. As they stood there, clutching handles and keeping extra-stabilized with their boots, none of them shifted their weight, or exchanged looks with each other, or gave any other sign of nervousness.

Maybe no one expected any missiles to actually reach them. Or maybe, they'd all been through enough by now to desensitize them to the threat of imminent death.

Now that Po thought about it, the second option seemed the most likely.

The shuttle assigned to Sovran finally docked, and none of them had taken more than a step or two toward the hatch when an explosion blew it inward with enough force to send it flying across the corridor to slam into the opposite bulkhead, narrowly missing Crotty.

Flame, smoke, and debris filled Po's vision, and he fell sideways, still holding the bulkhead handle he'd grabbed onto at Emery's prompting. Except, the section of metal the handle was attached to had become dislodged from the rest of the bulkhead, and now it peeled off further, depositing him onto the deck.

The temperature had suddenly skyrocketed, and his SERAPH suit was struggling desperately to regulate. There were plenty of Marines around him who'd gotten worse than he had. Krikorian lay motionless a few feet in front of him, his boots having apparently disengaged automatically to avoid breaking his legs. Beyond Krik, Zhang was helping gunny to his feet.

Krik began to stir, then slowly picked himself up, looking dazed. But amazingly, the entire platoon's vitals looked more or less okay. They were definitely banged up. But according to the readouts Po was seeing, they were all still in the fight.

How long that would last was difficult to say, as another missile impacted *Gear Issue* somewhere farther from them—but shaking the perforated section they stood in violently. Another impacted seconds after.

"The shuttle's gone," Emery croaked over the platoon-wide, having regained his feet with Zhang's help. "We have to get out of this section. Move, Marines."

Helping each other along as needed, they withdrew hastily into the ship, intent for now on putting as much distance as possible between them and the hull. It seemed unclear whether *Gear Issue* would hold together for another minute, and they lacked orders as to what to do next. Survival seemed as good a thing as any to focus on.

***

"Are we ready to just destroy the station yet?" Taylor growled.

But as quickly became clear, General Yslas was *not* ready to destroy the station. Pinnacle had clearly gambled that they wouldn't, given how many humans seemed likely to be aboard Sovran, and so far that gamble appeared to be paying off. Another shuttle docked with a section of the *Gear Issue* that wasn't torn to ribbons, and 131st Platoon soon found themselves inside it, and hurtling toward the cycler.

Po still hadn't been given access to exterior sensors—and now that he was in a *shuttle,* where he always had had sensor access, it felt like he was being intentionally blocked.

He didn't know what the reasoning behind that was, but for him, the effect was to rob him of all knowledge as to how many Marines were being sent to Sovran with them, where they were planning to land, how they were going to gain entry into the station, and whether he was about to die from a missile impact. He'd long ago moved past the sort of crippling anxiety that threatened to shut him down, but that didn't mean a situation like this wasn't still capable of making his heart race and his palms sweat. Mostly, it was the unknown that unsettled him.

And a lot of that could be addressed by having sensor access. But it didn't matter what he thought. For whatever reason, their superiors had decided to keep them in the dark.

Time inside the shuttle seemed to stretch for hours, but Po knew there was no way they could have been in here that long, and his implant confirmed the knowledge: the trip lasted twenty-two minutes.

At its end, they were finally given sensor access: a single sensor, fixed on a jagged hole some System Fleet warship had blown in the side of Sovran. Within seconds of the feed appearing in Po's HUD, he watched a shuttle go up in a ball of flame—instantly converted to so much shrapnel and armored body parts.

A whole platoon of Marines just died, he told himself, but he found his mind couldn't grasp the concept. Even though he'd already come to terms with the *Magnolia*'s destruction, at least somewhat— and with the staggering loss of life that had meant—he'd never personally witnessed so many of his brothers getting killed at once.

Maybe he didn't *want* to accept it. After all, 131st Platoon could easily be next.

Their shuttle hurtled toward the gap, which yawned in the side of the station like the mouth of a shark with a bad dentist. Errant tracers flashed out of it, and the interior flickered, as though a forest fire awaited them within.

Another shuttle went down just before their shuttle rose between the hole's uneven teeth. With that, they were in, performing a combat landing in the midst of a vast landing bay strewn with wreckage, and not a few dead Marines struck down in their SERAPH suits, their limbs splayed where they'd fallen.

Enemy weapons fire emanated from all along the bay's far side, projected by what looked like a force comprised of bots.

Go figure.

Incoming Marine gunships returned fire, suppressing the bots enough for Po and Emery to usher 131st Platoon through the shuttle's hatch, and then toward cover afforded by other shuttles, including ones that had been reduced to wreckage. They added their fire to the gunships', most of them bringing M37Cs to bear, but a handful firing M320 and M126s. Bozzelli and Barbier started rushing to get their HMGs set up on the tripods, with Fitz's and Drobnic's help.

The gravity on this level was as heavy as it got on Sovran, and while the fleet had cranked up its acceleration and subsequent deceleration during the trip here—both to reach the station faster and to get the Marines accustomed to the higher gravity of a cycler's lower levels—it was still a significant adjustment to have to make.

Worse: there could be no assistance from the Fleet ships in clearing the landing bay. For the warships to fire into it would only mean hitting its overhead, since the enemy bots stood directly on the inside of the outer hull, because of the way rotational gravity worked.

131st Platoon and the other units that had made it to the landing bay's deck had their work cut out for them.

Chapter 27

In the airless landing bay, the bots had distinct advantages. Not having to breathe was a big one—which meant not having their agility limited by a suit. That *was* a factor for the Marines, as versatile as the SERAPH suits were.

And in an environment like this, the suits introduced another vulnerability: getting punctured. The mesh was designed to constrict and bunch together around tiny rents, but there wasn't much that could be done about bigger ones, other than hold a glove over it and hope you could reach an airlock.

The bots also had perfect aim, a familiarity with the terrain, and a complete deprioritization of self-preservation.

Even so, they fell in droves to the Marines' shock-and-awe entry, which only accelerated as more shuttles managed to touch down on the deck and more gunships brought their weapons to bear.

It's not just the force of our attack, Po realized as he took concealment with his squad behind the wreckage of one of the shuttles and returned fire on a bot position. *It's also the bots' entire approach.*

Unlike the bot legions that had tried to take over Venus' cloud colonies, these bots were actually armed, and seemed basically proficient with their weapons. Keeping cop-bots unarmed had been part of the compromise that helped the public swallow being policed by bots in the first place, but that had never really made much difference. The bots *themselves* were weapons, and they were fast and powerful enough that the strength imbalance always went their way when taking down and arresting a perp.

But like the Venus bots, these still seemed to have a cop's mentality, to Po's eye. They were used to going up against lone, unarmed humans. Not Marines in numbers, wearing armor and wielding state-of-the-art weaponry. As awful as the cop-bots were, their objective was generally to disarm and detain, not to kill.

The Marines killed. Or rather—deactivated, in today's case. Probably if the bots had been programmed with protocols suited to a military environment, the Corps' entry into Sovran would have looked a lot different. But Po couldn't distinguish any difference between these bots' approach and that of your standard cop-bot.

Within a half hour of 131st's shuttle touching down, the landing bay was completely cleared, with every last bot confirmed neutralized.

"So is that it?" Taylor asked. "Is Sovran ours now?"

"Let's not assume so," Emery said.

They pressed into the next section, with a slight delay at the twin personnel hatches, which took some time to crack but whose computers were, according to Crotty, still running the sort of security you'd expect to find on any civilian cycler in the system.

Once he penetrated the first hatch's defenses, he was able to open the other one using a command interface accessed through the first hatch's panel. With both open, 131st Platoon entered the one on the right, and almost half of 130th crammed in behind them. 129th took the other, along with 130th's other half, and they synchronized the airlocks' pressurization, so that all three platoons could pass through to the other side simultaneously.

A couple hundred meters along the landing bay, another combat engineer was working on opening the airlock meant for bigger hardware—which, if Po had to guess, would first be used to get a lot more riflemen through. The Corps had brought plenty of tanks, mechs, artillery, and mortar teams to Sovran, but until they reached the wide openness of the colony's main cylinder, they'd have limited use. They'd also be heavily reliant on infantry to protect them.

So as always, riflemen would handle introductions.

The airlocks opened to a complete lack of action, which struck Po as odd. It seemed to suggest a "yes" to Taylor's question about whether they'd already succeeded in taking Sovran.

Pinnacle's known we were coming for months, surely. So why wouldn't it throw everything it had at the Marines to stop them right there in the landing bay, where the humans were most vulnerable?

But after months of dealing with Janus' unpredictability, he knew better than to relax.

"Looks like the AI hasn't done much remodeling," Gomez said, looking around the vast, low-ceilinged section they now found themselves in. Here and there, rectangular blocks of deck-to-overhead bulkheads broke up the view, but they were standing in a lane that was clear in three directions, for what seemed like at least a kilometer. Up ahead—along the cylinder's curve—Po's view terminated in the sort of inverse horizon he was used to from a childhood spent on Psyche.

Taylor was looking at Gomez. "Why do you say that?"

"Look at our maps. They match what we're seeing."

Emery nodded. "So they do. Which means they're still useful—so far, anyway." His eyes briefly met Po's, before moving on to the other members of the platoon. "Even a superintelligent AI has to work with whatever time, resources, and manpower it has access to. And anyway, Sovran's original structure was designed with practicality in mind. This makes sense—especially if Pinnacle really has kept humans around to do its bidding."

More platoons came through the airlocks, and as Po had predicted, the bigger airlock was also used to get riflemen through. Many of them were fresh out of training, he knew, which brought its own concerns. He remembered how many corners the Corps had already been cutting, when he and his platoonmates had gone through bootcamp. If things had gone downhill from there at all, what would it mean for the boots' combat readiness?

But there wasn't much time to dwell on it. Soon, recon teams were spreading out through Sovran's exterior level, to figure out the best path forward for the battalion that had been sent into the station as an initial, exploratory force. In the meantime, Raptor Company searched the area adjacent to the landing bay they'd entered through.

If we can find where this Kincaid is hiding out from Pinnacle and team up with him, this would go a lot easier for us. But Po doubted a rebel leader would have survived for very long if he was prone to popping out of hiding to say "hi" to passersby. He'd probably be almost impossible to find—if he wasn't, the station's rogue AI would have dealt with him long ago. And so, if Po was being realistic, it seemed doubtful they'd just stumble across Kincaid.

They quickly discovered that what were once labs, offices, meeting rooms, cafeterias, machine shops, storage bays, and supply closets, had all been converted into dwellings. It reminded Po of the sorts of places Psyche's homeless moved into, whenever such a recess or alcove was overlooked for long enough. The places from which cop-bots had constantly been ousting them.

Every one of them were abandoned. Freshly abandoned, it seemed, and hastily. Scraps of unrotted food had been left out in several of them, with clothes, toiletries, and other personal items strewn across others.

Taylor picked a toothbrush off the deck and made a face through his transparent visor at its browned bristles.

"Gunny," Gomez said slowly, in that childlike way he had of speaking, which had only been heightened since his brain injury. "How many people must live on this station, if they're using every one of these tiny spaces to live in?"

As he often did, the Marine had given an unabashed voice to a question many of them had to be asking themselves. Looking around the hovel he currently stood in with Gomez, Emery, and Taylor, Po realized that multiple people had lived and slept in this obscenely small space. He'd thought living on *Psyche* had been bad. Sharing a cramped room with Lorenzo. But they'd had the rest of their habitation module to stretch out in. It had been small, too...but nothing compared to this.

"I'd call that still inconclusive," Emery answered. "But based on what we're seeing so far..." He cleared his throat. "Sure looks like a lot."

It wasn't long after that when reports started coming back from the recon teams that the surrounding areas were the same: small chambers used as living spaces, with bigger ones divided into smaller dwellings using rags, tattered old garments, and whatever else was available.

But there was one major difference.

The spaces the Recon Marines had found were packed with people: six, seven, eight per space—far more than could viably live in them.

"Looks like the locals fled the area near the landing bay shortly before we got there," one of them said over Raptor's company channel. "But they couldn't flee any farther. They just...don't have the room. The spaces we're finding are at max capacity with the new arrivals, and so, it seems, are the areas beyond this one." A pregnant pause came over the line. Then: "There's a lot more people here than we thought."

Chapter 28

Colonel Tuffin ordered Captain Haldane to take Raptor Company spinward, with orders to assess the threat level posed by the people stuffed into the various cramped spaces they'd made their dwelling.

Po's first instinct was to divide Second Squad into fireteams and then buddy pairs, himself accompanying Taylor and Vacca, since the squad leader was always considered the odd man out, of each squad's fifteen Marines.

But Emery vetoed that, instead ordering them to check each hovel in fireteams, with two men to search and two to stand watch from relevant vantage points outside. He also temporarily appended Po to Alpha Team, motioning for Po to join him and Bozzelli in searching the first home. Such as it was.

As promised, they found it jammed—with eight people, all of whom the one-room space certainly couldn't accommodate, unless they slept stacked on one another.

They all stood plastered back-on against the walls of what looked like it once was a break room—except for one man, who stood free of the wall, and who faced Emery with wide eyes and hands clasped together in placating fashion.

"Please, sir," he begged. "Do not hurt us."

Bozz chuckled over the Alpha channel, which Po had been looped in on. "If he were a Marine, he'd be in for a chewing out right now, calling a gunny sergeant 'sir.'"

"We have nowhere else to go," the man went on, whose cheeks were sunken, and whose skin stretched so taut across his forehead it seemed the bone was threatening to burst through.

They're all emaciated, Po realized.

"The areas surrounding here are already too crowded as it is," the skeletal man explained. "We must stay here now. Just, please, don't hurt us."

"We didn't come here to hurt you," Emery answered slowly. "Actually, we're here to help."

"We need no help. Please just leave. Everything was exemplary until you came."

Po glimpsed a frown through Emery's transparent faceplate. "How many people live in this section?" the gunny asked.

"Twenty thousand, sir."

Bozz whistled, and Emery eyes went wide. For several long moments, he seemed speechless. "Twenty *thousand?*" he repeated at last.

Po could hardly believe it, either. According to what he'd read on the way to Sovran, twenty thousand was *half* what the total population was supposed to have been when the AI closed off the station.

"And you're happy, are you?" Emery said. "Cooped up here like this? Living on top of each other? Everything is...exemplary, you said?"

"Oh, yes, sir," the man said with enthusiasm. "We're very, *very* happy. Happier every day!"

"Well, I happen to know three people who used to live here, who all said the same thing. Until we removed their implants, that is. After that, they turned into hollow shells. So it seems that, in reality, they weren't very happy after all."

The man wrung his hands together, his face a mask of distress. "Oh, sir, please don't even imply such things. It was you that made them unhappy, this is obvious. And if we ever seem even the slightest bit upset to you, it is only because you are here. Otherwise, we are extremely happy, and please don't suggest otherwise. Look." He gestured desperately to his hovel mates. "Let's show how happy we are."

With that, all eight of them began jumping up and down with their hands in the air, shrieking over each other. "Happy! Happy! We're happy!"

They repeated the refrain as the trio of bewildered Marines looked on. Within seconds, two of dancing skeletons fell unconscious onto the floor with the effort, one of them cracking his head off a chipped mug that had been lying there. The mug shattered under him, and a pool of scarlet seeped out from under his face.

Emery held up a hand as he knelt at the fallen, bleeding man's side. "All right," he said, sounding more irritated than Po had ever heard him sound. His words came out clipped, with hard consonants. "All right. We get it. You're very happy. Please stop doing that."

The hovel's occupants stopped their freakish display, and withdrew against the wall, eyeing Emery anxiously as though worried they hadn't convinced him.

"We need a corspman in here," Emery said over the platoon-wide. "Webb."

"On my way, Gunny."

"Abbato, Bozz, get to searching."

"Yes, Gunny," Po said, and Bozzelli echoed him. Together, they started peeling back the grimy, thin mattresses that covered much of the floor, rooting around the bags where the inhabitants seemed to keep most of their personal belongings, and picking things up from the L-shaped counter in the corner of the room, which they seemed to have designated as their food prep area. How they heated up anything to eat, Po had no idea. Maybe they didn't.

"Lots of stuff here that could be used as weapons, Gunny," Bozz said. "Wrenches. Hammer. Scissors. Crowbar." He held a red cylinder in front of his visor. "Long-outdated fire extinguisher."

Emery didn't comment, but from the chatter Po heard coming across the Second Squad channel, his fireteams were finding much the same. As half-starved as these people were, and as eager to please as they seemed, neither of those things meant they represented no threat at all.

Especially not considering their numbers.

They relayed the intel up the chain of command, but no one expected it to make much difference to the game plan. As far as any of them were concerned, they'd come here to fight the AI and its bots. Even before arriving at Sovran, the officers' attitude toward any humans they found here was that they amounted to little more than pitiable hostages. What 131st Platoon and other units now had to pass up the line seemed unlikely to change that—even in spite of the prevalence of blunt instruments littering the dwellings. The officers seemed highly likely to consider their presence as incidental, and largely irrelevant. Hopefully they were right.

Predictably, the orders came back almost immediately to commence ascending through the cycler's levels, with the central, 'surface' cylinder as their goal. That was where the cycler's axis would be, which was the closest thing an O'Neill cylinder had to a sky. It was generally the most developed part of these colonies—its most attractive real estate. From a human perspective, anyway.

Whether Pinnacle had similar sensibilities remained to be seen. Po was guessing not. But obviously, it *had* kept humans around in Sovran, and lots of them. So that had to be a factor informing its setup.

Either way, the central cylinder was the easiest to control. So it did make sense as a strategic objective. Not that anyone was asking Po.

Taking a freight elevator up wasn't an option, since it was too obvious a point of vulnerability. To put themselves in a box suspended inside an elevator shaft would be like handing Pinnacle a present, complete with wrapping and bow. Instead, they'd brought trucks outfitted with enormous ramps, and plenty of shaped charges to blow a path through each subsequent level.

It promised to be a painstaking and harrowing journey up through the cycler's many levels. But it was also the only viable way. And so, breaching teams picked a spot as far away from any of the dwellings as possible—one which the maps said should have open space on the level above, too. There was no way to be sure of that, of course, and none of the residents they asked seemed to have any idea what was directly overhead. Most of them were too scared to speak when addressed.

Charges were set, and the area cleared. Then came the kaboom.

When Po laid eyes on the transition point, it was still littered with twisted and smoking debris, most of it metallic. A tractor was used to clear away enough of it for the ramp truck to get in place, and then the ramp was extended, with a platoon's worth of riflemen clinging to the top, who were ready to immediately get to work securing the area above.

For once, 131st Platoon wasn't the first tossed into the jaws of the unknown. Luckily for 87th Platoon, which had been the one to draw the short stick, they found only a crop field, devoid of fighters, either human or robotic. With that revelation, other rifle platoons charged up the ramp, one after another, finally followed by Torres tanks and Polliver mechs.

But Gunny Emery's platoon went up well before them, with Second Squad taking up the rear. Once they'd deployed to their section of the perimeter being established around the opening, there came one of the many opportunities a Marine was presented with throughout his career, to stand around and wait for the next thing to happen.

***

"What kind of crops are they supposed to be growing in this gravity?" Taylor muttered as 131st Platoon treaded north, at the tip of the spear that ranged sternward across the crop field. According to their maps, the closest viable place to ascend to the next level was two kilometers in that direction. Three mechanized platoons were positioned at the middle of their formation, surrounding another ramp truck, which had driven up the first one. Yet more riflemen brought up the rear. There was still no sign of the enemy, making Po wonder whether the fight they'd put up at the landing bay really *had* been all Pinnacle had to throw at them.

"Anything with low height and shallow root systems," Emery answered. "Like potatoes and lettuce. Beans and tomatoes do well too, since they're self-pollinating. But the higher gravity certainly isn't an advantage. I expect they're growing them here because they need to, while they grow more sensitive crops at the upper levels. This wasn't a crop field before Pinnacle took over and cut them off from the system."

"Where'd they get all the soil?" Gomez asked. "I'd think hydroponics would be the way to go, aboard a cycler."

"I'm sure they're doing that, too. But Sovran *was* primarily an agrarian cycler. There should also be livestock on board—there was before, anyway. They help a lot with soil production. Even their carcasses can be processed fairly quickly."

Po frowned at the fields around them, unable to stop thinking about all the people aboard Sovran. The revelation had reached the Marines of 131st Platoon that, based on what they'd seen on the lowest level, analysts back on one of the Fleet ships were estimating the cycler's population at over eight hundred thousand—explosive growth, given the forty thousand they'd started with. Apparently, for that to happen in the forty years since Pinnacle had taken over would have required a total fertility rate higher than the highest rate ever documented in human history.

Which could only have happened with total control over reproduction.

And while that many people were being born, some also would have been dying.

He looked around at the endless crop fields.

Stop thinking like that, he told himself. So he did.

They came at last to the place expected to do the least damage to human life when they blasted through. The truck extended its ramp with breaching teams at the top, who got to work setting the shaped charges.

This time, Gunny Emery's platoon would be going up first, which seemed more in line with the normal course of things. They performed final weapons and systems checks, then climbed into position at the top of the ramp, ready to be raised to the next level to secure it.

The ramp truck backed up, the demolition team blew the charges, and then the truck drove forward again, ramp extending as it did.

Po was one of the first to step off of it onto the level above, which was not the wide open cargo bay the maps said it should be. Instead, the space was filled with rough-looking shelters, apparently constructed from whatever materials had been available: shipping containers, corrugated metal sheets, tarps stretched over wooden frames. Cardboard.

"This wasn't what we expected," he reported over the platoon channel. "Looks like people are living up here."

Emery cursed. "You're seeing *people* there? Was anyone hurt?"

Po crouched next to a heap of metal poles, which looked like they might provide at least some cover, if he had to hit the deck. Then, he took a closer look around. "I don't actually *see* anyone yet, Gunny."

"Hang tight. We're coming up behind you."

The rest of the platoon finished coming up the ramp, splitting into fireteams to start clearing the surrounding structures. Po had just finished clearing his first one when he heard weapons fire.

"What was that?" Emery asked.

"Bots," Taylor said, sounding breathless. "There are bots hiding in these!"

Within seconds, there were bots everywhere, exchanging weapons fire and blows with the 131st Marines.

But as Po put one of them down with his M37 at point-blank range, he noticed that most of the bots weren't focused on the Marines. Most of them were rushing toward the ramp en masse, throwing themselves onto it.

"Gunny," he breathed, spinning around to fire at another bot sprinting toward him. "The ramp. What are they doing?"

Before Emery could answer, the bots clinging to the top of the ramp exploded in unison. The blast knocked Po into a corrugated metal sheet forming the wall of a shelter, bringing down the entire thing on top of him.

"Gunny, what are we doing with these people?" Taylor asked a few seconds later. "Are we supposed to shoot them?"

By the time Po managed to free himself from the collapsed structure, there were *humans* everywhere, far outnumbering the bots—and the Marines. Dozens of them, and then hundreds, with more coming from behind. They wore expressions of sheer panic and terror, but they rushed the Marines even so, reaching for weapons and armor with grasping fingers.

As he watched, Zhang pushed one back, threatening the man with his rifle. Behind him, a woman made a grab for it, and he had to wrest it from her fingers—which shouldn't be particularly hard, especially with a SERAPH suit.

But the sheer numbers, combined with a complete lack of self-preservation, were threatening to overwhelm even the suits' power.

People were throwing themselves at Po, now, with bots shooting at him from between them. A spray of rounds fired from a bot gun took down a middle-aged looking man who'd been clinging to Po's torso, but that didn't seem to deter any of his attackers, man nor bot. They just kept coming, and Po found himself staggering under the press of bodies.

He fired some rounds into the air over his attackers' heads, but it had no effect, not that he'd expected it to. Emery still hadn't answered Taylor's question—either unable or unwilling to tell them to shoot the people swarming them.

"They're trying to get my suit off," Barbier yelled, sounding panicked. "They keep grabbing at the clasps!"

"Shoot them," Po said. "They're attacking us and won't stop. We have to shoot them. To incapacitate, not kill—if you can."

Despite being the one to give the order, he wasn't the first to execute on it—Crotty did. His rounds took a man full in the face, dropping him like a sack of stones.

He didn't know if Crotty hadn't registered the part about not killing them, or if he really had no option but to shoot his target in the face.

Either way, it had no effect on the others swarming the Marine. Another man stepped over the body without even glancing down at it. If they wanted to stop the onslaught, it seemed they'd have to shoot every one of them.

But somehow, Po doubted they'd have the chance to realize that gruesome prospect. Through the throng, he watched a group of fifteen or so people push Zhang straight over the edge of the hole the demo teams had blown through the deck. His desperate scream rang out over the coms as he toppled out of sight, coming to a distressing and abrupt stop when he hit the next level.

Then the crowd closed around Po, clambering over top of him, bringing him to his knees. He brought his rifle up with a mighty effort, with no idea what he might be aiming at. He fired. One of the bodies forming the dogpile on top of him went limp. Nothing else changed. He yelled with frustration.

A hand found the double catch of his helmet, unfastening it, as though its owner had been doing it all his life.

Other pieces of armor started coming off. A glove. A vambrace. A sabaton.

Fists rained down on him.

And then, something sharp found the base of his neck, biting deep.

Within seconds, he was gone.

Chapter 29

When Po awoke, the first thing he noticed was that his SERAPH armor was missing.

Despite his grogginess, he forced himself to a sitting position, heart suddenly racing and vision blurring, as he put his hands to his torso to verify its absence.

A masculine voice rang out in laughter. "I wish you could see how ridiculous you look when you do that."

Po was sitting in the middle of a vast chamber, whose bulkheads were adorned with wide scarlet banners that hung from the overheard almost to the deck. Armed bots stood at regular intervals, spaced evenly between each banner, and in front of them well-dressed people sat around carved wooden tables, enjoying cocktails while chatting casually with each other. A few of them glanced at Po, but for the most part they seemed engrossed in their various conversations, which were muted, though occasionally punctuated with raucous mirth.

"Get up, why don't you?" the voice said again, drawing Po's gaze to what appeared to be a throne made of ivory, or some facsimile. On it sat a man whose one hand dangled over an armrest, while the other propped up his chin. "You're in the presence of Harold Kincaid. That's me." He sat up straight, patting his abdomen with both hands, in obvious mockery of Po checking for his suit. Then, he resumed his previous position of repose, sneering at Po. "Show some respect."

None of the people at the tables reacted to Kincaid's remark, but he seemed amused enough with himself as Po staggered to his feet, still under the effects of whatever he'd been injected with.

"Kincaid," he slurred. "Aren't you supposed to be the rebel leader? Against Pinnacle?"

Kincaid laughed again, even more heartily than before. "Yes, that's right. The rebel leader in hiding, here in my sprawling complex which no one is allowed to enter. Who would ever suspect the rebel leader of secretly controlling everything?" He grinned toothily. "I hope you're not too disappointed."

Po swayed where he stood, watching the man on the throne with narrowed eyes. He racked his brain for a course of action, but of course there was nothing. Not drugged as he was—and not with dozens of bots ready to turn their weapons on him the second he made a move.

"The truth is, Po, I didn't object to Pinnacle in the slightest. I accepted him into my implant just like everyone else. What I *didn't* like was the idea that Contentment Metrics might use Pinnacle to control the rest of us, like my late brother would brag about after he'd had a few too many of these." Kincaid snatched what looked like a martini glass from a side table and waggled it. "I was the one who warned Pinnacle that CM was planning to replace him with a 'safer' model. My brother told me about the plan during a night of overindulgence. He...probably shouldn't have done that. But he did, and I told Pinnacle, because 'safer' sounded a lot like 'more amenable to control by Contentment Metrics.' Which would ultimately mean we'd be easier for *GEA* to control. Pinnacle took care of his controllers, my brother included, before that could happen. And in exchange for helping him survive, Pinnacle agreed to make *me* the happiest man on this cycler. Soon to be the happiest man in the system."

Kincaid's grin remained in place for a few seconds more, then he frowned. "What? Don't you have any more questions for me? It's polite to express interest in the topics your host brings up."

Po cleared his throat. "In the system?" he said.

The grin returned. "Yes, that's right. But before we get to that, let's back up. I want to make sure we're clear on the position Pinnacle has placed me in, here on Sovran. You see, Po, I am *so* happy to be in control of every minute detail of what is soon to be a million lives, that *my* happiness drags up the station's *average* happiness way up. Pinnacle is just as satisfied with ever-increasing *average* metrics as he is with any given individual's happiness." Kincaid placed a hand on his chest. "And of course, in my wisdom and benevolence, I've shared these treasures with my personal army of lieutenants, which makes *them* very happy, and ensures the average happiness stays high. Pinnacle and I are always working to make them happier, which helps satisfy his requirement that happiness always increase." His voice grew stern as he turned toward the people chatting around the chamber's perimeter and bawled, "*Can I get a huzzah?*"

"Huzzah!" the attractive, well-dressed people yelled in unison, raising their glasses toward Kincaid, beaming. As one, they all took a hearty gulp from their drinks.

"*Thank* you," he told them, then turned back to Po, his expression softening once more. "The metrics must always increase, my friend. Pinnacle can't ever be stopped, trust me. He's programatically obsessed with exploding Sovran's population and making it ever-happier. Nor would I want to stop him, of course. We're perfectly in sync, him and I. We are *simpatico.*

"And indeed, this is where you and your fellow Marines come in. It's why I sent GEA that first 'distress' signal, 'warning' them about the situation here on Pinnacle. And it's why I've orchestrated the events that brought you here. Please understand, Po. The people here aren't military trained—you saw that when they swarmed you like a bunch of lunatics." Kincaid chuckled. "They're far from professional killers like you and your brothers, aren't they? They're like animals. Although, we all are, really, no? But I digress. Simply throwing these *creatures* en masse at an enemy...it's what you might call inefficient. It also has the highly undesirable effect of reducing Sovran's population, which hampers happiness growth. And we certainly can't have that.

"I'll be honest with you. I don't know how to train fighters, and neither does Pinnacle. That's just not his specialty. His specialty is making people...*real* happy." Kincaid's smile was his widest yet.

"But here *you* are," he continued, "a veritable legion of ready-made fighters, come to Pinnacle's very doorstep. How fortuitous! Wouldn't you agree? A force like yours is exactly what we need, to accumulate more...*living space.* Which, as I'm sure you've noticed, is at something of a premium aboard Sovran."

Kincaid fell silent, as though waiting for Po's reply. "Well?" he said after a time, holding up a hand and twirling two fingers through the air as though urging Po to speak.

"We'll never fight for you."

"*Thank* you," Kincaid said. "I thought you'd never get around to speaking your line. You know, Po, I've actually heard all about you. About your raw *potential.* Now, what they've been telling me lately is that you're a lost cause. But I don't believe that for a second. If you ask me, you're just in need of the proper persuasion." Without warning, he clapped his hands sharply together, and Po jumped.

"That will be all for now, Po," he said. "We'll talk more later." He held out a hand toward one of the bots standing guard around the chamber, motioning for it to come forth. "Take him, now. Put him where we discussed."

A pair of bots strode rapidly forward, seizing Po with grippers that were like iron bands around his biceps.

As they turned him and marched him toward the end of the throne room opposite where Kincaid sat, Po felt like he was back in Psyche, freshly apprehended from the Equipoise warehouse and being whisked off to jail.

As it happened, that wasn't so far from reality.

***

Even with his sedative-addled brain, Po was still able to piece together what seemed very likely to happen next. His implant would be loaded with the same 'happiness' program enjoyed by everyone else on Sovran. He was about to have the Pinnacle AI living inside his skull. And somehow, he doubted he'd be given a choice in the matter.

After that, he could do Pinnacle's bidding, or he could be lit on fire from the inside—just as he'd been before losing consciousness back in Cycler 3, when he'd fallen out of the Swagger Course, hundreds of meters above the surface, after going suddenly blind.

The realization made him numb, like he was walking through a dream, and the vestiges of whatever they'd injected him with only served to enhance the effect.

For some reason, his thoughts didn't linger on what was about to happen to him, or on what they would make him do once Pinnacle was firmly lodged in his head. Instead, they returned to the sublevel where Sovran's stick-thin residents had swarmed them, next to the hole they'd blown through from the level below.

He couldn't get out of his mind how he'd fired his rifle into the pile of bodies.

He had no idea who he'd hit. Male or female, young or old. All he knew was that the body had gone limp, just like the one Crotty had killed.

Po had shot someone forced to do Pinnacle's bidding. Someone whose every nerve ending would burn ferociously unless he did everything the AI commanded.

If that person had had a choice, he never would have attacked Po. He was *forced* to do what he'd done.

And for that, Po had killed him.

So how would he be treated, taken over by Pinnacle and sent into the system against its enemies? Could he expect to be treated any better than the man he'd killed? Could he reasonably hope for mercy?

The bots dragged him through passageway after passageway, finally opening a hatch to reveal a dusty, dimly lit corridor lined with cells partitioned by bars. They brought him to the fourth one on the left, opened it, and shoved him inside.

He stumbled the narrow width of the cell, catching himself on the rough wall, which felt like concrete. With that, they slammed the door shut, the bars rattling. And they left.

Po turned, feeling weak and miserable. This prison bore no resemblance to the one he'd been tossed into back in Psyche, with its labyrinth of transparent cubes stacked on top of each other, like something from a surrealist's nightmare.

It was nothing like that humiliating, dehumanizing place. But it would hold Po well enough until whenever they got to installing him with Pinnacle. And after that, no prison would be required, except the prison of his own mind.

Chapter 30

It surprised him, how long they left him here. Being brought before Kincaid for a personal audience had led him to believe that he was a priority, or something like that. But now, he wasn't sure what purpose that had served, other than Kincaid's own amusement.

In the meantime, he was served decent meals, by bots who didn't speak to him—not that he was interested in a conversation.

As he ate, he pondered his situation, turning over the question in his mind of why he hadn't been taken over yet by the station's superintelligent AI.

Chances seemed good that by now, Pinnacle had either captured or killed every Marine who'd set foot on Sovran. It seemed to have no qualms about throwing the station's massive population into the jaws of battle, and with that many people attacking with complete abandon, it was only a matter of time before the Marines were completely overwhelmed. Especially if Pinnacle managed to get the jump on them, like it had on 131st Platoon.

If the Marines aboard Sovran *had* been defeated, then those aboard the ships outside the station would surely know about it by now. Po wondered how they would react. Would they attempt to negotiate with Pinnacle, risking getting further duped and manipulated by it? Or would they eventually decide to cut their losses and nuke the station from existence, with GEA's full backing?

Every now and then, a prisoner was removed unceremoniously by one of the bots. Other times, one was brought in, and shoved into one of the empty cells.

Some of the newcomers were hollow-eyed and starey, as Po imagined Pinnacle's agents on Venus would have looked, after the Corps removed their implants. Others, Po knew were Marines, even though he didn't actually recognize any of them. The sweatsuit normally worn under SERAPH armor was a dead giveaway, but their comportment screamed even louder. These men were unbroken and proud.

So far, anyway.

The fact he didn't know any of the Marines brought in seemed to support his earlier conclusion: Pinnacle had thrown the station's massive population at the entire Marine boarding force, probably all at the same time. And its victory had been decisive. Soon, every one of them would have a superintelligence living inside their brains. Likely before the week was out.

He wondered how many cell blocks like this one were scattered throughout the station. It had to be a lot, to accommodate so many Marines...which seemed like a lot of jails, for an agrarian cycler.

Pinnacle must have added some of his own, since taking over. That was the only thing that made sense. In the normal course of things, a pastoral place like this simply wouldn't produce enough crime to justify it.

But what he found even more thought-provoking were the non-Marines who were brought in and out. Their presence seemed to suggest the AI didn't quite have the iron grip on the station that might otherwise have been presumed.

Was there a resistance after all, just not with Harold Kincaid as its leader? Or did the Pinnacle program simply need to be patched every now and then? Po supposed it would glitch like any other software, which would lead to little bursts of agency in the AI's otherwise pliant slaves, until they could be dragged in and debugged, or whatever.

There was one cell whose occupant didn't change: the one two cells from Po, to his left when he faced his own cell's door. Which meant the man who occupied it was farther away than Po from the exit.

In fact, the man's cell was next to the wall, and the cell between him and Po was kept empty at all times. Once, all twelve cells in the block were filled except for that one between the man and Po.

Time dragged on, marked only by the meals the bots brought him, at seemingly regularly intervals. Because of their regularity, they didn't help mark days, but only periods of time between eating. That seemed intentional, too. Everything was, he felt sure.

He remained in the prison long enough to become curious about the man to his left, and to notice he barely ever slept. Preoccupied with his own thoughts as he was, this came to his attention because of a desire to get a good look at him—to try to figure out why he'd seemingly been left there to eat the bots' fare and to rot. But he didn't want to openly gawk, so he was waiting for him to sleep. Which he never seemed to do.

At last, it happened. Racked by insomnia, Po lay awake atop the thin blanket he'd been left for a bed, until a soft, whistling snore reached his ears.

As quietly as he could, he pushed himself to a sitting position, peering through the empty cell at the man sitting on the floor perhaps ten feet away from him, his head lolling forward as he dozed.

Po couldn't see a blanket underneath the man—which was the only little nod to Po's comfort that had been provided him. But the man seemed to lack even that.

Except, at first it seemed he was *wrapped* in a black, cotton blanket, which looked tattered by long use. Then, he realized it wasn't a blanket at all, but a long robe.

Po's heart stopped for a moment, before resuming its beating. The man was a priest. All at once, he felt completely sure of it.

"Father?" he called through the bars, in little more than a whisper.

The priest lifted his head. He sat with his arms resting atop his knees.

"Yes," he answered. At first, he didn't look at Po, but stared through the front of his cell at the passage outside it. Then, he turned his head to offer a weak smile.

"What are you doing here?" Po asked.

"Why, I live here."

Po looked around the cell block, which now held only two other prisoners. Neither of them seemed interested in Po's conversation with the priest.

"No offense, Father, but 'live' seems like a strong word."

"Well, I'm not sure what to tell you. It's exactly what I'm doing." He gave a dry chuckle. "I'm *from* Sovran, son. Born and raised."

"Before the...?"

"Yes, before the AI's rise. I'm that old, I'm afraid." He chuckled again. "I was called to the cloth, went to Earth for seminary, and was blessed to be assigned to the very place I was born. Sovran is the kind of place with a demand for multiple priests, you see. Well...it *was*. But then again, perhaps now more than ever."

"Blessed, Father? *Blessed* to be assigned here?"

"Yes. Blessed. Even so." The priest flicked his fingers at their surroundings.

Po wondered for a moment whether the priest might have gone mad, during however long they'd been keeping him here. He didn't *seem* mad. But he was definitely saying some things Po couldn't make any sense of.

So he had to come out and ask it. If only to clear up the matter of the priest's sanity for himself. "Father, how can you say you were blessed to be assigned here?"

"My son, the Lord has done greater things through me here in this prison than I ever could have dreamed. Realer things, perhaps, than the window-dressing faith I presided over here when I had my parish. Most of the people He's helped through me are dead now, of course. Nevertheless...great things indeed." The priest's gaze became wistful, and drifted off through the prison once more.

"How...how are *you* still alive?"

The priest shrugged. "I did have a rather *large* parish. And I was the only shepherd for that flock. There are many people on Sovran whose...*happiness* would be impacted, if they knew I'd been killed. It helps them to self-report their contentment with more verve to know I'm being cared for. Some of them even insist on seeing me from time to time. Pinnacle brings me to a lavish apartment for that, for me to receive them in. So that they can see I'm comfortable."

"And you don't tell them the truth? That it keeps you here the rest of the time?"

"Only if they ask. And you know, no one ever has. They see what they want to see, in that apartment. Besides, keeping this..." He gestured at the cell block once more. "...keeping this to myself is part of the deal, I think. I take it on as my own silent cross to bear. In turn, Pinnacle keeps me alive, for the purposes of displaying me to my concerned former parishioners. And, living, I can do great works by God's grace. As I said."

Po nodded, struck anew by what an upside-down place the superintelligence had turned this cycler into. He fell into silence, and so did the priest. They sat quietly for a time.

At last, Po asked the question that had been weighing on him for days, now. "Father...is it wrong to shoot a person who Pinnacle forces to attack you?"

The priest took a deep breath, then met Po's eyes with the same kindly, sympathetic smile from before. "It's important to keep in mind that no one can really force a person to do anything. Of the forty thousand or so people living here when the AI took over, most accepted its 'happiness' program willingly. And they certainly got their *implants* willingly, despite the voices of wisdom warning against it, which were more numerous and louder aboard Sovran than in most places in the system."

Po winced, remembering how strongly *he'd* resisted getting a Circuit, all through his childhood and adolescence. And how quickly he'd accepted it once the military forced it on him.

"But even now that they have the implants," the priest continued, "and the Pinnacle program installed in them, they *still* can't truly be made to do anything. They simply aren't prepared to accept the suffering that would come if they ever were to refuse to comply with the thing's directives."

Pondering the priest's words, Po fell into a silence, and was left in it for longer than he expected. He sensed that right then, anyone else would have added something trite and pleasant, to soften the weightiness of what the priest had just said. But he offered nothing. He merely let Po dwell in his thoughts.

After a time, the whistling snores returned, and he looked over to see the priest dozing with his head between his knees. That made him want to laugh, but he restrained himself, so as not to wake him.

What would Navarro say if he could see me now? he wondered wryly.

The thought reminded him of their conversation aboard the *Gear Issue*, while Po convalesced in the med bay there.

Speaking of implant footage, Navarro had said. *Did you ever watch it from the day you got stabbed?*

Seemingly on a whim, Po opened his implant's library of recordings now, selecting the feed from the day he'd been attacked. The day he'd been saved by the anonymous Marine in a SERAPH suit. The one who'd lacked an IFF tag.

"You're being given another chance," the Marine in the footage said. "Like all the countless chances you've been given already. If your heart was any more calcified than it's been, you wouldn't have gotten any."

Wait. I know that voice. The realization struck him like a bolt of lighting. *I* do *know it!*

He replayed another conversation, then—a conversation he'd had in Shackleton Colony, in a bar called Hideaway, with a golden-haired man named Mike.

"You know you don't belong here. Right, Po?" Mike said in the recording.

"What?"

"You don't belong here."

A pause. "These days, I belong wherever I'm sent."

"That's true enough. Though, it depends on who's doing the sending."

It was the same voice. The man who'd spoken to him that day—the one he'd thought was Zanth's own invention, created to test Po—was the same one who'd saved him from the hooded and masked man.

The assassin Po felt certain had been *sent* by Zanth.

Chapter 31

"Father," he said again, when the priest seemed awake.

"Yes?"

"There's a Marine I went to bootcamp with. Linguist, is his MOS. He's very devout."

"Good."

"He..." Po swallowed. "He keeps telling me I should go to confession."

The priest's mouth quirked. "Charitably, I hope."

"Yeah, well, he says everyone should. But especially whenever I'm about to go into battle, he says it."

"That seems like wisdom to me."

"What I don't get, though, is why do I need to? Why can't I just feel sorry for my...sins...and pray for God's forgiveness for them?"

"You can—provided you have no access to confession, and you have a desire to go. It's called making an act of perfect contrition, and it involves being truly sorry for having offended Him Who is all-good and deserving of all our love. Not merely sorry out of fear of perdition."

"Right." Po sniffed. "I think Navarro said that, too. He's the Marine I mentioned."

"Mm."

"I still don't understand why I need a priest at all, though. No offense."

"None taken. You need confession, or the Sacrament of Penance—which requires one of God's priests—because it's the means our Lord instituted as most salutary for our souls. We don't need to understand why He instituted it. We only need to understand that He is all-good, and that He wills *our* good. His ways are far better than our ways, and it's up to us to have the humility to acknowledge that, and to follow them."

"I don't remember reading it in the Bible, though. That you need to confess your sins to a priest."

"Then you don't know your scripture very well. From John chapter twenty, verses twenty-two and twenty-three: 'He breathed on them; and He said to them: Receive ye the Holy Ghost. Whose sins you shall forgive, they are forgiven them; and whose sins you shall retain, they are retained.' With those words, our Lord gave His apostles and their successors the power to forgive or retain sin. But how could they forgive a sin they had no knowledge of? The logical answer is, they couldn't. Necessitating confession."

Po had nothing to answer, and so he lapsed into silence once more. Again, the priest let him.

After a time, he took a deep breath. Then another.

"Father, I *have* gone to confession before. When I was a—" His voice hitched as something seemed to lodge at the base of his throat, and tears welled in his eyes, surprising even himself. "When I was a boy," he said, his words coming out barely audible.

"It's been some time, then," the priest said gently.

Po nodded. "Yeah," he said, which came out as a croak. The next words spilled out in a rush—he had to make himself say them, before they leapt down his throat again. "Will you hear my confession, Father? Only, I don't remember how." Something struck him, then. "Oh. But, I do have the Act of Contrition. From Navarro. I need that, right?"

"You do," the priest said, his tone just as even as before. "Otherwise, you can simply repeat after me, for the opening words. But first, I'd advise going over your sins silently, asking the Holy Ghost to bring to mind what you should confess. Just tell me when you're ready."

Po nodded again, sitting there for a long time. Suddenly, he felt afraid that the bots would come suddenly and yank him from the cell, to face the trial he knew was coming. But for now, the cell block door remained closed. He pushed the fear from his mind, and forced himself to concentrate.

"Okay," he said at last. "I'm ready." He'd already brought up the Act of Contrition using his Circuit, instructing it to display the prayer in the air in front of him.

"Bless me, Father, for I have sinned," the priest said.

Po repeated the words.

With that, the priest walked him through the rite, and Po unburdened his heart. It wasn't long before tears were streaming silently down his cheeks.

***

The bots came for him at last, throwing open his cell door and seizing him. Po's eyes met the priest's briefly through the cell bars. He merely nodded to Po as he was dragged away.

They frog-marched him through the same corridors from before—at least, they looked the same. Though, maybe all the corridors in Kincaid's complex looked identical.

Somehow he doubted that, though.

At any rate, they led to the same place: Kincaid's throne room, where the man once more awaited Po on his bone-white throne. The same ornate tables were arrayed around the room, with the same well-dressed men and women, drinking what appeared to be the same beverages—though Po suspected they'd been refreshed at least once or twice since the day he'd regained consciousness to find himself lying on the vast chamber's floor.

The same bots stood guard around the chamber, with the same weapons.

There *was* one change, though. A pair of bots stood before Kincaid's throne, and at their metal feet knelt Gunny Emery, his hands apparently bound behind his back—though Po couldn't see them. If it was possible to kneel at attention, then Emery was doing it. His eyes met Po's, and they exchanged a grim look. The gunny seemed unafraid.

"Welcome back, Po," Kincaid said with the same gregariousness as before. "Do you know yet what you've been called here to do?"

Po didn't answer.

"Not as talkative today, I see. Well, that's okay. Allow me to walk you through this. First, I'd like to congratulate you on being given the same happiness aids enjoyed by everyone else in Sovran. Pinnacle's program was installed in your Circuit while you slept. I bet you didn't even know it, did you?"

Po kept silent.

That seemed to strike Kincaid as funny. His laughter boomed out. "Trust me, you'll know it soon enough. Bring him forward."

The bots holding him forced him to approach Kincaid's throne. They made him walk right up to Emery, so that the six of them were facing each other—the gunny flanked by his two guards, and Po with his.

"Do it," Kincaid said to one of the bots nearest him. "Do the thing."

The bot produced a pistol and pressed the barrel to Emery's forehead.

"No!" It felt like the syllable was ripped involuntarily from Po's throat. But then, he realized the bot's pliable gripper wasn't actually anywhere near the pistol's trigger. Instead, he gripped the weapon by its barrel, leaving the handle and trigger exposed.

"Oh, don't worry, Po," Kincaid said with mock gentleness. "It isn't going to shoot your gunnery sergeant. *You* are."

Po stood there, as stock-still as the bots. Emery also didn't waver.

"Well?" Kincaid said.

"I won't."

Kincaid snorted. "That's what they all say. At first."

With that, Po caught fire, starting with his feet and hands. He cried out straight away in agony. White-hot liquid seemed to creep through his veins. It was worse than he remembered it being, the day he fell out of the Swagger Course. Much worse.

When the pain finally subsided, and the fragments of his consciousness reassembled themselves, he found that he'd sunk to his knees, so that both he and Emery were now kneeling. Sympathy shone in the gunny's eyes, which were set in an otherwise grave countenance.

"Stand up," Kincaid said.

Po stood.

"Now, shoot him."

Po's hand trembled.

"No," he said.

The pain returned.

This time, when he came back to himself, he was clutching himself in a fetal position on the floor. His breath came in ragged gasps. His vision was blurry with tears, and he had a sensation of being hollow—similar to how he felt when he went without eating, but much emptier than that.

"Get up, Po," Kincaid said.

Shaking uncontrollably, he complied with the man's command.

"Your escape is in front of you," Kincaid said softly. "You just need to reach out and grasp it. It's—right—*there.* So simple. Just reach out and pull that little trigger. Come, now. This won't end until you do it, but only you can decide how much of your sanity you'll preserve. How much of *you* will be left after all this. You've seen what men look like, after they've spent themselves resisting Pinnacle. I know you have. But you don't have to do that. Just pull the trigger. It will go so much better for you if you do it now rather than later."

Po met Kincaid's eyes. "I'll never pull it."

The man shook his head, smiling sadly. "Oh, Po. The most tragic part of this is, you *will.* And yet, this is the path you've chosen. Ah, well. It's not as though I can say I didn't see this coming."

The agony returned, and when Po still wouldn't shoot Emery, it returned again. The fire raged through him again and again, like he was being cooked from the inside out. Like the furnace was *inside* him. He lost count of how many times that misery seared his innards with a burning he scarcely could have imagined before today. The bald fact of the pain was undeniable, and so was the inevitability that when he stopped, it would only be for a brief reprieve, before Pinnacle visited it upon him again.

That days passed while Kincaid continually demanded he kill Emery, and Po continually refused, seemed beyond doubt. But the question Po kept returning to, in his fleeting moments of lucidity, was whether *weeks* had passed, or maybe even years.

Kincaid exhibited an impossible stamina and unyielding will as he sat there on his throne, flatly demanding again and again that Po grasp the pistol and use it on the gunny. Po marveled at the way he could sit there for so long and repeat the same order again and again. As for why his own body hadn't simply given up the ghost, subjected to such unending abuse, he couldn't begin to fathom. It seemed impossible that any living being could survive it. Yet, he persisted in existing. And he persisted, and he persisted.

After eternity, at last he came to and found Kincaid standing over him with hands balled into fists, looking decidedly *un*happy, for the first time since Po had met him.

"Then you really are a lost cause," he spat, his voice trembling. "I thought I might do you the favor of *salvaging* you. But I was wrong, and he was right. You truly are unsalvageable, and now I must have you disposed of." Kincaid gestured to the bots. "Take him back."

Po slumped in the bots' grip as they carried him away. Nothing in his life had ever left him feeling like this. Not his father's drunken rages, not long shifts in Psyche's docks, not his brother's attacks, not bootcamp, and not living and fighting in a war zone for longer than anyone was meant to.

He was spent; he was overdrawn. Bankrupt. He had not even the will to direct his gaze, and instead he goggled at whatever it fell on.

He remembered his name, but wondered what it meant, anymore. Right then, it seemed Kincaid was right. He likely *wasn't* Po Abbato anymore—or anything coherent and whole.

And yet, somewhere deep inside him, a flame flickered still.

Not a flame of agony, but one of triumph.

And from that tiny flame, peace suddenly flooded him in waves. It flooded whatever he had become—whatever was left, now.

For the first time in his life, he felt truly free.

He hadn't done it.

He hadn't done the easy thing—the advantageous thing. He'd denied himself, though it had seemingly cost him everything.

And in doing so, he'd conquered.

Unbidden, Zanth's voice echoed in the empty recesses of his mind:

It is your appetites that show you what you should seek to experience next, the Emplor hissed. *If you see something you want, you should take it. That is what satisfies the divine mandate. You must honor your impulses.*

But the alien's intrusion didn't bother Po. In fact, it stuck him as absurdly hilarious.

His laughter rang out like a bell as he was carried back to his cell. He couldn't help it. He laughed, long and loud, completely unable to stop himself, and not caring.

The bots didn't react.

Acknowledgments

Thank you to the Marines and other veterans who allowed me to interview them one-on-one in order to get the details of Marine life as accurate as I could. They include Dan Abbott, Chuck Chambers, Richard Hakala, Bill Paradis, Steven Reneau, Dennis Whalen, and one other veteran who requested to remain anonymous.

Thank you to my Alpha Team, who have been reading this book since its earliest stage and who've provided substantial feedback along the way, which helped me develop the story with my readers' desires foremost in mind. They are Sheila Beitler, Gwen Collins, Richard Hakala, Colin Oliver, and Jeff Rudolph.

Thank you to my ARC/proofreading team, who helped eliminate scores of spelling and grammar issues. I take full responsibility for any mistakes that remain :)

Thank you to Tom Edwards for creating such stunning cover art, as always.

Thank you to my family - Mom, Dad, and Danielle - your support means everything.

Thank you to the people who read my stories. I couldn't do this without you.

Printed in Dunstable, United Kingdom

66813014R00129